MY BIG GOBLIN SPACE PROGRAM 2

ALSO BY SCOTT WARREN

War Horses Series

Chevalier

Ymir

Serpent Valley

Dog Soldier

Grand Melee

The Sunstone Imperative

Union Earth Privateers Series

Vick's Vultures

To Fall Among Vultures

Where Vultures Dare

Standalone Fantasy Novels

Oathbreakers Anonymous

The Dragon's Banker

Ought to be Dead

MY BIG GOBLIN SPACE PROGRAM 2

SCOTT WARREN

Podium

This is a work of fiction. Names, characters, places, and incidents are either products of the author's imagination or used fictitiously. Any resemblance to actual events, locales, or persons, living, dead, or undead, is entirely coincidental.

Cover design by Mary Cruz

ISBN: 979-8-89539-405-2

Published in 2026 by Podium Publishing
www.podiumentertainment.com

THE STORY SO FAR

Chris was intended to be the NuEarth company's first double-amputee astronaut to walk on the moon. Instead of a smooth launch and a four-day tour in space, he found his rocket exploding around him. He awoke moments later in a new world and a new body—that of a goblin king with access to an advancement system called the Goblin Tech Tree, granted by an enigmatic System.

The world and the moon might have changed, but Chris was never one to be so easily deterred. Armed with the ability to rapidly iterate on primitive technology, Chris assumed the name Apollo and began recruiting local goblins to help him achieve his thwarted goal of reaching the moon. Together with the unruly mob of manic goblins, Chris brought his new tribe through the Stone Age, developing primitive technology with modern ideas in order to speed-run through human civilization.

Along the way, he met a well-traveled wildkin trader and scholar, Rufus, as well as a fire elemental Ifrit named Taquoho. But he also encountered a hostile group of pig-dwarf hybrids called the javeline, and a reclusive tribe of bog-dwelling goblins led by a rival king. Through growing his tribe, he also unlocked various goblin variants, who specialized in things like bossing other goblins around or taming local creatures.

With the javeline hunting the goblins of Tribe Apollo, Chris set out to unify the local goblin tribes and push technology even further, developing simple firearms and gliders in order to defend the tribe. Together with the rest of his goblins, including a new variant specialized in blacksmithing, he mounted a desperate defense against the javeline and pushed them out of the jungle for good. But more danger loomed on the horizon, as the javeline turned out to be mere hunters peddling goblin parts to a larger human settlement, Habberport. And a growing tribe means more mouths to feed. Chris sets his eyes on the badlands to the southeast of the village, seeking to hunt the creatures that dwell there in order to feed his tribe.

MY BIG GOBLIN SPACE PROGRAM 2

CHAPTER 1

FUN WITH HOMOPHONES

<6 Hobgoblin Scrappers have been added to your tribe.>
<5 Hobgoblin Wranglers have been added to your tribe.>
<2 Noblin Igni have been added to your tribe.>
<3 Noblin Canoneers have been added to your tribe.>
<1 Noblin Canoneer has been promoted to taskmaster.>
<Your tribe has increased to 226 members.>
<Unlocking Noblin Canoneers has automatically unlocked several technologies of the Goblin Tech Tree.>
<Goblin Technology Unlocked: Deification>
<Goblin Technology Unlocked: Idolatry>
<Goblin Technology Unlocked: Downy-scratchers>
<Goblin Technology Unlocked: Sequential scratchings>
<Goblin Technology Unlocked: Iconography>
<Goblin Technology Unlocked: . . .>

What the hell?

I groaned at the bright sun, already high in the sky, stabbing my retinas through the slit windows, and rolled off the cuddle puddle. My mouth was dry and I was definitely not prepared for a deluge of System notifications. I dismissed them without reading most of them. The new noblins had come with some pretty bizarre technologies. Deification? Idolatry? Sounded more like cult practices. I struggled to the nearest rain cistern and washed the gunk out of my mouth, then stood under the water for a minute as the cool spray ran through my matted fur. This hangover wasn't as bad as the times here on Rava when I'd missed a full night of sleep. But it wasn't far off.

When I turned around, I was surprised to see Sally, agitated and fidgeting, waiting for my attention. While technically verbal, my lead engineer almost never spoke. Once convinced she had my attention, she turned and led me to the corner of the bluff where we'd made our first paper mill. She pointed at a blank spot on a table nearby and began to chitter.

I looked at her. "You . . . want another table?" I guessed.

She made a frustrated squawk and stamped her feet. I sighed. But I'd rarely seen the shy taskmaster so animated with me, so I concentrated.

"Something isn't on the table that ought to be?"

She waved her arms, and then made a square in the air, and then a crinkling noise as she balled her fists.

"Is this where you keep the paper?" I asked.

She nodded, exasperated.

"So, where's all the paper gone?"

Sally howled, having finally gotten her point across. She turned and stomped off to another corner of the bluff where a trio of pot-bellied noblins were leaning over a workbench. Dozens of discarded sheets of paper littered the ground around them, representing hours of work for Javier and his clothiers-slash-papermakers.

"What's all this?" I demanded.

The noblins looked up, blinked, and squinted at me.

"Whossat?" one asked. "Issit morning already?"

"Your king," I said.

One of the noblins sniffed. "Well, *I* didn't vote for ye!"

The largest one reached over and slapped the dissident, who squawked and acted appropriately chagrinned.

<Goblin Technology Restricted: Democracy>
<Goblin Technology Unlocked: Percussive reeducation>

"Sorrys 'bout that, King. I'll keep 'im in line." He squinted. "You sure you're Apollo? I thought ye'd be bigger."

I glanced at Sally, who vibrated with impatience.

"Look, I said. "I get that you guys are eager, but the engineers need paper, too. We're working on unlocking engines, motors, and batteries today, and we can't scribble everything on bark."

One of the noblins snorted. "What we're workin' on is way more great than whatever *engines* are, King!"

"Designs for new guns?"

"Wot? No! Way better."

"Artillery? Missiles?"

"Nothing like that!"

I marched up to the table and pulled over one of the wide sheets of paper, looking at the noblins' work.

"That's not finished, boss!"

I squinted down at the page where rough squares had been drawn in some sort of sticky ink. I didn't even know we *had* ink. And inside the squares . . .

"Are these . . . *comics*?" I asked.

"It's *histry*," said the largest of the pack. "Record of your kicking porkbelly butt wot at the battle of the bluff! How's folk gonna remember it?"

"It was *yesterday*," I said. I looked down at a crude drawing of a tall, heroic goblin atop a rough sloth. It was musclebound, with a large gun in each hand, and a crown. "Is this supposed to be *me*?" I asked. I shook my head. "I'm so confused. I thought you guys were supposed to be canoneers, but you've got terrible eyesight and you're sitting here making cartoons."

"But this is *your* canon we's workin' on," one of them protested. "I don't see wot the problem is."

"My . . . canon? Oh no. No, no, no."

I walked away from the group.

System!

<Awaiting query.>

Did you give me comic book nerd goblins?!

<Your selection of Noblin Canoneers was confirmed and granted.>

I tried to keep my teeth from grinding.

Show me the details of the Noblin Canoneer.

<Noblin Canoneer
Noblin: This advanced goblin variant is capable of speech and can reach level 6.
Short-Sighted: Noblin Canoneers cannot see far ahead.
Canon Keeper: Noblin Canoneers are skilled at keeping written records and maintaining information integrity. Note: Conflicting canon can lead to strife within the tribe.
Porcine: Noblins consume an extra choom of food per day.
Scratchy Specialist: Canoneers are exceptionally skilled at crafts involving writing or paper.
Codex Chaplains: Adding Noblin Canoneers to your tribe unlocks the Religion sub-tree of the Goblin Tech Tree and the Tribal Canon sub-system.
Big-Mouthed: Canoneers are adept at negotiations and swaying the opinions of other goblins—often through sheer volume.>

I fell onto my backside, dizzy, and not just from the hangover. What had I done? The potential destructive force of firearms in the hands of the goblin species was bad enough. Now I'd gone and given them *religion*! And judging by the comic panels squeezed in my hand, they were making me out to be some sort of war god. I felt sick.

System, can I go back and choose the partizans instead?

<All variant choices are permanent and binding.>

I rolled over, stomach heaving, and threw up.

When I looked up, Sally stood, little arms crossed and nose in the air. She sniffed loudly and then stomped off. Couldn't blame her. Alright. I guess we were doing this. Noblin Canoneers were now and forever a permanent part of Tribe Apollo. Unless I had them all killed as soon as they were born, which was unconscionable. After all, I'd been raised Lutheran, and even though for many years I had believed an omniscient supreme being to be scientifically impossible—ironic, I know, considering the System—I was pretty sure *murder* still equaled *bad*. Especially when the canoneers hadn't done anything wrong and it was my fault they were here. Unless . . .

System, did you take advantage of me while I was drunk and trick me?

<Denied. Timing of new variant selection was based on your victory over a formidable enemy, and your inebriation was coincidental. Tip: Large decisions made while intoxicated can lead to regret.>

No kidding. Not like it would have admitted tricking me anyway. I should have known the all-powerful calculator with a penchant for puns would eventually pull something like this.

Alright. Alright. Think, *Apollo.*

This was happening, and it was time to adapt and iterate. I was witnessing the literal birth of the very concept of religion among a growing civilization whose primary means of communication had, up 'til now, been chirps, screams, and physical assault.

Maybe this wasn't a disaster. On Earth, religion had historically done just as much good as bad. Mesopotamian religions tracked seasons, kept written records of crop yields, and wrote animal husbandry guides. Christian Churches in Europe had been instrumental in the distribution of the printing press and increasing literacy rates. The Islamic Golden Age had helped promote and spread algebra, astrophysics, and coffee.

God, I missed coffee.

CHAPTER 2

PRAISE THE STANDARD

I needed to clear my head and work on something sane for a while. I left the noblins to their own devices, for now, taking a few of the less scribbled-on sheets of paper as a peace offering for the engineers. As I walked through the village, I could already see goblins tucked into corners, alone or in pairs, squawking over little paper pamphlets with crude drawings. Just how early had the canoneers started working? Couldn't find fault with that ethic, at least.

I found Sally embedded with her fellow engineers, assembling the first test crankcase for a primitive rotary engine out of ceramic parts. I wasn't sure how well it would hold up to tests, but since every scrap of iron we had went into musket barrels, ceramic cases were our second resort. I could have those guns melted down, and part of me still wanted to. But it was a no-brainer to keep them for the next time a threat faced us, even if it would put a strain on our raw iron stores.

Huntsville, our settlement in the swamp west of Bluff Apollo, was producing about twenty-two chooms of raw iron a day, which melted down into about thirteen chooms of bar steel at the furnaces and anvils. Not a lot, by industrial measure. We didn't even need wagons for it yet. It could be brought on the backs of cliffords (as long as they didn't stay after nightfall and fall prey to strange red spirits). But just the fact that we had it was nothing short of a monumental leap.

That the pigs had forced me to divert almost everything we had into weapons of war just . . .

Ugh. Damage done. Neil's hunters, at least, were very fond of those rifles. I could hear the *pop pop* of them test firing even over the noise of igni hammering away at a rotor on the other side of the bluff. I was just glad the piggies didn't know about Huntsville, because hitting that would have really crippled our progress, not to mention our food supply of what swamp beasts could be caught.

Huntsville also supplied us with fuel. The icky-slicky oil I'd used to fry a few boglins and escape King Ringo's island didn't burn quite as cleanly as kerosene, but rotary engines are notoriously robust when it comes to burning even the worst bunker-fuel sludge. It would do. The boglins were eager to trade fuel for the meat and fish that we gathered. Until we could get well pumps up and running, and then we'd be self-sufficient.

Between the javeline leftovers from the battle and the goblins trekking back to retake Canaveral to the southeast to hunt the swarming lizards, we'd bought ourselves some wiggle room to address the looming food shortage. Ideally we'd get agriculture going—and we'd already started planting some fruit and nut seeds to form orchards near the base of the bluff. But that would take years to pay off. Livestock and herd animals, that was the fast solution. But we needed the tools for it. And that . . . was proving to be an obstacle.

Sally's engineers held up the two halves of the engine case and tried to get the uneven parts to marry up. I sighed. The problem with using ceramic parts is that they can't be reshaped after they are fired. I'd measured both halves before they'd gone into the kiln, and they'd both had molds. Yet the Goblin Tech Tree made them come out uneven. How would this thing ever run if it didn't even have a sealed combustion chamber?

I came closer and inspected the seam as the engineers chittered excitedly. If the shapes were at least similar, we might have sealed the gaps and re-fired it in the kiln. But I could see daylight through gaps that shouldn't have even been there, and it was beyond fixing. That meant another firing, another waste of clay and charcoal. Even *this* was frustrating me this morning.

Trying to explain standards and tolerances to the goblins was like speaking to a brick wall. I just didn't think their brains were wired that way. And nonverbal as they were, most of them couldn't ask questions to better understand. Sure, they could grasp the basic technology—and the variants had an even better understanding where their specialties were concerned—but your average forest goblin learned primarily by osmosis and experimentation, not lecture.

"Sorry," I said, letting the engine prototype tip over. "Won't work. Let's try again. Maybe check the molds and see if we can't get the ratios closer."

Sally's goblins all sighed with dejected slumps of their shoulders, until Sally started laying into them with angry chirps and flying fists. Then, they hopped to.

The pressure may have been lessened with the javeline off our backs, but it hadn't disappeared. We needed to figure this out.

I ran my hands through the fur on my face and thought about the words Hadfield had spoken on his birthday in Huntsville. *The System provides.*

I grabbed the nearest goblin. "Go get me the canoneers."

It jumped and chittered and took off in the direction of the central pavilion. I watched the blue furry streak disappear around a bend, then set to work helping Sally's team with the molds until the noblins arrived. It took them a while. Apparently, they weren't exactly coordinated and bumped into a lot on the way over. I made a mental note to invent spectacles once we got some high-quality silica, or else trade for some from Rufus.

The taskmaster came up to me with an armful of papers wedged against his side. "Boss! We chronicled your escape from King Ringo. Want to see it?"

"How?" I asked. "The only witness to that event is a dead scrapper."

"We might have, um, filled in some blanks," he said. He stuck the back end of his charcoal pencil up his nose and scratched it around. "Ya know, where details was light."

"You know what? No." I shook my head. "I won't be deified. I'm not God, I don't speak to any gods, and I certainly don't want to risk being smited if this world has one that's a little more active than the one I'm used to."

The taskmaster nudged one of the others. "*Write that down!*"

I snapped my fingers to turn his attention back toward me. "Doesn't mean I ain't the boss. Now, I need something to call you." I didn't add that I'd be damned before I named him after an astronaut like the other taskmasters. Well, work with what you know. "Luther. Your name is Luther. We're going to make our own reformations here."

Seemed equal parts blasphemous and appropriate.

Luther nodded. "I like it. So then, King, what's your decree?"

I considered. *System, how does codification of goblin religion work?*

<You can institute a wide range of theological philosophies, beliefs, permissive and taboo activities, funerary rites, belief in deific figures, symbology, spiritualism, methods of worship, litanies, mealtime prayers, gain bonuses through ritualistic sacrif—>

Okay, I get the picture. I scratched my chin with a claw. But how best to use this to my advantage . . .

"Let's start with some commandments," I said.

Luther and the other canoneers listened raptly.

"First, thou shalt be excellent to each other."

<Good start.>

I considered, running a hand through my fur. Religion was hard.

"Thou shalt maintain proper version control."

The canoneers started scribbling—doodling, I should say. Written language was still a foreign concept, it seemed, despite my attempts to introduce it. The Goblin Tech Tree simply had no place for syllabic written language, as far as I could tell. Which made a certain sort of sense, since non-variant goblins couldn't speak. Representational symbology was a different story.

"The scientific method is this: Question, research, hypothesize, experiment, analyze, and communicate."

We'd started to draw a crowd as goblins gathered to listen to our new religious edicts.

"Uh . . . to measure twice before cutting once is holy."

<You're reaching.>

It's important!

"When in doubt, thou shalt iterate and try again."

I looked around at the goblins nodding and chittering to one another. I was good at this. I held up my hands.

"Questioning work hours or safety standards is heresy!"

The goblins cheered.

I briefly entertained the idea of introducing a paradoxical commandment just for fun. But I didn't want to cause little blue heads to explode. That was enough for now.

I clapped my hands and grinned at Luther. "Alright. Let's start thinking about some religious iconography. Bring over that engine case and some paper."

CHAPTER 3

THE CULT OF THE RIGHT ANGLE

Personally, I thought it quite clever to make the schematics for a basic rotary engine our first religious symbol. Drawn on blue-tinted paper from the accidental goblin pulping at the paper press even gave me the feeling of working with actual blueprints—albeit ones with an unpleasant fuzzy texture. Codifying schematics gave the goblins working on it a religious incentive to create careful reproductions. The canoneers proved deft hands with their charcoal sticks and faithfully reproduced drawings as if they'd been sketching them their entire lives. Which, I suppose, technically, they had.

Within a few hours we had a functional manual for a hydrocarbon-powered motor, though entirely pictographic with representational iconography and all measurements in relation to the rough size and shape of a goblin head. But what was really wild was that Sally's engineers finally seemed to understand the more complex relationships between the various dimensions of the drawings when the canoneers canonized them. It was like a shortcut to introducing complex ideas for undeveloped technology through the Goblin Tech Tree.

New molds were hammered out for the various parts and fixtures of the engine and sent to the kiln. In the meantime, I also codified smithing and made sure taskmasters were revered figures in the new doctrine. Like village elders. Not that they needed any help. The various divisions of the labor pool already treated their respective taskmasters like rock stars.

Feeling quite satisfied with the day's work, I called a halt for dinner and joined the rest of the goblins in the central square for the communal mealtime. The igni were still working through the javeline meat and had repurposed the crank and impeller technology to invent sausage-making. All we needed was a little wheat flour and yeast, and we could start having brats and buns.

It took me a moment to realize that all the goblins were looking at me without touching their food, which was a completely new phenomenon. I looked around and spotted Luther waving for my attention.

"What is it?" I asked the lead canoneer.

"They want a mealtime litany, O King."

"I'm not a religious figure," I said. "You do it."

Luther bowed low. "That right is reserved for you alone."

I sat back, sighing. As if being king wasn't enough. Now I had to be pope, too. I raised my hands overhead and made a circle with my thumbs and index fingers. "Ever higher. Ad Luna per aspera."

The goblins aped my hand signal and then dug into dinner. I leaned back in my spot and considered. It's not every day you get to design a science-based religion. There was no way it could go horribly, horribly wrong.

<Your tribe has decreased to 221 members.>
<Your tribe has increased to 256 members.>

I woke up with the excitement of a kid at Christmas, pulling myself from the bottom of the goblin mound and jogging to the kilns. The crankcase sections having cooled overnight, I opened the hatch on the kiln and pulled out the parts now built to religious tolerances. My excitement grew as I started to inspect the results. Neither half looked to be deformed or misshapen—at least not to the degree I expected of goblin-manufactured parts. They were still a bit wonky and oblong, but they were *consistently* wonky and oblong. The two halves married up in a way that they could be sealed and bolted with a rotor and crankshaft in place. This was an engine that could potentially be fired up. And once this tribe had access to the power of angular momentum . . . the sky really would be the limit. The igni could use this as an example to hammer more—many more, hopefully—out of metal. Sally could make powered airplanes instead of just rocket-assisted gliders.

I was so excited that I had to be shaken out of my fervor when Eileen ran up to me with a report.

"What is it?" I asked.

"The Ifrit are on their way!" she exclaimed. "Caravan spotted coming off the badlands. Scout just told me."

That was fantastic news. The fire spirits from the desert in the southeast were masters of clockwork and fine crafting. They also had a knack for taking over devices and controlling them from the inside. I was eager to see what they would do with some of our newer technology. They were en route with a big pile of spare parts in exchange for some of our industrial ceramics.

"Make sure we're there to greet them," I said. "And get the Canaveral convoy on the move. We need to make some room."

System, how much clay do we still have?

<32 chooms, with an additional 43 chooms in discovered nodes.>

Excellent.

New technologies and new friends. This was going to be a big, *big* day.

I explained the next steps and then worked on my electric motor project until Chuck, my wrangle chief, woke up. I had the cliffords saddled up, and I mounted up on the back of Chuck's doggo with a few of my bodyguards. I felt bad for the poor clifford trying to hold Armstrong up. The scrapper taskmaster was almost as big as a noblin.

"Eileen says they found the road markings and they're following it north. Decent group, three or four wagons," I told Chuck.

"Alright, let's go bring 'em in," said Chuck, pulling his clifford around. He thumped its side with his palm and it took off, yapping and slobbering as it dug its claws into the turf. As we rode, I noticed the road.

"Buzz did a good job clearing a path here," I said.

"Makes it easier to bring in beasties," said Chuck. "But we're still eatin' 'em faster than my lads can rustle 'em up—at least the ones we can catch on the cliffords. They're not meant to hunt things that can run, not while carrying goblins, anyway. They get tired. Most of what we chase out here gives us the slip, even working together."

"You need something that doesn't get tired," I said.

"Got plans for somethin' like that, boss?" Chuck asked.

"The boss has got plans fer everything," said Armstrong.

I grinned. "Just wait and see."

We rode for the kilometer or so of rough road before a hulking figure in black cloth wraps leapt out of the woods in our path. Despite having its legs in a wide stance, it was twice my height at least, enough to make the javeline look small. It was broad across the shoulders and wore a horned brass mask that triggered the same part of my goblin brain as the night haunts. Its hand rested on the hilt of a curved sword at its hip, as long as I was tall, and—holy hell. Was this a *human*?

If it was, it was level 35. Chuck pulled the cliffords up, and every rifle and slinger with the welcome party was aimed at the new arrival. The brass mask scanned across our collected group, and several centimeters worth of steel slid from his scabbard.

"Boss, get behind me!" said Armstrong, stepping forward with his rifle—the same one I'd used to kill Hrott.

"Hold!" I said as the goblins around me tensed up. "We're expecting company, remember?"

"Yeah, little flame guys, not . . . *this*," growled Chuck. "I don't like it."

"I don't like *them*," added Armstrong.

"I don't think we're supposed to like it," I said. Then, raising my voice, "You speak? Are you with Taquoho?"

After a few more seconds of hesitation, during which I hoped none of my goblins would get trigger-happy, the masked man took his hand from the hilt of his sword and relaxed out of his readied stance. He moved to the side, and beyond him, two more like him flanked what I can only describe as a walking wagon, striding up the road on six spindly brass legs. I could hear the rhythmic whirring of gears and clockwork and the wagon glowed with a pale blue flame. The Ifrit were *walking*.

Several smaller clockwork creatures walked alongside or tended to parcels stacked high on the flat bed of the wagons that teetered dangerously on the ungainly gait of the heavy brass artifice. Each of them no doubt had an Ifrit pulling its strings, and they ranged from a dozen centimeters across to half the height of a goblin. Some had four legs, some six. But no two were the same size or proportion. Each of them made a bowing gesture as they passed me by, spreading their front two legs on the ground, though none spoke. It made sense that Ifrit, being able to possess devices from the inside, would create vessels like these to maneuver around. If anything, I should have expected it.

The goblins chittered and pointed—fingers, not guns—at the convoy. Those wagons were filled with goodies, and I wanted to dive in like a ball pit and swim in the Ifrit components that would soon be integrated into all our equipment. I scanned the convoy and the other wagons but didn't see the familiar face I was looking for.

"Is Rufus not with you?"

"*Ah, King Apollo*," said a familiar, whispering voice. I turned and looked at the small brass quadruped scuttling toward me. It was about the size of a cat, and had a wide, tapered body with pointed legs that reminded me of an origami frog. A pale blue flame clung to its surface, and the joint for its front right foreleg had been replaced with a ceramic bearing. *Huh.*

"Taquoho," I said.

"*Our friend Rufus continued on to the coast in an effort to secure more of the canvas you requested and pass on some of your ceramic tools. But we have brought additional supplies and Ifrit, as we had discussed and agreed.*"

"You've brought more than that," I said, eyeing the security detail. Seeing humans from this perspective . . . man, there's no other word for it but *terrifying*. I looked at one of my wranglers, trembling in the human's shadow with his rifle clutched in his fists. If the human held it, it would look like a child's toy gun—too small for him or her to even operate effectively. "You didn't say there were humans coming with you."

"*Did Rufus not explain? Apologies, King Apollo, I am truly embarrassed. These humans are our paladin—protectors and guardians of the Ifrit. We could not have crossed the desert without them and they shall be staying with us at the bluff. I trust this presents no problem?*"

I bared my teeth in what I *hoped* was a friendly manner. "None at all," I said.

CHAPTER 4

NO PROBLEM AT ALL

It strikes me as odd that you would trust human security, with your dislike of the newcomers," I said. I glanced up at one of the humans walking beside a trundling cart. They gave no indication of having heard me. All of them were between level 25 and 30, according to the System, except for the leader, who was all the way up at 35. I wondered what had triggered the ability to see that high of a level now. When I'd been able to see the croc levels, it was because we'd defeated the stone-sloth alpha. But neither Rotte nor Hrott had been higher-level enemies. Was it because we'd defeated the javeline as an organization? Because I'd invented guns? Or was it simply at the System's discretion?

<Yes.>

So helpful.

The artifice on the back of the clifford beside me twisted, though it had no eyes that I could see. I wasn't sure how creatures of smokeless fire interpreted visual animation, but clearly they could.

"*Herein lies the error of your assessment, O King. The paladin are not new to Lanclova. They are descendants of the first men to try to settle the land beneath Raphina's watchful eye. All that is left of them, in fact. Their camps, ports, and cities lay in ruins—taken by disaster, disease, and desertion. This land is not kind to outsiders. These humans have lived in the City of Brass for seven generations. Their loyalty to the King of the Ifrit is as unwavering as their bravery is resolute.*"

"It would have to be, to willingly assent to stay in a village of carnivorous goblins," I said. Individually, the paladins were terrifyingly powerful. But within the village, they could still be swarmed and overwhelmed. "Why don't they speak?"

"*They remove their tongues once secondary sexual characteristics begin to appear.*"

"That's barbaric!" I said.

"*Is it?*" asked Taquoho. "*I find that to be a crude and reductive description. They seem no worse for wear because of it, nor does it turn them into savages. I do not know why it is done, but they persist in the ritual.*"

"They do it to themselves?"

"*A keepsake of their previous culture—one of the few remaining traditions they observe that did not originate in the City of Brass. Along with their martial regimen and sword forms.*"

So those brass masks were hiding mutilated-mouthed lifelong warriors. Even if I could get a word out of them, they were probably too loyal to the Ifrit for me to learn anything useful.

We reached the bottom of the bluff and Taquoho stretched his mechanical legs to their full extent. "*The jungle has been pushed back. What are those towers at the corner of the fenced areas?*"

"Stationary defenses," I said. "We recently finished our war with the javeline. They attacked our livestock. It was the last time they'll attack us."

"*Curious. It is fortuitous that they did not exterminate you.*"

"I'd like to think so, too," I said, sliding down off the clifford. "We have a freight elevator cleared to bring your wagons up."

"*There is no need,*" said Taquoho. "*Observe.*"

The walking wagons moved to the base of the bluff and put their spiked legs up, slowly transitioning to a vertical climb. Their security hooked small brass loops onto the sides of the wagons and allowed themselves to be lifted. The smaller spider-bot Ifrit shifted to the front of the cargo as the orientation changed.

I grunted. "Huh. That's a lot of power in those walkers. Is it Ifrit moving them, or are they getting energy from some other method?"

I moved over to the freight elevator with Taquoho and my goblin guards. A goblin counterweight of a half-dozen furry blue menaces descended, pulling us up level with the walkers. Each wagon had a drum built into the back of it. I pointed at one. "Is that some sort of power source?"

"A well of potential kinetic energy. The Ifrit only directs the movement. Energy to move the limbs is stored in wound springs and must be rewound periodically."

"Clockwork, then. Is that how yours works, too?"

Taquoho lifted one of its legs. "*This form is small enough that we can manipulate it at will. We are used to it.*"

The elevator reached the top of the bluff and two of Buzz's builders hooked us and pulled the boom over the ground. The first of the Ifrit walkers reached the top of the cliff and pulled itself over. The goblins started to take notice, and a rising tide of chittering brought a decent portion of the tribe running—until they saw the humans.

Their reaction was much the same as mine had been: visceral fear and panic. In their case, this caused a surging tide of goblins to flee as far from the southern elevator as they could. In many cases, that meant flinging themselves from the top of the bluff.

"*What an unfortunate degree of friction,*" observed Taquoho.

"They'll come around," I said, hoping I was telling the truth. Still, having humans at Village Apollo made the goblin side of me nervous. Part of me felt it was like inviting night haunts to roost in the eaves of the buildings. I had wondered how I'd feel when I encountered humans here. Would I feel a sense of camaraderie, having been human myself? Maybe loss or longing? I hadn't spent much time in this goblin body. Though the days ran together without my cell phone keeping the date for me, it couldn't have been more than a few weeks? A month? Two? And unlike Ringo, who'd apparently gone native quite quickly, I still felt that my mind was mostly human. But this pint-sized perspective and innate fear of what were, ultimately, the apex predators of my old world, put into no uncertain terms that any vestiges of my humanity would most likely matter little to *actual* humans.

I was a blue, fuzzy goblin. Not a man. A level 1 nuisance at best. Humans were tall, strong, and agile, and they didn't fall over if a predator looked at them funny. They had hands that could break as easily as build, and how many of my tribe could this handful of warriors cut down before they were stopped? More than a javeline mauler, or even a croc-knocker, I was sure.

"I wasn't prepared to host humans," I said. "I'll have to have some larger quarters arranged. If you'd like to rest, we can carry on later."

I whistled for some of Buzz's builders, at least the ones who hadn't flung themselves off the cliff. They returned with the task-master, who took one look at the masked humans and shook so bad that his knees clacking together sounded like a woodpecker going to town on some pine.

"Buzz, they're going to need somewhere to sleep," I said. "Dry and warm. Presumably a latrine as well, and maybe facilities to cook and wash."

Buzz just stared at the humans. I snapped my fingers in front of his face, and when that didn't work I gave him a solid smack. He squawked and finally turned in my direction.

"Buzz! They're guests."

My lead builder considered. "We could knock in a few walls what to make rooms longer. I'll get the lads onnit, boss."

Buzz beat a hasty retreat, casting the human warriors a fear-ful look over his shoulder. But a moment later, I saw several of his builders with flint saws and mallets.

"Buzz is the one to talk to if you need any kind of facilities managed or constructed," I told Taquoho.

"*We are humbled by your accommodation,*" said Taquoho. "*However, my kin are eager to see the village I've described—though it has changed much from my description. I believe, even, that I hear the ring of a steel hammer. And do not think I failed to observe that several of your tribe now carry metal tools.*"

I grinned. "What can I say? We've been busy."

Taquoho tried to keep their excitement under wraps, but apparently Ifrit get the tippy-taps and it wasn't exactly subtle. "*The speed at which you have progressed through the rudimentary sciences continues to impress. May we see the work area, and perhaps the artifice you're working on?*"

"I thought you'd never ask," I said. "We'll get your people and gear situated soon enough. I—" I stopped as a group of shouts drew my attention to a building that had slumped over. It fell in on itself as a handful of builders scattered for cover.

<Your tribe has decreased to 254 members.>

I caught some of the paladins exchanging what I imagined were nervous glances underneath those masks.

"Not there, obviously. Someplace still standing. Shall we, Taquoho?"

CHAPTER 5

INFERNAL ENGINES

Armstrong and his scrappers tried to stay between me and the humans in much the same way the paladins tried to stay between him and Taquoho. Mostly this resulted in the two groups of bodyguards bumping and jostling through the village as I took Taquoho and a few of the other Ifrit to the north side, where the igni and engineers worked in tandem.

"I'm not as far along as I'd hoped we would be when you returned," I admitted. "Getting the iron from the swamp turned out to be more . . . challenging than I'd anticipated and the javeline making their move threw an extra monkey wrench into things. We were forced to focus on making weapons both to defend ourselves and make progress in the swamp. But now, we're back in development mode. Without the javeline causing trouble for local goblin tribes, I can focus on unifying and feeding them to transition them into working on the Space Program."

"*A clever use of bio-lightning, to be sure,*" said Taquoho, eyeing one of the tesla wasp spears being tested by two goblins on an unfortunate (or perhaps kinky) third member. "*The City of Brass employs a similar defense using magic artifacts.*"

I debated telling the Ifrit about King Ringo being the source of the know-how on the wasp larvae but decided that wasn't my story to tell. "Huntsville ended up being a veritable treasure trove of resources. It'll be a launch pad that extends our reach to encompass the other bluffs and wrangle more livestock. Mostly thanks to this."

I tapped the steel springs at my legs. "Do the Ifrit use much steel? Or do you stick to brass?"

"*We are familiar with steel, though we find it ill-suited to our purposes, so we seldom trade for it. Copper and zinc are much more plentiful near The City, and brass is more malleable at lower temperatures. Our true forms adhere to zinc especially well, which makes brass ideal for our vessels.*"

Taquoho lifted one of his vessel's forelegs, waving it about as if to demonstrate. Several other Ifrit vessels of varying sizes scuttled about, investigating the smithing area. The igni stopped work to watch them, eyeing the clockwork bodies with hammers close to hand in case the little spirits got a little too curious.

I approached Promo at his workstation, and he quickly made a show of shuffling papers around, but it wasn't hard to tell that the whole charade was an effort to hide a piece of paper with little boxes on it. I sighed. Those canoneer comics were spreading.

"Boss! Good to see yeh, and yer, um, friends." He caught sight of the humans and patted around behind him on the table until his fingers wrapped the familiar handle of his own hammer. "Big jobs, ain't they?"

"Taquoho, this is Prometheus, the boss of my smiths."

Taquoho performed a bow, spreading his forelegs. "*Prometheus. We are humbled to meet you.*"

"Call me Promo," he said.

Taquoho tilted up toward me. "*Familiar brevity!*" he whispered. For a creature from such a formal society as the Ifrit, being invited to use a nickname must have been like getting invited to the inner circle.

One of the noblins squawked as an Ifrit vacated its vessel and flowed into one of the forge impellers, stoking the flame and nearly singeing the ignis's fur. Good thing they were resistant to heat damage. Others examined ceramic receivers for unfinished rifles. I saw one gun cock itself and the hammer drop. Thankfully it hadn't been loaded.

"I'd have your kin be careful around those," I said. "And refrain from possessing any of the ammunition. I wouldn't want someone to set off a rockette by accident and get separated." I considered for a moment as I pictured one of the fire spirits leaping into a basket of rockettes. "I have to ask, do Ifrit produce heat?"

"*No more than you yourself do,*" said Taquoho. "*The subtle fire of our beings consumes the magic substrate that infuses all things. It is an elegant way to take sustenance. Unlike our paladin friends, and yourself, who must crudely masticate nutrients and cycle them through an excretory system.*"

I wasn't sure if I ought to be offended that the Ifrit was appalled at the concept of digestion. I shrugged. "Goblin scat actually has quite a few applications, I've found. Like flying balloons, rocket fuel, and blasting powder."

One of the Ifrit near Promo's workstation flared blue, and then a shade of light pink.

Taquoho straightened and observed, shifting his own flames from a pale blue to a shade of orange, violet, and then back to blue. He turned to me.

"*Basha Delton Rathraha Ithius Fayad wishes to know, what is the purpose of the angular shaft with the rounded triangular plate?*"

"Ah," I said, moving over to inspect it. "Promo, you should have told me it was ready," I said.

"Din' want to be rude, King," said Prometheus. "Do yeh like it?"

I picked up the rotor for the prototype engine with the small offset shaft that would make up the core of the engine. It was . . . surprisingly accurate, for goblin work. I glanced down at the desk, where Luther's first canon build manual for the Church of the Right Angle showed the ordained dimensions for the prototype rotor.

I turned to the Ifrit who had asked the colorful question. "This, erm"—I thought hard for a moment—"Baderaithifa."

The Ifrit in question, and several others, flared at the shortened name. I didn't understand why, as I'd made a mental note to make sure I caught all the first syllables. Taquoho waved his forelegs frantically. "*Please do not shorten Basha Delton Rathraha Ithius Fayad's name! You are not yet familiar enough with them, nor are several others in our company. This is offensive to their union.*"

"Oh," I said. "Isn't that your custom?"

"*It is* my *custom*," said Taquoho. "*Based on this union's dealings with outsiders and their needs for brevity.*"

I bowed. "My apologies."

The Ifrit seemed placated for the moment, so I continued. "This is the next step in our technological progression: an internal combustion engine." I looked at the rotor. "Well, technically this is just *part* of the engine. My chief engineer, Sally, has the outer shell. It still needs work, but we'll be firing up the first prototype here in the next couple days once I'm convinced it won't explode."

"*Your desire for caution is laudable*," said Taquoho. "*May we see the ceramic kilns? And this prototype engine powered by internal flames?*"

"Of course," I said. I slung the rotor over my shoulder. "Promo, I'm taking this with me."

"Give the engineers my best," said the noblin chief.

I waved and led the party to the northeast corner, past the air traffic control tower and the landing strip. The strip had been cleared, with all the aircraft returned to Canaveral with enough goblins to fend off the lizards. We passed the paper press next, where fresh sheets were being pressed under flat stones and cut into sheets. Javier stood waiting nearby with the tribe's only pair of metal shears, waiting to cut it.

"*You have developed a paper process?*" asked Taquoho.

"We have," I said. "We're not exactly hurting for timber, so the cast-offs can be pulped and pressed." I pulled a fresh sheet off the stack. "I imagine you don't get enough trees in the desert to make paper on the regular. If it's something you'd be interested in trading for, we already have plans to set up another cask."

Taquoho waved his leg dismissively. "*The Ifrit keep no written records. Paper is for wealthy newcomers to fan themselves in the summer.*"

Hmm . . . "I bet I could give you a reason to want paper," I said. "Give me two days."

We moved on to the ceramics workspaces. Sally was overseeing one of the kilns being fired up, with a pair of noblins stoking the charcoal flames beneath the blower. I waved to her, and she caught sight of the rotor in my hand and began to chitter.

"You want to see how this fits in the outer case?" I asked.

She jumped up and down. I held out the triangular rotor. My chief engineer snatched it out of my hands and ran to compare it to the crankcase. By divine providence, the two looked compatible.

"I'll be damned," I said, looking at the canoneer drawings on the bench nearby. I suppose divine providence wasn't too far off. The new noblin canoneer variants were doing what I couldn't: establishing and maintaining manufacturing standards. The would-be religious nuts might end up being useful after all. "My new friends, you're looking at the first prototype engine case and rotor. All it's missing now is some spark plugs."

Taquoho approached the engine. A small lid on a reservoir concealed within his vessel slid open, and the formless fire slipped from the tiny spider-bot into my prototype engine.

"*Fascinating*!" his voice echoed from inside. "*You say this will produce angular torque?*"

"For the gliders, boats, tools, and other purposes." I pressed my hands against one side of the case. "Hold the case together!" I called out. A few of the goblins dropped what they were working on and ran over, putting their weight into the two ceramic pieces to help me hold them together with the rotor in place. I knocked on the ceramic. "Taquoho, see if you can spin that rotor. It should have very little clearance."

The metal scratched as it began to rotate, but it didn't take long for it to slow again. Taquoho slid out of the exhaust port in the crankcase and back into his walking vessel.

"I'm afraid it's too heavy," he said. *"As I said, steel is difficult for us to move. Perhaps if it were zinc."*

I shook my head. "With the abuse this thing is going to take, I don't think zinc is going to be hard enough to cut it. That's alright. We have a liquid fuel we're going to try." I turned to Sally. "Seal it up. The Ifrit brought bolts to lock everything down. By tomorrow night, we should be ready for the first test-fire."

One of the other Ifrits flashed and chirped a series of musical notes.

Taquoho stretched his limbs out. *"Behern Galt Muya pays you a compliment and reminds me that it is time for our prayer, and is also excited to see your gliding apparatus."* He sighed. *"Would that I could look upon The City from one of your gliders, but alas, the creatures in the deep desert would be quick to attack anything with wings."*

"That explains why you never developed flight," I said. "Wait, the Ifrit observe a deity?"

Taquoho raised his leg in warning. *"You should not ask about it. It is taboo for many unions to discuss it with anyone from outside The City."*

I nodded. "See no evil, speak no evil, hear no evil."

"Just so," said Taquoho. *"Wise words. But it is missing the most crucial command of all."*

"What's that?" I asked.

"Practice no evil."

"Ah," I said, running a hand through my fur. "I'll have to consider adopting that one."

CHAPTER 6

TRINKETS

<Your tribe has decreased to 246 members.>
<Your tribe has increased to 268 members.>
<Your tribe is consuming more food than it produces by a deficit of 11 chooms per day.>
<Goblin Technology Unlocked: Fire-wrought pulpers>
<Goblin Technology Unlocked: Flaming crane>
<Goblin Technology Unlocked: Forge spirits>
<Goblin Technology Unlocked . . .>

The next day I awoke to frantic squawking and another hail of notifications. I brushed them aside and raced out to see that Ifrit had taken over one of the cranes and pulleys and were working the mechanisms. Others had settled into the gearing for the drop hammers, and yet another was roasting in the test balloon over the scat pile. Others were spinning augers and pottery wheels or stoking forge bellows. The whole village looked to be possessed by pale sprites.

I relaxed. The tribe was excited, not panicking. Armstrong ran up, rifle at the ready, fur matted where he'd been sleeping. Becoming my bodyguard had given him the benefit of being able to sleep and wake when I did, instead of being beholden to the typical hobgoblin hours. I waved him down. "It's alright, Armstrong."

Some of the tribe fussed, but mostly they were amazed at tools suddenly moving by themselves. Most of them hadn't been on board the heavy glider when Taquoho took over controls from Eileen. I had to imagine she was sitting smug watching other goblins have their devices co-opted.

The small spider bot I recognized as belonging to Taquoho scurried up. "*I apologize for this,*" he said. "*My kin can be quite incorrigible.*"

"It's alright. I was hoping this would happen," I said, laughing. "I *wanted* your Ifrit to integrate into the tribe, feel at home with our technology, work with my tribe to get the most out of our engineering." I watched a pair of goblins getting pulled along by the paper-pulper jig lines.

Taquoho worried at the ground with his front two legs. "*I suppose with your leave, it is alright,*" he said. Then he flared a moment, which I had to assume was the Ifrit version of clearing his throat. "*We have unpacked much of the trade brought for you.*"

"Lead the way!" I said.

Armstrong whistled for a few more bodyguards as we trotted to the Ifrit/human quarter of the bluff. Buzz had erected a few buildings that looked more accommodating to human scale, though it seemed like the paladins weren't quite ready to trust my chief builder's efforts just yet. They'd erected their own tent pavilions and cooking stations. It also seemed that not all my goblins held on to their innate fear of humans, because at least two cuddle puddles had made their way into the tents, settling onto the sleeping humans for warmth. The paladins seemed at a loss for how to deal with them.

A few Ifrit were present as well. Some of them had abandoned their vessels for the light gauze wraps Taquoho had used last time—the equivalent of using a pair of camp sandals after a long hike in boots, I supposed. I spotted at least one human thumbing through what looked like a blue-tinted paper brochure with hand-drawn art alongside a pair of Ifrit in their gauze getups and narrowed my eyes. Friggen' canoneers.

The strange walking wagons had been unloaded. I spotted stacks of brass piping, crates of threaded bolts and associated tools (clearly meant to fit on Ifrit vessel connections), two brass casks, three barrels of coal, solid rods of copper, brass, and zinc, various rings and gears, and their own versions of bearings. I also spotted spools of copper wiring, springs, more lodestones, and a variety of powder compounds I couldn't identify at a glance. And some stacked canvas—which I realized had been the canvas covering the supplies on the wagons. Ironically, the simple canvas covers used to weatherproof and secure the cargo were perhaps the most important thing the Ifrit had brought.

I went and lifted the canvas, testing the weight and thickness. It was light and had a little bit of give, perfect for our needs. Then I moved on and took a look at the metal fixtures. There were a variety of arms, ball joints, sockets, connectors, hinges, flanges, brackets, and a lot of what would amount to cast-offs in most workshops but was a gold mine here. Plenty of pipe sections and joints filled one barrel, and I was sure I'd be able to find a use for them.

"Our friend Rufus is acquiring more sailcloth and other items from the coast for you. The leader of our delegation hopes this offering demonstrates our good faith and interest in incorporating ceramics into our artifice."

It was the richest treasure trove I'd seen since coming to Rava. All the scraping and scrapping we'd had to do for a little metal, some sulfur, and some magnets, and these guys had dumped a crate of it into my lap. I could have jumped for joy. I could have wept. And yet . . . something about their phrasing bothered me. *Incorporating ceramics into our artifice.* Nothing about friendship, or alliance, or a relationship with Tribe Apollo. Despite their presence here, they weren't here for a goblin king or his enterprising tribe. They were here to further their own material sciences. And that was fine. Trade and equivalent exchange would promote shared learning and friendship between our two cultures. But it wasn't everything I wanted out of the partnership.

"Taquoho, you honor me," I said.

The Ifrit vessel bowed. "*The honor is mine, King Apollo.*"

I whistled for the goblins in the human tents, and they came to wakefulness like a slow tide, if the water were furry and groaned and scratched its butt.

"Let's go! We've got goods to distribute." I pointed at the piles. My goblins' ears perked up when they realized it was their king giving instructions. "Canvas to Javier, metals to Promo. Nuts, bolts, cogs, and springs to Sally. Nails and piping to Buzz. Let's go, go, go!"

The goblins gained their energy back and swooped in on the goods like a pack of ravenous vultures. I was surprised half the goods didn't get destroyed before they made it out of eyesight. I watched them go.

"*Quite industrious creatures. I never imagined . . .*" said Taquoho.

"Well, they take after their king, I suppose." I turned and faced the Ifrit. "The seals on the engine need time to cure. They won't be strong enough today, so I've got some free time for an old idea I toyed around with for a design contest once. Why don't you come find me after the eclipse? Until then, your people can get with Sally or Promo with designs for any ceramic parts you want."

"*As you say, King Apollo,*" said Taquoho, bowing. He waved a foreleg goodbye.

I trotted off, trying not to let my shock and glee show, lest the Ifrit realize they could have demanded much more in trade than they had. The treasure he'd just dropped at my feet, all for a few chooms of crude industrial ceramics that would get rejected by the quality control department of any factory on Earth. And for the first time in what felt like weeks, the sword of Damocles that was the javeline wasn't hovering inches above the back of my neck. Though how long had I actually been here? The moon on Rava was tidally locked, so without counting individual days, I had no way of knowing whether a month had passed, and the thought of keeping track of time hadn't even occurred to me while flitting from one crisis to another. Did Rava even observe a custom of discrete months?

Never mind that. Today, I had time to *tinker*. I looked up at the skyline of the village and the self-moving artifice that scraped the rooftops. I knew why the Ifrit had chosen the cranes, the drop hammers, and the balloons. Their squat walkers were stuck close to the ground. They wanted a better view.

Well, I had the means to give them one they'd never want to give up.

CHAPTER 7

COAXIAL MOTIVATION

They say idle hands are the devil's playthings, so I put mine to work in the engineering quarter on the northeast side of the village. I'd confiscated more of the noblin comics this morning, ones that appeared to depict me designing a divine rocket to smite the javeline—a very different sequence of events than I remembered. I started cutting and shaping sheets.

The nice thing about paper is that it's light, even if it's not very strong. But there are various ways to increase its strength, and then it gains a lot of versatility as a material. We had adhesives, and I was going to use those to turn paper into lightweight rigid structures.

The brass parts from the Ifrit included several globular and cylindrical vessels I had to imagine were originally designed to *hold* Ifrit. When I looked closely, I noticed that every piece of metal had been inlaid with geometric patterns or designs, all of it possessing some form of radial symmetry. I puzzled at their purpose for a moment. Then it hit me, and I giggled. I was looking at Ifrit fashion, or at least their clearance section. The *Autumn Trapezoid* collection. I selected a light bottle, and then took some copper rings and a handful of brass gears and rods, and went to work.

Drones had been the new hotness back on Earth. Devices with four or eight motors dominated college robotics labs and flying fields—and with good reason. They were cheap, had easily replaceable parts, and their lithium batteries came in all shapes and sizes with enough voltage to spin multiple brushless motors. But what they weren't, was *efficient.* Aerodynamically, they were about as wasteful as a design could get—four motors, four small props working double-time to make up for a lack of surface area and multiple wingtip vortices, and having no swashplate meant motors had to accelerate or decelerate constantly to change pitch or heading.

A swashplate is what makes a helicopter a helicopter—i.e., an abomination unto aviation, unlike a much more reasonable fixed-wing aircraft. In a nutshell, the swashplate converts stationary control inputs into outputs on a rotating plane. It's a way to have the helicopter blades pitch up when they're at the back of the aircraft for more lift and flatten out by the time they get to the front of the aircraft. That simple transition tilts the whole thing forward, and the helicopter is able to accelerate.

Granted, there's a whole lot more advanced physics involved, like gyroscopic procession, blade flap, and yada yada boring helicopter stuff. *Yawn.* But the basic principle is, mechanically, not all that complex. A few push-pull rods, a pair of matched discs that move up and down, and some bearings to make it all smooth. I'd often wondered what you could accomplish with having a main rotor without a helicopter attached. You'd need a pretty advanced autopilot to be able to stabilize it.

Or, alternatively, a pilot able to intimately feel and understand the aircraft itself.

I went to work sketching designs and laying out parts. Then I started to tinker. The rings formed a central hub, from which the brass bottle hung. Above that, push-pull rods connected to a stationary plate, and a spinning plate above connected to a short rotor mast.

The Ifrit had given me all the brass tubing I needed, and a four-way connector made the base of the rotor head. Gearing let me create an assembly and bearings let me mount it with almost zero friction in the whole system. I had the frame nearly done and started folding paper over the rotor blade sections.

<Your tribe has decreased to 264 members.>

I looked up as the sun passed behind Raphina's closed eye. The daily eclipse, already. I blinked and looked around. An audience of both goblins and Ifrit had gathered, watching me work with interest. Even one of the canoneers madly scribbled something on a bit of paper. The only one not interested was Armstrong, who dozed in the corner, who was primarily interested in my inventions that went *boom*.

The Ifrit were here for ceramics. I had no illusions about that. Taquoho might personally have a passing curiosity as someone who found newcomers and their trinkets a novelty, but the other Ifrit weren't interested in *Apollo, goblin king and inventor*. I had to give them something they couldn't ignore. Clay and kilns would only take this relationship so far.

Taquoho was in a group of several larger Ifrit vessels, likely discussing what it was I was building—and I doubt it went unnoticed that I was using primarily parts they had brought. It meant I was designing a device they could *almost* reproduce. But human know-how and goblin tech insanity were the missing puzzle pieces. The Ifrit refused to speak to any goblins, choosing (or capable only) of communication through a mediator who I was beginning to realize did not actually have much pull within the greater Ifrit social structure by the way he bowed and supplicated to several of the others. Time to elevate his standing.

"Taquoho, I've got a gift for you," I said.

Several of the Ifrit around the fiery translator flared various shades. The little vessel skittered forward. "*You should refrain from interrupting conversations between unions. Many among my kin find such things offensive.*"

"So you don't want what I've got to give you?"

Tippy taps. "*I did not say that, King Apollo! I only wish to help you navigate the complex social norms of my culture so that you don't unintentionally offer insult. I'm very curious to see the artifice you've wrought. But . . .*"

One of the larger proxies strode forward. It had masterwork geometric patterns inlaid on the bronze parts, along with detailed jewel inlays at intervals that represented, as best I could tell, the Fibonacci sequence. It flared a series of colors.

"*Haut Voclai Behen Mira Do is the ranking member of the delegation here. Gifts should be offered to their union, and they may distribute them among the other Ifrit if they see fit to do so.*"

I looked at the gaudy vessel. Clearly any gifts offered to the "ranking member" would stay squarely in his . . . claws? Spikes? Never mind. He didn't even know what it was, and yet he'd take it away from Taquoho just to swing his weight around.

The Ifrit in question stepped forward, ready to receive the gift.

Wasn't happening. "Ah. Well, please inform Mr. Haut Voclai Behen Mira Do that this isn't a gift for the Ifrit delegation. It's a gift for my friend, Taquoho, with whom I share familiar brevity. I find attempts to diminish that distinction crude and reductive."

"*King Apollo!*" Taquoho said. He stopped short of outright gasping in shock, but it was certainly implied.

So be it. I continued. "Now, Taquoho, where I come from it's considered rude to keep a host waiting when they offer a ride to their guest."

"*A ride?*" asked Taquoho. He inched closer. "*This is some sort of new vessel? The legs don't look to be articulate.*"

"They don't need to be. It doesn't walk. Take it for a spin."

The lid on the reservoir in Taquoho's vessel slid open, and a small cyclone of flames streamed from one vessel to another. The pale blue fire tucked itself into the brass bottle built into my newest device and then spread over the assembly above.

"Zinc paddles and reciprocators. Married plates on bearings moving on three axis. This part . . . freely rotating. This is like the device you were testing when last I arrived. Yet . . . it is designed for one of my kind."

"Is this one too heavy for you?"

By way of answer, the blades began to spin. I'd designed a stacked set of coaxial counter-rotating blades to eliminate the counter-torque problem. Without an engine or motor to speak of, the only noise it made on the smooth greased bearings was the air being displaced. Taquoho raised the swashplate a hair and the individual blades took an angle. The vessel tipped to one side, but the Ifrit caught it and tilted the rotor the opposite way until it leveled out. Then it raised the pitch higher and slowly lifted into the air through only the power of the Ifrit itself.

<Goblin Technology Unlocked: Fire fliers>
<Goblin Technology Unlocked: Pulpy props>
<Goblin Technology Unlocked: Brassy bodies>
<Goblin Component Technology Unlocked: Push-pull'ems>
<Goblin Component Technology Unlocked: Coaxial spin'ems>
<Goblin Component Technology Unlocked: Swashy bucklers>

The device was so light that the blades didn't really need to move incredibly fast to leave the ground. The paper-covered wings offered very little durability for harsh aerodynamic conditions or crashes but were very efficient in their thrust-to-weight ratios at small scale, which was something a device like this needed.

Taquoho lifted himself above head level and then clear of the structures. He got the hang of it quickly, thanks to his innate feeling for devices Ifrit possessed. I've been told that hovering is the hardest part of flying a helicopter, sometimes taking a week or more for a new pilot to manage. But Taquoho acted like he was born in the cockpit when he drifted around in a lazy circle, seeing the village from the air.

He dropped back down, arresting his fall with a quick pull of pitch on his rotors, which scattered a half-dozen sheets of paper from my workbench that a few of the Ifrit were quick to chase after. Probably hoping to glimpse the designs for this new flying vessel. Good luck with that, since those sheets were just the leftover comics that I'd used to paper the rotor blades.

Taquoho didn't land but instead hovered above the gathered crowd. "*King Apollo, I thank you for this gift and opportunity. I'm sure other members of the delegation would also appreciate gifts such as these, if such is your inclination.*"

Unsurprisingly, Haughty Vocal Bear Mirror Do, or whatever his name actually was, stepped forward. He spoke in a voice much scratchier and crackling than Taquoho's, and clearly less practiced in conversing with non-Ifrit.

"*Give gift vessel.*"

I looked across at the Ifrit. "Any goblin in my tribe is capable of building what I just built. If other members of the delegation are interested in receiving such gifts, then I suggest they consider forming friendships with other goblins capable of offering them," I replied, offering a grin. "This was, after all, a gesture of just that. Friendship."

With no ulterior motive whatsoever.

CHAPTER 8

TURNED OVER

Once Taquoho translated my words, I'm sure it wasn't lost on the Ifrit that, if they wanted similar treatment, they would have to learn to communicate with words, befriend goblins, and earn their favor. After all, every hobgoblin and noblin understood the fundamentals of flight thanks to the quasi-gestalt nature of the Goblin Tech Tree.

With one swoop, I'd turned them from obstacles to goals in their own right and given more Ifrit a reason to leave their xenophobia at the door. Sustained flight is a powerful motivator. Sure, an Ifrit could copy the design, and probably even improve it. But I'm betting it would lack that Goblin Tech Tree special sauce that greased the applied sciences on Rava. Gliders and coaxial Ifrit vessels were, for the moment, a monopoly of Tribe Apollo. And soon, we'd have another.

I checked on the engine seals for our first rotary engine and found that they had cured enough for a test, and now we had a forged-steel rotor for our rotary engine. It was time to put them together.

There are a lot of advantages to Wankel-style rotary engines that make them ideal for material-starved goblins. They could be built small and light, they had only a handful of moving parts, and they could burn the gnarliest, filthiest crud-laden bunker fuel mixes. Which meant a rotary engine should gobble up the impure raw bog sludge and come back for seconds.

If they're so great, why aren't they more popular, you might ask.

Well, just like my first roommate in undergrad, they're weird and a bit gross. It's tough to get their output clean enough to pass emissions standards without reducing the output below a useful level or making the engine prohibitively expensive. Luckily, I'd not yet encountered Rava's version of the EPA. It was time to get our rotary on.

I watched Sally get the engine bolted to the test block with brass bolts the Ifrit had supplied, while two wranglers came up with the custom spark plugs held at arm's length as they cracked and popped. The spark plugs were small ceramic jars with a pair of tesla wasps inside, ornery and sparking. The bog had supplied everything we really needed to create an engine. Ringo didn't know the gold mine upon which he sat. He had been using the slick-sheen oil to grease down his *hair* when I'd met him. He was lucky he hadn't gone up like a chimney when I pulled my escape.

The engineers took the plugs from the wranglers and fitted them to the side of the engine casing. The pops and snaps grew muted. With the business end of the tesla plugs pointed toward something inert, Sally brought up the bladder of fuel. And, fun fact, it was an actual bladder from some poor creature. I fitted it to the valve on the fuel intake and gave a little squirt to make sure the flow was good.

"Promo!" I called. The burly noblin trundled up with a leather band that he wrapped around the shaft of the motor. Our throttle was just a simple brass wrench the Ifrit had given us, connected to another valve. I pulled on it to open it up.

"Ready, boss," said Promo.

"Pull it!"

The noblin chief yanked on the leather band, spinning the shaft, and with it, the rotor.

Pop.

A tiny puff of smoke came out of the exhaust port and the engine went still.

Prometheus leaned down and looked at it. "What went wrong?" he asked.

"Nothing," I said, practically giddy. "It turned over first try!"

I flipped the fuel valve choke to *on* and had Promo repeat the process until it *popped* again to clear the fuel left in the system. Then I gave it slightly less fuel.

I learned a lot about small engines when I'd gotten my motorcycle—a hunk-of-junk old Triumph that had been neglected by its first owner. It wasn't a rotary engine, of course, but most of the principles were the same. The hardest part was getting the fuel-air mix right. Too much fuel meant not enough air. I needed to *lean* the mixture—that is, reduce the amount of fuel and increase the amount of air entering the combustion chamber.

Unless you want to give it to me based on theory, I suggested. *It did turn over, after all.*

<Practical applications only.>

Stingy System. I gave the nod to Promo, who took the belt again. This time, when he yanked it, nothing happened.

I frowned. "Hmm. Armstrong?"

"Yeah, boss?" my bodyguard asked.

"Help him out, put those muscles to use."

Armstrong flexed his arms and cracked his knuckles, strutting over to the eccentric shaft and taking the belt. Despite noblins being bigger, hobgoblins were still stronger. It seemed like noblins were more suited to cerebral pursuits, while hobgoblins tended to be the more physically skilled variants. Armstrong let out a grunt and yanked on it, and I heard the wood of the stump strain under the mounting bolts.

Pop, pop.

Closer. But we needed more torque on the shaft. At the flying field I'd seen more than a few old timers hand-start their planes, be it via strap, handheld starter, or just grabbing the tip and whipping the thing down. Seen a few broken fingers, too.

I had a second belt brought up, and this time Promo and Armstrong stood on opposite sides of the engine and yanked at the same time. Unfortunately, I'd been fiddling with the engine and didn't realize they'd wrapped in opposite directions, so all that happened was they both slipped and bonked their skulls on the shaft.

Once the two knuckleheads got that issue sorted out, and I double-checked to make sure they were spinning the rotor in the right direction, I had them try again.

Pop pop pop POP POP pop pop . . . pop

I moved the throttle, trying to give it enough fuel, but it still just didn't have the initial gusto with only goblin muscle. I could tie a longer band around it and have a few goblins take a swan dive off the bluff, but we weren't going to be able to rely on blue fuzzy counterweights every time we wanted to crank an engine up to idle. A decent chunk of the crowd started to disperse, interest waning. But Taquoho hovered nearby in his new ultralight helicopter vessel. He'd been flying around in it almost since I'd given it to him, with only brief breaks to rest. He'd been a bit of a menace with the thing, flying all around the bluff and nearly crashing as he learned to control it.

"*I'm not sure what the issue is from out here. Would you like me to investigate from within?*" he asked.

I cocked my head. "Would that be alright? I don't want to put you at any risk."

By way of answer, Taquoho touched down and slid from one device to the other, infusing the rotary engine with a pale blue flame. We went through the startup procedure again, getting a handful of pops.

"*I'm afraid I'm not an expert at this manner of artifice,*" said Taquoho. His voice came out of the exhaust port sounding like he spoke through an iron pipe. "*But it seems that the angular piece is struggling to gain enough speed from the manual rotation for the expansion of hot gases to sufficiently sustain the cycle.*"

"Yeah," I sighed. "That's what I figured."

Armstrong and Promo were huffing and puffing after their multiple attempts. Even with two strong variants working together, it was looking like the early attempts at a pedal-powered glider: Goblin muscle just wasn't up to the task. Even Armstrong was only matched in strength to maybe a twelve-year-old boy, and he was the strongest goblin in the entire tribe. And when I was twelve, I'd had a hell of a time trying to pull-start our battered old lawn mower. This rotary getup wasn't nearly as well-refined as a gas mower engine. I kicked the stump in frustration. What I wouldn't give for a battery-powered starter. But turning our raw materials into a battery and brushed motor was, if anything, a more technically challenging task than just figuring out the solution. The javeline threat might have been dealt with, but I didn't know how much time we had until the next crisis. I didn't want to start chasing down a different technical rabbit hole. I wanted to work the problem I had, not introduce new ones.

Taquoho streamed out from the exhaust port and back into his little aircraft, as though worried one of his kin might steal it if he left it idle too long. The blades began to spin, and after a moment to gain momentum, he was off the ground again. I watched him climb into the air. At least *something* had worked today.

I had worried that the static friction of his rotors would be too much to overcome. I'd considered co-opting an old mid-1900s design from before they really got helicopters and gyrocopters figured out. People had tried all sorts of novel ideas to try and get rotary aircraft off the ground, most of which had failed catastrophically. There'd been one gyrocopter design in my history of aviation class that was really ridiculous. Instead of torque from a central hub to get the rotor going, the rotational energy had been provided by pods at the tips of the rotors that had . . .

Huh . . .

They'd had *rockets.*

CHAPTER 9

SPUN UP

Sally! Sally!" I yelled. The chief engineer had left the boys to their toys and gone back to work on her own projects about the time Armstrong and Promo decided to put their heads together with an eccentric shaft between them. She looked up from her workstation and shuffled the mix of bark scratching and paper, not-so-subtly shifting a cartoon-covered page to the bottom. At least she had the decency to look guilty.

I narrowed my eyes. "What's that one about?"

Reluctantly, she pulled it out and handed it over, looking down and away as she did.

I took the canoneer comic and turned it right-way up, perusing the panels.

"This is about me and Chuck," I said.

Sally nodded.

"Scouting the bog."

She nodded again.

"We're sitting awful close together on this clifford."

Nod.

I handed the page back. "There sure are a lot of these featuring me and Chuck."

Emphatic nod.

If I was still able, I'm sure my face would be turning red. The canoneers were just *the worst.* I cleared my throat. "I need some of those spare rockettes that came out too wonky to fit in the guns."

Sally went to her stores and fished around until she pulled out a small case containing mismatched rockette shells. The primitive self-propelled rocket bullets we'd designed were extremely forgiving when it came to caliber and consistency. But there were still plenty that had defects so extreme they'd been deemed worthless for ammunition. They were just hollow shells, so I had to fill and pack them myself. While I did that, I explained to Sally what I needed, and she got to work with a brass fixture the Ifrit had brought with them and a couple of our ceramic bearings.

When Sally was done, we had a free-spinning arm with two handles on the back. We had to carry it between us back over to the test area. Promo had left to baste some javeline chops with bomb fruit juice, so I sent Armstrong to bring him back.

The potbellied noblin lumbered up with his mask raised and saw what we were holding. He waddled over to take it from us, easily lifting what had taken both Sally and me to carry. I envied the noblin for being able to level up, a fact of which the System handily reminded me with the *5* superimposed above his head.

"What's this gubbin do?" he asked, tilting it this way and that, and giving the spinning arm a smack. "Making more of those spinners for the hotheads?"

"Nope, it's a rocket-powered engine starter," I said. I pulled a pair of the rockettes from my pouch and stuffed one of them into the sleeve on the spinning arm. "That socket on the face should marry up to the engine shaft and the rockettes should give us a few seconds of high-speed rotation, if you can hold on."

Prometheus grinned. "Oh, I'll hold on, hoss. What's to stop the engine from turning *me* once it comes alive?"

"It's a free-spinning flywheel," I said, giving the arm a tap. "The grips are just so you can push it against the engine. When it comes on, make sure you pull back and get clear."

Prometheus nodded, hefting the starter and fitting it to the shaft on the engine. "Ready."

Armstrong scratched his chin. "How are you going to start the rockette?"

"I . . ." I stopped. "Good question."

"Gotcha covered, boss," said Promo. He whistled another goblin over. "Go get the unfinished blast'em on my workbench. Go on!" He gave the goblin a little backside boost with the top of his foot. The goblin ran off, rubbing its backside, and returned with what looked like a mostly disassembled rifle receiver without a breech, barrel, or stock. Just the grip, trigger, and striker.

Armstrong took it and held it up. "No stock? No lever?"

"Ah, was working on a smaller one, what for close-in fighting," said Promo. "Some of the lads complained about the long guns being unwieldy when the porkbellies got within arm's reach. But bring it over, yeah?"

Lord help us, Promo had already figured out pistols. Armstrong brought it over, manually pulling back the tab on the striker to cock it, then lined up the striker with the rockette in the starter.

"Perfect!" said Promo.

<Firing a rockette outside a blast'em. No way this could end poorly.>

Shaddup! If you're not going to unlock the engine 'til it starts, you don't get to claim you're helping.

<Goblin Technology Unlocked: Starter blast'ems>
<Goblin Technology Unlocked: Spinny-sparky start'ems>

Dammit, System!

Armstrong pulled the trigger and a shower of sparks and smoke exploded, followed by the freewheeling arm taking off like, well, like a rocket. I opened the throttle and turned off the choke as the rotor spun, the rockette tracing a circle of flame in the air.

Pop pop pop POP POP POP pop pop POP POP pop pop pop

The flame on the rockette flared out.

Promo spat on the ground. "Not enough fuel?"

I hemmed and hawed for a moment and ran my finger on the inside of the exhaust. It came away black and wet.

"Too much fuel," I said. "Not enough air."

Drawn air through the intake manifold wasn't going to be enough, and the fuel was too thick. I needed to aerosolize it, and to do that I needed a carburetor.

I won't bore you with the details of how we rigged up the main shaft to power an impeller that would draw fuel and air into the engine intake. It involved a few gears, bearings, a chain we'd taken from the javeline, and a lot of swearing on my part. I'd even rigged up a clever little release valve so the intake system wouldn't over-pressurize.

When it was done, it looked even more impressive, with the impeller strapped to the case and tubing made of cured gut feeding air and fuel in. But dammit, I'd built an engine, and I was going to run it. Well, technically Sally and Promo had done most of the building. All of it, really. But I told them *what* to build!

A shadow passed overhead and I looked up at Taquoho hovering nearby. "*Another attempt, King Apollo?*"

"Hopefully not an *attempt*," I said. "Don't jinx it."

The color of Taquoho's flame flickered slightly. "*The superstition of believing a disaster will come to pass by speaking of it is an imagined fancy.*"

"Next you'll tell me the power of positive thinking is a myth."

I fed another rocket into the sleeve and took my place by the throttle, turning the choke on and having Armstrong spin the rotor until the remaining fuel inside burned off. Then I opened up the choke and the throttle and gave the signal.

Sally had the starter pistol now, and she angled it up in order to reach the rockette in the starter and held her other hand in front of her face as she pulled the trigger. The miniature rocket flared to life and the freewheel started cranking the engine.

Pop pop pop pop pop

I opened up the throttle a little more, letting more fuel into the mix.

Pop pop POP POP POP

I hauled back on the lever. Over the sputtering engine I could hear the impeller whistling as it worked overtime to draw fresh air into the narrow intake throat. Blue smoke began to billow out of the exhaust. I eased up just a little. The starter kept spinning, but I knew the rockette would fizzle in seconds.

POP POP POP BRRT BRRRT BRRRRRRR

"*It is working!*" said Taquoho, excitement creeping into their voice.

"Now, Promo!" I shouted. I cranked the throttle all the way open as the noblin yanked away the starter and dove for cover. The engine rattled and vibrated, and at least one of the brass mounting bolts popped out, sheared from the vibration.

I eased down on the throttle, and the noise subsided to a dull rumble. The thing bucked underneath me like a mechanical bull, but I held on and kept adjusting, trying not to lose it. It was going to destroy itself at this rate.

Taquoho's vessel landed so hard it nearly bent one of the brass struts it used as landing gear. The Ifrit streamed out of the brass bottle and into my engine, and I felt the throttle move under my hand.

"Hey!" I said, but ceded control to the Ifrit. If anyone on the bluff knew fire . . .

The throttle adjusted itself under the touch of the Ifrit until the elemental being found the idle, and then the engine started to *purr*. Taquoho fled the engine for his bottle, but didn't immediately spin up and take flight. "*That,*" he said, "*was a very dizzying experience.*"

"You did it!" I said, laughing. "It's working!"

In the grand scheme of things, this thing wouldn't be winning any F1 races. It was putting out a couple of horsepower at max and was probably just one loose counterweight shy of flying apart and flinging the rotor into the stratosphere. But it was running. An internal combustion engine was running, *on Rava*, in my village!

I started to think something was wrong as a whine began to mount, until I realized that it was the collective cheer of almost two hundred goblins.

But there was one voice conspicuously absent from the celebration.

System?

<Awaiting query.>

CHAPTER 10

BACKFIRE

I shut the throttle. The rotary engine died, and I looked between Sally, Armstrong, and Promo, confused. "Do any of you know how to build or operate one of these yet?"

Promo cocked his head at me. "Reckon I could maybe run it, but ye lost me in the build."

"Boss, I don't even know what it's supposed to be," admitted Armstrong. "I just know it's loud and it spins and I want one."

Sally shrugged and pointed to the build guide she'd followed. I ran both hands through my fur. Somehow, the technology hadn't unlocked yet.

System!

<Awaiting query.>

What gives? It ran! It's a working engine. Where's the unlock?

<Device parameters do not meet requirements of any locked technology in the Goblin Technology Tree.>

Why?!

<Information on locked technologies in the Goblin Technology Tree is not available.>

I buried my face in my hands. I didn't understand it. The engine worked. And not just *goblin*-worked. This thing was running on pure physics—would run on *Earth*, for maybe five minutes before seizing up. It should have been enough to unlock the node in the Goblin Tech Tree.

Was it because Taquoho jumped into it?

<Ifrit do not interfere with technology unlocks in the Goblin Tech Tree, save for technologies involving the Ifrit themselves.>

Then why didn't internal combustion unlock?

<Information on locked technologies in the Goblin Tech Tree is not available.>

I pulled the lever off the throttle control and chucked it, screaming out my anger. All the goblins immediately screamed and made throwing motions, many of them throwing whatever was close to hand—including mud, bones, a few rocks, and at least one tesla bomb with a half-dozen angry wasps inside. That did a fine job dispersing the crowd as everyone ran to get away from the shocking, hissing wasps.

I sat down and thumped the back of my head against the stump.

"Boss?" asked Armstrong.

"Just go," I said. I waved a hand. "*All of you!*"

"Even us?" said a voice to the side. I looked over at a Noblin Canoneer hunched over a piece of paper on the ground.

"*Especially* you!"

The portly, oversized goblin scurried off, papers wrapped up in his arms. I groaned. Luther's canoneers chronicled everything I did at all times. I didn't need comics made of my failures.

I just didn't understand it. Based on everything I'd experienced so far, it should have worked. The engine had a working fuel intake system, a properly counterbalanced rotor, a heat sink, throttle controls, and good seals, and if the sounds from the spark-plug jars were any indication, the wasps were alive and popping. Our fuel was clean-ish burning, with more than enough power and a smooth flow.

We'd had combustion. It had been internal. As far as I was concerned, we had *internal combustion*. How was this even an issue? The System wasn't volunteering anything, either. It was being its usual recalcitrant self, probably sitting back and laughing at me on the other side of its sysadmin terminal.

The sun dropped low, and Chuck brought by a bark tray full of kilned pork. Apparently, wallowing made me ravenous, because I tucked in and didn't realize I'd finished until I was licking the grease off the bark. I handed the tray back to Chuck.

"Take it you heard?"

"Problems you can't punch or ride. Not my forte, boss," he replied, taking the bark and spinning it off into the night. "But you'll figure it out. You always figure somethin' out."

I sighed. "I just don't get it. If engines aren't a part of the Goblin Tech Tree . . . well, we're dead in the water. Does the tree *end* at the pre-industrial age? Was this whole moon thing a pipe dream?"

Chuck lifted his hand and put it in front of Raphina. "She's so close I feel like we could get her with a good thermal, boss."

"Orbital dynamics are a bit more complicated than that," I said.

"Do they gotta be?" he asked, climbing to his feet and shrugging.

I laughed, drawing my legs up so I could rest my chin on them. "Would make my job easier if they weren't."

"Maybe you just think too much," Chuck countered. He loped off into the night.

Nothing seemed to deter Chuck, or the rest of the goblins, for that matter. I *was* their king, and I *would* get them to the moon. They had absolute confidence in me—as long as I stood behind them. I'd learned the hard way that their *absolute loyalty* to a goblin king came with caveats. They'd follow me to the moon so long as I was the one leading. But if I couldn't even get internal combustion engines off the ground, how would I ever reach Raphina?

System, why do goblins follow kings?

<Refer to the Goblin King class menu, in particular the Undying Loyalty skill. Would you like me to give you the skill's description?>

No, I want to know why goblins show undying loyalty in the first place.

There was a pause.

System?

<Goblins follow goblin kings because they believe goblin kings will lead the tribe to greatness.>

And what happens if I don't? What happens if I never reach the moon?

A longer pause.

<There exists more than one metric for greatness, Apollo.>

Is this a simulation?

No answer.

Does anything I do here matter?

Nothing.

<Your tribe has decreased to 255 members.>
<Your tribe has increased to 285 members.>
<Your tribe is producing less food than it consumes by a deficit of 11.5 chooms per day.>

I had fallen asleep at the stump and woke up at the very bottom of a sleeping mound with goblins pressing in on all sides. I pulled myself out and showered off at one of the casks. In the distance I could hear the *crack crack* of rifle fire already, and the deeper *whump* of a bomb fruit going off. Some of Neil's hunters must have been getting some target practice before going out in search of game.

It was surprisingly easy to tune out the explosions, crashes, shouting, and general mayhem of the bluff village sometimes. Amazing how quickly you get used to the strangest of circumstances. Even working for a rocket company, I'd never expected explosions to be a daily part of my life. Of course, the first explosion I'd encountered had been the rocket with me riding it.

I took a look at my engine, still silent from the night before, and sighed. Maybe I hadn't refined the fuel enough. I could run it through another filter to increase the purity. Maybe I needed another wasp in the spark chamber. Maybe the throat of the carburetor was lowering the temperature too much. And maybe goblins were just meant to ride cliffords forever. There was no way to know.

Armstrong was still sleeping at the top of the pile, so I took two of my other bodyguards and went looking for Taquoho. The Ifrit had begun to integrate ceramics into their workflow, and I wanted to see how he was doing. It wasn't hard to spot the Ifrit, since he was hovering—or rather, wobbling—in the unstable air above the kilns. I worried the paper on his rotors would catch fire with the smoke and cinders starting to rise from the massive ovens.

I waved him down, and he descended. Surprisingly, he'd already modified the design with articulated legs from his old vessel and hinges along the blades that allowed them to fold up to save room. The Ifrit dropped onto the ground and scuttled over.

"Ah, King Apollo! I noticed that the sheets with which you chose to paper my airfoils have small sequential renderings of your tribal history. I wanted to ask about them."

I put a palm to my face. "The comics. I'm sorry, Taquoho. It's what I had handy while I was working. I'm sure you find it crude and reductive."

Taquoho raised a placating leg. "*On the contrary, O King! The Ifrit are formless fire and do not practice representational art, so are often perplexed by its meaning. But the format here is so intuitive to follow! Truly, I am grateful for these drawings, and some of my kin have taken notice of the history of your tribe circulating in the village. I wondered if we could perhaps see more of it.*"

"You want *more* comics?" I asked, incredulous. "I can't believe I'm saying this, but I'll talk to the canoneers."

Taquoho dipped his vessel. "*Thank you, Apollo.*"

I stepped around him to a tray of fired parts from the night before. I didn't recognize some of them, which I assumed meant they belonged to the Ifrit and were destined for delicate clockwork. "The first orders are going well?"

"*Indeed!*" said the flame spirit. "*The material has all the properties that our friend Rufus promised, and then some. While we cannot manipulate it as easily as brass, it is proving to be a most robust material, well-suited for gearing and artifice. The only problem is, well . . .*"

I got the impression of his gaze shifting and followed that impression over to the row of kilns. "Huh," I said, counting. "I thought we had at least one more."

"*You did. Until last night.*"

"Ah," I said. And laughed. "You get used to it. Ifrit tech doesn't blow up in your faces sometimes?"

"*We do not have faces in which to blow up. But I believe I understand the crude and reductive metaphor you are using to convey the normalcy of catastrophic failure. In fact, Ifrit artifice is known for its meticulous attention to detail and precision. You would be reasoned and wise to say that it is the defining characteristic of what makes a piece of artifice Ifrit, as compared to say . . .*"

"Goblin artifice," I said. "Which is the opposite. Ramshackle, loose, and . . ."

I looked at the remains of the kiln, and the ceramic parts that had been embedded halfway into the neighboring kiln.

"One bad kick shy of exploding."

"*I daresay, yes,*" said Taquoho. "*A philosopher might describe it thus: If it is not about to explode, is it truly goblin artifice?*"

I looked at the Ifrit. I looked at the kiln. I looked at the Ifrit.

"Taquoho," I said, backing away and looking around for my taskmasters. "I'm going to get you all the comics you can read, you absolute genius!"

I grabbed the nearest engineer and told him to find Sally and Promo and have them meet me at the stump.

CHAPTER 11

SAFETY NOT GUARANTEED

Give me that prybar," I said.

Prometheus handed me his new favorite tool—a metal prybar that he'd fashioned out of a ruined section of rifle barrel.

"Thanks."

I smashed the clay jar of tesla wasps off the connector, ducking as the ornery insects flew out, so disoriented and eager for freedom that they didn't even bother to sting anyone on their way out.

Promo laughed. "Giving up on your combust'em project already, boss?"

"The opposite," I grunted. I dug the prybar into the mount for the counterweight and managed to work the small plate off the back of the engine.

Sally watched in horror as I smashed the relief valve. There would be no relief.

"I don't get it," said Promo, scratching his head. "You said we needed the wasps. *And* the relief valve. And that doo-dad in the back."

"I did say that," I said. "They were very practical and very foolish."

The noblin chief cocked his head at me.

"*Too* practical. I built a *working engine.* A fully functional prototype engine. Something a human or an orc could have made with the knowledge and a good enough forge."

"And it woulda worked?"

"Yup," I said. I disconnected the fuel bladder and opened the throat, pulling a popper from my pouch, along with a small ceramic auger. I drilled two small holes through the outer layer and then tipped the globe so that the bomb fruit juice mixed in could drain out through the hole. It didn't take long until the dribble of red juice began to empty into the fuel bladder.

"Is that what I think it is?" asked Prometheus. "You sure you don't want me to do that?"

"Does your fire-crafting skill extend to contact explosives?" I asked, then said, "Forget it, don't answer that. If this blows up in my face, that's a random goblin dead. If it blows up in *your* face, that's my ignis chief gone. You're too important to the tribe. I'm not risking that."

Promo dropped his ceramic mask in place. Whether it was to keep me from seeing his expression or because he thought the concoction might explode inside the bladder made no difference, really. Not in the end. In fact, if even the *goblins* were worried, then I was on the right track. The dribble petered off, and I tossed the damaged popper over my shoulder where a bunch of squawks alerted me that it probably wasn't the best place to have done that. A small *pop* and a few angry chitters later, the System didn't alert me to any lost goblins, so we were still in good shape. I began to cackle.

"What's got into him?" asked Armstrong, backing up a bit and whispering down to Sally. She shrugged, just as confused.

"This whole time, I was trying to design the wrong type of engine," I said. I banged on the case to loosen the seals a bit. "Armstrong, get the starter."

The scrapper looked to Promo, who scratched his head.

Eager for a chance to make himself scarce, Armstrong retreated to a safe distance and retrieved the rockette-powered starter. I fished out a rockette from my pouch and passed it over, then busied myself with hooking up the fuel bladder.

"Sally, how's it look?"

She made the goblin gesture for *explodey.*

"Perfect. Armstrong, you're up!"

Armstrong reluctantly approached with the starter, and Promo pulled out the starter pistol beside him. I climbed atop the engine and squeezed the choke shut.

"Promo, give it a few spins," I said.

The noblin twisted the shaft a few times, until with a *BANG*, it nearly jerked out of his hands. He backed off to a safe distance. Or, at least, what he probably thought was a safe distance.

I opened the choke and moved the throttle to the halfway mark, then motioned Armstrong forward. "Let 'er rip, my friends."

Armstrong fitted the starter to the shaft and had Promo hit the rockette with the pistol. The tiny rocket booster ignited and started to swing the ensemble around. The engine rattled and shook underneath me, popping and hissing. Great gouts of angry, black smoke puffed out of the exhaust and a few weak spots in the seals.

Pop pop pop clank pop clang pop pop

I yanked the throttle all the way open.

The engine barked and bucked so hard underneath me I worried that it had already come apart. Metal shrieked and protested, and a small plume of smoke pushed its way out of what was once our relief valve. "Sally, plug that!" I shouted. My chief engineer ran up with a hammer and pounded the opening flatter until the leakage dropped to a small puff.

The starter began to fizzle out and Armstrong pulled it away.

Underneath me, the engine bucked, growing hotter and harder to hold on to, struggling to stay clamped around the throttle. One of the mounting bolts snapped, and the thing began twisting on the stump. It was like trying to ride a full-size mechanical bull as a toddler, but I held on to the throttle lever for dear life. The shaft was a blur. My ass was numb from the vibration.

POP POP BRRRRT POP BRRRRRR . . .

"*Come on, baby!*" I shouted over the racket.

A huge gout of black smoke and orange flame erupted out of the exhaust, thumping in time to the shaking of the motor

BRUM BRUM BRUMMMM . . .

"*Come on!*"

POP POP BRRRRUUUUMMMM . . .

<Goblin Technology Unlocked: Infernal combust'em engines>

"*YES!*"

<Goblin Component Technology Unlocked: Icky-slicky vapor>
<Goblin Component Technology Unlocked: Forced torque power>
<Goblin Component Technology Unlocked: Icky-slicky additives>
<Goblin Component Technology Unlocked: Internal press'em buster>
<Goblin Component Technology Unlocked . . .>

I cleared away the notifications to focus on what I was doing. The heatsink on the *very, very goblin* engine was glowing red hot and a heat haze had started to shimmer on the metal. I tried to push the throttle closed, but the abused valve screw snapped off in my wrench.

"Uh-oh!" I yelled.

<Congratulations.>

"Oh no!"

"Apollo, get out of there!" shouted Promo.

Sally just screamed and dove for the deck, wrapping her hands over her head. Now that she understood the motor, she definitely understood that it was about to blow sky-high. And I was sitting on top of the damn thing! Worse, I couldn't bring myself to let go!

"Help!" I yelled.

I felt a big, furry body tackle me off the top of the engine, and we tumbled across the dirt. I ended up face-down and tried to raise my head, but Chuck shoved my face back into the dirt. "Get down, Your Highness!" he yelled over the screaming whine of the engine. The canoneers were never going to stop drawing this.

The whole ensemble finally gave out with an earth-shaking clap of thunder that left my ears ringing and caused at least one building in the village to collapse. Chuck finally moved, and I pulled myself out from under him, looking around. Every goblin and Ifrit in the square was on the floor, ducked and covering, and most were stacked behind hard cover where it existed.

On the stump was a warped piece of glowing metal with a gaping wound where the internals had torn their way out of the housing.

"Where'd the rotor go?" asked Armstrong, looking at the sizzling hole.

A heavy object crashed through the roof of the air traffic control tower a hundred or more meters away, scattering goblins from the rise. The entire thing collapsed inward in a plume of adobe brick dust and wood splinters.

"Found it," said Promo.

"Boss! Booooossss!"

"Hey, boss!"

I looked over. Eileen and Neil were practically coming to blows over who would be the one to reach me first. They tripped each other up and started rolling in a knot of blue limbs and plausibly deniable sucker punches. When they finally stopped and untangled themselves, both of them jumped to their feet.

Eileen took a deep breath. "HeybossIhadacrazyideawhatifweputthatonnagliiiiider?!"

Neil just spread his hands apart. "*Combust'em boats.*"

I looked up at Promo and grinned. “Ready to build the next one?”

Promo made the moon-sign of the Church of the Right Angle over his chest and grinned back. “Forges are already fired up, boss!”

CHAPTER 12

INDEPENDENT SUSPENSION OF DISBELIEF

<Your tribe has increased to 344 members.>

<Food requirements continue to exceed supply by a deficit of 19.2 chooms per day. A spawning penalty has been applied.>

The week or so following the reinvention of the internal combustion engine passed in a frenzy of activity that saw renewed vigor in the bog iron collection and the first pumps pulling swamp kerosene out of the wells. The first powered vehicle came in the form of boats to scout and collect more ore and fuel. Wheeled vehicles weren't far behind, and powered flight was still the second priority behind food security.

But it's tough to worry about anything, even a food shortage, when you've got an engine to redline. Village Apollo started to sound more like a rat-rod car show than a medieval blacksmith's forge. Internal combustion had been leveraged to create not just our first generation of gas-powered vehicles, but other various tools and processes as well. Lathes were turning to mill out rounded parts, a motor-driven blower with brass piping had taken over for the crank teams on every forced-air kiln, and the friggen' canoneers were busy enforcing quality standards under threat of branding deviants as heretics.

But a food shortage meant we couldn't afford to rest on our laurels. And while the first generation of gas vehicles had been nautical, the second generation was meant to broaden our range and let us navigate the savannah to the south.

I watched Sally and her team assemble the frame for a five-goblin buggy. Other frames lined the yard, swarmed by goblins with hammers, wrenches, knives, and saws. We were making everything from two-wheeled motorcycles for pairs or trios of riders, to big six- and eight-wheeled monsters that carried fifteen or more goblins. I wished we had some rubber for tire-making, but you can't have everything.

After the rotary engine struggle, the rest just kind of fell into place. Basic automobiles aren't exactly complex machines, when you think about it. Rotational energy from the motor goes back to the gearbox, which sends power through the drive shaft, and a simple rack-and-pinion gear set allows for steering. These vehicles didn't even have batteries, airbags, or windscreens. Forget power steering or automatic shifting. They were the kind of bare-bones rigs you'd see in a post-apocalyptic flick, complete with hooligans hanging off at odd angles. Every type of resource we had was being utilized, from the metal frames and wheel banding to wood paneling and rims, to bone armor and suspension, to ceramic gearing.

The scent of exhaust fumes and the rumble of fresh engines reverberated through the ground. My hunters and wranglers especially had been suffering the wait for our first push out from the bluff on wheels ever since we stuck a prototype engine into something with four wheels. Can't say I blamed them. I had my eye on one of the trikes myself. Admittedly, after the accident on Earth, I'd somewhat lost my taste for riding motorcycles—not that I really could, without legs. Plus, these rough riders had little in the way of creature comforts, and sitting on the motorcycles with the engine burning below felt a bit too much like sitting on top of the kiln for my tastes.

The resident Ifrit showed great interest in our work. They flitted around, many having convinced my igni to make them versions of Taquoho's coaxial vessel. Some of them remained distant and aloof, but a dozen or more unions had come around to Taquoho's way of thinking and began ingratiating themselves with the noblin smiths and even learning bits of the common language. Besides, they got better ceramic parts from goblins who liked them than from goblins who were indifferent. They continued to possess and try out every new piece of tech we developed while the paladins looked on, probably unsure how to properly guard a possessed buggy doing a lap around the bluff five times faster than they could run.

"King Apollo," said a voice behind me. I turned to see an igni, somewhat smaller and wider than Promo—though a few of the igni were looking a bit slimmer with the food shortage.

"We have a buggy ready for a test drive. Would Your Majesty care to do the honors?"

"Of course," I said. I rubbed my hands together and grinned. "In fact, I insist on it."

I followed the igni over to the forge yard, where a group of noblins and their non-variant assistants were securing the last bolts on a three-wheeled buggy. *Secure* is a bit of a strong term, since the vibrations on goblin engines were so bad that almost all bolts eventually either sheared or worked themselves loose. Luckily, a few missing bolts didn't seem to adversely affect the vehicles much. The Goblin Tech Tree was built on the loosest of tolerances.

As with the rest of our technology, as soon as the tribe unlocked it, every goblin in it gained an innate understanding of how to use it. But *building* them was still too much for the average goblin to wrap their soft heads around, so the igni led the charge on that front. They were hammering out variations on engines from steel and ceramic in different shapes and sizes to fit the vehicles. But they were all variations on the Wankel engine we'd started with.

I climbed up in the saddle of the trike buggy, which had been designed for a taller, lankier wrangler, so it was a bit big for me. Three other goblins climbed aboard, including Armstrong, who was manning the rear rifle position. A double-barreled lever gun had already been mounted to a pintle, and Armstrong swung it around, sighting down the bore. I reached into the ammo hopper behind the seat and pulled out one of the rockettes.

The igni had made a modification to the starter that was rather genius, in that they'd affixed a permanent flywheel. Simply dropping a rockette into a slot on the engine and stabbing down with a tamping rod would start the engine up. I stuffed the rockette down the hole and one of the other goblins was ready with the tamping rod. I manipulated the throttle pedal as it went down, giving it enough gas to get the ignition going. The trike rumbled to life underneath me, and I revved the engine to get it warmed up.

Promo leaned in. "You got enough fuel for a couple laps. Break 'er in good, boss."

I gave him a quick salute and threw the trike into gear. The buggy lurched forward, nearly tossing two of the goblins off as torque hit the wheels. The whole thing tilted back as it shot forward, and I worried it would immediately tip over backward. But the front wheel crashed down and we were off, churning dust and gravel under the primitive wheels.

I peeled out of the forge area and navigated my way through the narrow lanes toward the edge of the bluff. Goblins dodged out of our way, squawking as we roared past, and then chasing and cheering behind us. They loved the engines and had all taken to making *vroom vroom* noises as they stomped invisible gas pedals. The bikes and trikes were almost as popular as the good ol' classic of throwing themselves off the edge of the bluff.

Speaking of the edge, it started coming up fast, so I cranked hard on the handlebars and brought us around to skirt the perimeter instead of careening off the side—which had happened more than once to test drivers already.

The trikes didn't have brakes. Oh, I'd invented them, and the System acknowledged that they had entered the Goblin Tech Tree. But every goblin in the tribe had staunchly refused to admit they understood the concept. So, either there was a dedicated brake-tech variant of goblin that I'd yet to unlock, or we had the tribe's first conspiracy—which seemed much more plausible now that I knew the goblins followed my orders voluntarily out of a sense of collective ambition, rather than just as a biological imperative.

I swore I'd give them a reason to follow me. Well, this trike was about four horsepower worth of reasons. Not much by Earth power standards, I know. But on Rava, it was bleeding-edge stuff. And goblins didn't weigh much.

We rode north until we hit the perimeter wall. I glanced over at the newest extension on the northwest corner of the bluff, where Javier's tailors were hard at work stitching the Ifrit cargo canvas sheets together to prepare for the launch of our first powered aircraft. I swung us around, riding in the shadow of the wall as the sentries atop it hooted and hollered down. A bit farther down, one of them kicked over a pole fixed to the top of the wall, on which a wooden target dangled.

"Armstrong!" I called out.

I heard the scrapper load the gun and close the action. The barrels thundered, and two rockettes zipped out on thin trails, punching two new holes in the target. My side goblins angled spears down toward a pair of low targets, and one cheered as the tip smacked into the target. The other's pole dipped too low, hitting the ground instead, and then launching the goblin out of his seat with an *EEEeeeeee* when the side of the trike turned the spear into a flex-a-pult.

I had to turn the trike so hard to avoid squashing my spearman that it rode up on two wheels and another goblin toppled out of the sidesaddle. Armstrong roared with laughter, barely able to hold on himself. We passed the pond and the kilns and turned south toward the airstrip. The goblins had gotten one of the launch ramps turned around, because of course they had. I got us lined up and jammed the throttle as high as my little prosthetics could push it. We hit the ramp at probably 40 kph, if I had to take a guess. Faster than a clifford could run, but not as fast as some of the revved-up bikes could go.

I let up on the gas to shift the trike's weight forward just as we hit the ramp, then stomped down hard. The iron-banded wheels shrieked for a moment on the wooden ramp, and we hit air, suspended for just a moment at the apex of our parabolic trajectory. Then we crashed back down and fishtailed. It was all I could do to hold on, let alone steer us.

"Boss!" shouted Armstrong.

"I see it!" I said, as we drifted perilously close to the edge of the cliff. I hauled right on the bars and applied more throttle to get some positive steering. The back of the trike swung out over the edge of the bluff, but momentum carried it round and the wheels bit into dirt and gravel again.

Armstrong whooped and pumped his fist in the air as I angled us back through the engineer workshop and toward the motorpool. *God*, I loved that we had a motorpool! Even if it only had a dozen wheeled vehicles in it so far, and they were so basic and bare-bones as to barely qualify as such.

I pulled the trike into a cleared spot and cranked it back to neutral, then choked the motor. I had to work some feeling back into my hands and my butt from the vibration. Goblin transportation did not make for a smooth ride.

Promo came up and gave me a hand down. "How's she handle?" he asked.

I grinned. "Like a feral hog in heat."

Promo laughed and then hem-hawed.

"What is it?" I asked.

"Speaking of hogs," he said. "We're running real low on meat. Can't run on pulp-slurp forever, boss."

"You're right," I said, looking at the assortment of vehicles. "Once Big Hoss Rig is up and running, we'll make a run at the badlands. How soon?"

"Tomorrow, earliest," the ignis said. "Day beyond more like."

"Guess we'll be cinching up belts another two days, then," I said.

CHAPTER 13

SEQUENTIAL DISTRIBUTION

Armstrong nudged me as we walked out of the motorpool. "There's always the . . ."

"*No*," I said.

Armstrong groaned. "Aww, boss, I ain't had nothing but bird bones and pulp-slurp for three days. I can't believe yer savin' all that good lizard meat for them scrawly nobbers."

"Those scrawly nobbers need food for their mission," I said. I walked to the northwest side of the village, where the platform extended over the edge of the cliff. "Besides, the longer their mission, the less they're here making those awful comics about me and Chuck."

Armstrong guffawed. "Haw! You seen that one wot with him and you and the big fish yet?"

"A long, *long* mission," I ground out between clenched teeth.

"It's *histry*, boss! It's important."

As cool as the bikes, trikes, and buggies were, this part of the bluff had been dedicated to the new pride and joy of Village Apollo: a powered wood-and-canvas airship. It would be kept aloft with canvas envelopes filled with air heated by burning scat, and we'd already tested it with eighteen goblins. On the back, it had two gas engines with paper-covered props. Two heavy slingers on each side and an armory of rifles would protect it from night haunts. While they hadn't troubled the bluff for some time, the night skies of Rava were still unfriendly to goblins. Soon the ship would be loaded with food and crew and sent northeast, to scout bluffs and see if any goblins were left after the javeline raids.

I would have liked to hop on and join the expedition. But I'd already been taught too many times that a goblin king's place is surrounded by his people. I'd go to the savannah and the badlands, instead, with Neil and Chuck and Armstrong all able to watch out for me along with as many other goblins as the rigs could carry and still move. And I wouldn't be climbing any signal balloons by my lonesome this time, either. If I'd learned one thing from King Ringo, it was that a goblin king doesn't fly solo. They roll deep.

I approached the first prototype airship (well, air *boat*, really), already floating against its restraints as some of Eileen's pilots carefully managed the scat burners under the envelope. What would have taken a thousand lizard skins was being done with the canvas the Ifrit had been using to cover their wagons. Strange to think that the cast-off canvas tying down the Ifrit trade goods was almost as valuable as what was underneath them. We were so starved for composite materials; yet one more shortfall that needed to be addressed. At the back of the ship, the first engine was being fitted with its propeller shaft. The airship was getting the lightest engines we had—lighter even than the ones going on the two-wheeled bikes. It still had to be able to fly, which meant every ounce counted.

Why couldn't the canoneers have at least been regular goblin-sized? I watched as my portly noblin chief, Luther, argued with the engineers. I came close enough to catch the tail end of the conversation—which involved Luther shouting, while the nonverbal engineer was chittering away and making rude gestures.

"What's the problem?" I asked.

"Ah, King Apollo," said Luther, turning my way and making the circle sign over his head. Despite their argument, the engineer made it too. And yes, if you're wondering, the irony of the Church of the *Right Angle*'s holy sign being a circle was not lost on me. "I'm trying to make sure there is space allotted for icons of Your Highness."

"Icons?" I said.

Luther gestured behind him, where two more of his canoneers worked at what appeared to be a clay statue of, erm, *epic* proportions. I approached it, looking up at the crown. "Is that supposed to be *me*?" I asked.

"It's how the tribe sees you!" said one of the canoneers.

"It's got more muscles than the Masters of the Universe."

<*Goblin Technology Unlocked: Artistic liberties*>

Stop helping!

I ran my hands through the fur on my head. At least it was a statue of *just* me. This was probably the kind of thing someone like King Ringo would go mad over, the narcissist. "Obviously you can't take it with you. It probably weighs as much as both of you combined. And talk about a waste of clay. How many engine cases do you think we could make with that much ceramic?"

"Oh, that's the best part," said one of the noblins, spinning the whole thing around to reveal a cavity in the backside. "It *is* an engine case!"

I stared. That explained the hole in the front side where the, erm, *shaft* would protrude. And the exhaust outlet? Well, I'll leave that up to your imagination. I covered my face.

"Absolutely not. Take the comics. Take the tools. Leave this . . . *monstrosity*. Break it down, use it to make shovels, and then bury any ideas like it."

Luther tapped a hand against his chin. "His Majesty, King Apollo, has decreed that his image be destroyed that the common goblin might know the use of the spade. There's probably a metaphor in there."

"I can assure you, there's not," I said. I turned to one of the igni working on the platform. "How soon 'til she's ready to fly?"

He glanced up at the ship straining against its anchors. "Uh . . ."

"How long until she's ready to make the voyage?" I corrected.

The ignis brightened. "Oh! That's easy! Soon as the glue on the prop dries."

"Perfect." I turned and clapped Luther on the shoulders. "I'm counting on your boys to hit every goblin village from here to the mountains, Luther. We're going to see if that big mouth skill can be used to convince other goblins to join our tribe."

"Your will, Highness," said Luther, bowing deep.

I turned my attention to the goblins crawling on top of the envelope, stitching patches over leaks. Armstrong came up beside me.

"It really is an important mission," I said.

"I know ye want to be on it," said Armstrong, patting my shoulder.

System, tell me about the Big-Mouthed skill again.

<Big-Mouthed: Canoneers are adept at negotiations and swaying the opinions of other goblins—often through sheer volume.>

They'd certainly spread their antics through Village Apollo like wildfire. Even the Ifrit were getting in on the comic book action. If they could act as emissaries to persuade other goblins to come join the tribe, that could go a long way toward unifying all the goblins in the area. Maybe I could even assimilate new variants. Feeding them once they got here was my problem to solve in the interim. But so long as the canoneers didn't put a foot wrong and get themselves Captain Cooked . . . well, even if they did . . .

The only thing that worried me was the possibility of running into another society with a goblin king. I had thought I was an isolated case until I met Ringo. Rufus and Taquoho had said that goblin kings were extremely rare, but maybe there was another one hiding up on one of those distant bluffs. If there was, and he was hostile, I had to hope his tribe wasn't bigger than mine. And if it *was* bigger than mine, I had to hope they had no way of getting to this part of the forest.

It was a literal application of the dark forest theory. If there were other tribes out there, the jungle was so hostile that broadcasting their own position only invited disaster. Every announcement was a dinner bell. And I was about to make the biggest announcement of them all.

I looked up at the sky and tugged on the anchor rope.

"Alright. We've got enough daylight for a test run to Canaveral and back. But I want clifford support on the ground and two gliders in the air."

"Yer goin' on this test run, then?" said Armstrong.

I nodded. "With you and a half-dozen other scrappers."

Armstrong tried counting to twelve on his fingers and, failing that, included two toes and then worked backward until he only had six. He nodded decisively. "More'n a handful is enough. Okay, boss. I'll round up the lads."

"Grab Eileen while you're at it. She's piloting this shindig."

"Truly momentous," said Luther.

I stabbed a finger at him. "You're coming too. Gotta make sure the blimp can even lift your fat ass."

"As you say, my king," he said, deflating. Clearly he didn't share the smaller version's love of heights.

It took a few minutes to get the crew assembled and climbing aboard. Besides Armstrong, we had Eileen as captain, an ignis for engineer, two of the canoneers, maybe eight other goblins as crewmates, and the half-dozen scrapper bodyguards. I could hear the barks from below the bluff as Chuck took off toward the hot springs. The gliders would launch to monitor as well. Each of the crewmembers also had a personal glider to help get them as close to home as possible if we had to bail out. I wasn't taking any chances—or at least I was trying to mitigate the risks of the chances I *was* taking.

That's all aviation is, really. It's an inherently risky business, and if I was going to stay on the ground just to be completely safe, I may as well have not been reincarnated at all. But the key to aviation safety is acknowledging those risks, not avoiding them. You spot them, you *plot* them, and then you come up with mitigations to make sure that whatever happens, you have a plan B, C, D, and enough backups that scrappers need to start using toes to track them.

And if all goes well, one of those plans keeps you safe when the scat hits the fan.

CHAPTER 14

GERTRUDE

There's certain imagery I've always associated with certain names. Part of it is the meaning behind the name itself. Diana, for instance. It just screams poise, class, and wisdom. Likewise, Cooper sounds like someone who can sling a couple of barrels around the farm and then fall into a black hole.

Then there are names like Melvin. You just know Melvin is going to play *Dungeons & Dragons*. Just like you know Chad is going to get a visit from campus police after pledge week. And then, at the prow of the unfortunate name boat, is Gertrude. It's a weighty cudgel of a name. It's the name of someone whose ankles look like salamis. It's the name of someone that no amount of caked-on makeup can disguise their bloodhound jowls and cigarette-stained teeth.

It's the name of our first and currently only airship. I don't make the rules. It's just what her name was. It's a fundamental law of the universe. And if you don't believe me, you can ask System.

<It's not.>

Ignore System. It doesn't know everything. The point is, when Gertrude belched to life, she was fat, slow, and she was damned ugly. I'd still have married her, though. No prenup.

The engine sputtered to life with a dangerous-sounding *BANG* before settling into an unsteady rhythm. With the throttle at idle, the paper-covered prop created very little thrust. But once we cast off the anchor lines and started to rise, Eileen turned up the RPMs and I felt the airship tug against the hot-air balloons keeping it aloft. Eileen turned the engine mount to change the thrust vector, and we pivoted as we climbed.

It seemed like half the goblins on the ground raced us to the eastern edge of the bluff, whooping and cheering. More than half of *them* followed us right off it, plummeting to the ground below.

<Goblin Technology Unlocked: Sticky-skinny combust'em zeppelins>
<Goblin Component Technology Unlocked: Thrust vectrin'>
<Goblin Component Technology Unlocked: Multi infernal engine airy-knotics>
<Goblin Component Technology Unlocked: Cluster 'bloons>

"*Gertrude's maiden voyage*," I said to no one in particular as we gained altitude. Several of the crew were in the rigging below the envelope openings, managing the scat fires that kept the conjoined balloons aloft. There were three balloons, lashed together like a snow pea, so that if one failed, the airship would *land* instead of *crash*. I wasn't worried about the goblins, of course. So far as I knew, they could fall from space and be completely fine thanks to their System-given fall damage immunity (though they'd probably burn up on reentry). But the airship was a tremendous investment of resources and goblin power. Plus, it was just so darn cool.

Admittedly, even if we were calling this an airship, it was more of an air canoe. It didn't have niceties like cabins or a galley, just floorboards that could be lifted up in order to access stores and the armory in what would be the bilges if this were a water vessel.

For the next hour, goblins scrambled all over the rigging and the tops of the envelope, checking for leaks with a complete and total lack of fear. Several swung off the side of the gunwales for little more than a lark. A few of the scrappers were arm-wrestling. Even with empty bellies, spirits soared high whenever new technology was on the docket. Wasn't too long ago that the bleeding edge was a blunt rock for this tribe. Now we were conquering Rava's skies.

Or at least contesting them.

"Sighting, boss!" shouted Eileen from the helm. I followed her pointing to where one of the gliders had burst a popper of colored powder. The scrappers all rushed to the side and leaned so far over the rail I thought they might tip the whole thing over.

"I don't see anything," I said, shading my eyes with my hand. "Must be a wrangler in that glider. They've got better eyes on the wing."

We'd been in an uneasy truce with the night haunts ever since we'd gotten pretty good at trapping and killing them and spawned enough wranglers to keep watch through the night for their attempts. But they were still out there, and we competed with them for food. That made us a threat in more ways than one. Not to mention that when we *did* trap one, we turned it into a glider. And they knew it, too.

Most of the monsters on Rava, it seemed, possessed at least rudimentary intelligence. You could see it when they looked at you. The croc-knockers held grudges. Night haunts could work out traps and sneak into even the most well-defended shelters. Even the stone-sloths and the swamp turtles were more than just base beasts. I wondered if that was a result of the System or if Ravan creatures simply evolved better brains naturally.

After a few minutes with no excitement, my crew lost interest and returned to what they were doing. I dropped my hand from where it rested at the new pouch at my hip.

It took another two hours before we made it to Canaveral. One thing Gertrude was not, was *expedient*. The eclipse was underway, and what light did emerge reflected off the photosensitive lizard frills as they swarmed up the cliff.

At the top of the bluff, my goblins had rebuilt much of the defenses, and they had upgraded weaponry to make up for the abused fortifications. The *pop* and *flash* of shock spears rippled up and down the cliff.

"Eileen, bring us in for the assist!"

Last time, we'd come by with a meager handful of poppers haphazardly thrown from a glider on the wing. This time, the scrappers broke out rifles and loaded up the portside heavy slinger with a clay ball. Eileen bled off some hot air from the envelopes, dropping us into a controlled descent until we were level with the climbing lizards.

"Grease 'em," I said. The hobgoblin on the slinger tilted it up and fired. The ball flew out in a lazy arc and shattered against the cliff face, where it spread a stain of oily grease. Lizards who tried to cross it scrabbled for purchase and fell back. On either side of the slinger, rifle barrels erupted with flame and smoke and tiny trails of exhaust. Goblins aren't accurate marksmen. Even if our rifles were capable of reliably keeping shots within a forty-five-degree arc of the shooter, goblins would still have a tendency to shoot directly behind themselves, somehow. But with a half-dozen scrappers under Armstrong's direct supervision, and about a dozen other goblins working in teams of two, we knocked twenty or more lizards off the wall in a matter of seconds. But that wasn't the only surprise we had in store.

Our ignis came forward. His mask was down, and he had a brass cask on his back, which a smaller goblin stood on top of, furiously working a pump. The ignis had an apparatus in his hand with a length of brass and a nozzle, and he held it up to the airship burners to ignite the tiny ball of scat near the tip of it. Then he leveled the pipe and opened a valve. A jet of flaming fuel shot out, splashing against the side of the cliff and igniting the oil patch already there. The flaming oil spread, creating a barrier that funneled the lizards up a narrow corridor where the ignis proceeded to roast them. I could smell the cooking meat from where I stood. Even five or ten meters away, the heat was intense.

The brass cask couldn't maintain pressure, though, and the goblin pumping on it began to get tired. Eileen brought us around, trying to hold our position in the air. But then the sun peeked out from behind Raphina, and the lizards abruptly changed their course before the natural light could harm their skin. We'd only caught the tail end of the daily battle.

Gertrude's maiden flight was a success.

CHAPTER 15

CANAVERAL

Canaveral was more organized than Apollo, to be sure. Part of that was the resident taskmaster, John, who had the unusual skills of organization, motivational speaking, and battle tactics. Unusual for a goblin, anyway. The larger variant goblins still looked up to him, despite him being a head shorter than any hobgoblin or noblin.

He greeted us as we brought Gertrude in for docking by running up and offering a stiff salute beneath the brim of his tortoise-shell helmet.

"The men'r ready fer inspection, sir!"

"At ease, General," I said, returning the salute. I hopped down from the side of the airship and clapped my commander on the shoulders. "Good to see you well."

John grinned. "Aye, got the camp up and running right enough. Piggies left it a mess."

"Well, we did the same to them," I reminded him.

John beamed.

Wood creaked behind me. "Oy! Is that who I think it is?" Armstrong shouted down.

John grinned and shaded his eyes. "Armstrong!"

Armstrong jumped down, laughing, and pulled John into a hug. Tight as brothers, those two. They'd defended Canaveral together and then stood shoulder-to-shoulder against the maulers when Rotte and Hrott attacked Apollo.

"Now he's just a couple hours by airship," I said. "Should be able to get over here more often."

Armstrong looked at me, a question in his eyes.

I sighed. "Fine, let's go see the new defenses."

The two goblins whooped and ran off. I looked back up to Eileen. "Keep the engine warmed up. We want to be back before nightfall."

"Aye, boss!"

The Noblin Canoneers struggled down—mainly due to the fact that their arms were filled with sheafs of papers. I eyed them warily.

"Just what's in those?" I demanded.

Luther had the decency to look chagrined. "Erm, tech manuals, Majesty?"

"They're comics, aren't they?" I asked.

The smaller noblin piped up and squeaked "Important histry!" before Luther could clamp a hand over his acolyte's mouth, somehow managing to keep from dropping his load of papers.

"King Apollo," he said. "The goblins of Canaveral don't get to witness your daily deeds or see the marvelous machines of the Church of the Right Angle. It's only fair they receive records to inspire them in their fight. You cannot always be here, after all. And where you are not . . ."

I sighed. Goblin loyalty could falter, especially during combat—which was a daily occurrence at Canaveral. "That's those persuasive skills at work, I suppose." I looked around. "Still, I wish I knew why the lizards are so persistent here. They were winning before, but they must know they can't make headway against our improved defenses."

The smaller canoneer managed to free its mouth from Luther's hand. "Oh, that one's easy, boss!" he said. He shuffled through his papers and pulled one out, handing it over. Sure enough, it was a comic. And it depicted an event that must have happened long before the bluff assimilated into Tribe Apollo: a group of goblins venturing into the plains, finding a nest, and taking some eggs back to the bluff for dinner. Apparently, the lizards had never stopped trying to get them back.

Okay, so maybe recorded history in comic book form wasn't so bad. But they could have at least drawn the lizards with the right number of limbs and not ten times the size of the goblins.

"I guess that explains it," I said, handing the comic back. "Fine, spread the good word. Tech manuals first. *Then* 'histry,' okay?"

Both goblins made the circular icon over their chests and trundled off (since it's quite impossible for noblins to scamper).

I was left to my own devices with a handful of bodyguards. I spent some time just wandering around Canaveral, looking at how these goblins had managed their shelters. We'd reinforced and mixed the tribes, but here and there I still spotted one of the Canaveral originals with their green-tinged fur from before they'd hitched their wagons to Tribe Apollo. The history of Canaveral *was* the history of Tribe Apollo. And as much as I didn't care for comics, the canoneers were making sure that our tribe didn't stay prehistoric as it advanced into the industrial age. Armstrong, likewise, had colored striations on his arms and back that matched *his* original tribe before the piggies had reduced them to only three members.

It was also much, much quieter at Canaveral. Village Apollo was now constantly humming with the low roar of engines, the crackle of gunfire, and the ringing of steel hammers. Canaveral still sounded like a jungle, filled with bugs and birdsong and, yeah, some light construction.

At the airship, a couple dozen goblins worked to unload the supplies we'd brought on the test run. We'd brought rifles and raw materials, and even the pump-action flamethrower was staying, along with the ignis to wield it and work a local forge. The piggies may have been gone, but Canaveral was still the central hub of our martial might, where goblins were turned into warriors. Having the lizards back and basically throwing themselves into our larders helped with the food supply problem, but it didn't abate it completely.

In the distance, I could see more bluffs to the north and east. That's where this airship was really meant to go, and I wondered what the noblins would find there. Wayward tribes looking for direction? More goblin kings? Or just the smoking ashes of the goblins we were too slow to save from the porkbellies? Was there something I could have done differently to get there faster?

I'd already run the first few thousand years of human history in a short time—though the days blended together without a lunar cycle, so it was difficult to say just how long I'd been here. I guessed it had been a couple of months. Progress would slow in the preindustrial age as development became more reliant on complicated tools and processes, and it might become a trickle when it came time to make things that normally required computers.

The basic principles of organizing a computer weren't actually that arcane. Turning binary into useful logic is primarily a function of yes/no/maybe/sort-of questions filtered into an output. Granted, that's an extremely simple explanation of a very nuanced discipline. But it had only taken forty years for humans to turn that concept from punch-card machines to personal computers, and a huge amount of that time had been spent refining and miniaturizing those gates and switches to something that could fit on a microchip instead of a small bus.

I stared down from the edge of the bluff for more than a few minutes and tried to imagine the forest cleared into a great field, whereupon hundreds of thousands, or maybe even millions of goblins stood with flags, simulating the various *why*, *and*, and *for* gates that would comprise a basic program. Each individual gate doesn't need to understand the whole process, just its individual part.

God, could you imagine trying to build a computer out of goblins? It would somehow manage to overheat and explode, I'm sure. It would be more bugs than features, and half the goblins would probably eat their own flags. And somehow, it would *still* spit out useful data thanks to the Goblin Tech Tree.

But I digress. The point is, now we'd unlocked gas engines, we'd likely be moving into a period of refinement and expansion as we moved toward laying the groundwork for the infrastructure a Space Program would require. Metalworking, assembly lines, and tools to make processes more efficient and effective. More tools to make the acquisition of resources more efficient. Tools to make *tools* more practical and useful. And without OSHA anywhere in sight to gum up the works. Workplace safety was heretical to the Church of the Right Angle, after all. Safety inspectors were likely to be burned at the stake.

And eventually, it would all lead back here. How could it not? Village Apollo was becoming a sprawling town, and if the goblins continued to reproduce, it would eventually develop into something of a cliffside metropolis. So, this would be where the rockets would launch. Oddly prescient and prophetic that I'd named it *Canaveral.*

I whistled for attention and spun my finger in the air in a *round up* gesture.

Armstrong reluctantly parted ways from John with another bear hug. The canoneers finished handing out the rest of their religious literature and rejoined us at the airship. Eileen had her crews stoke the burners and get the engine ready to spin up again, checking the various lines and simple pipes that supplied the primitive engine with fuel.

We climbed aboard, and my air delivery captain started up the props with a *bang* and a gout of angry black smog. I patted the side of the rumbling engine as it whumped and thumped, spinning the paper-covered prop and pushing the airship against its anchor lines. Within a few minutes, we had enough lift and the engine was warmed up enough to start pushing us back east toward Village Apollo.

One of the Canaveral gliders took off to escort us back, rocketing up to high altitude for a view of the land. Most of the Canaveral goblins came and waved at us as we began our slow ascent, though it was much faster than our takeoff from Apollo now that the cargo holds had been emptied of supplies. Not entirely empty, though, as the Canaveral goblins who had stowed away below deck were only mostly managing to stifle their giggles and only occasionally bumped their heads on the floorboards beneath my feet.

The golden hour approached as we rode west, with the sun slipping low enough to start opening Raphina's eye. I watched the pink surface and verdant forests of the moon begin to sparkle, and I narrowed my eyes at its surface. Hadn't it had more water before? What I was looking at now seemed like a desert lined with long, narrow fissures that had claimed some of its landmass. Maybe I was just seeing a side I wasn't used to looking at as the moon rotated on its axis.

The *crack* of a popper directed my attention lower, where our escort had detonated one of the warning signals. Night haunts had been spotted on the wing, and this time I caught the silhouette below us. The early evening flights had spurred at least one of them out of their nest.

And it was drawing closer.

CHAPTER 16

ACTIVE DEFENSES

"Battle stations!" I called out. I stomped on the floorboards as well, signaling our stowaways to come out and be useful. Goblins started crawling out of every hole, nook, and cranny on the airship until we had about two dozen strong. Not so long ago, this would have comprised the majority of the tribe.

"Rifles and slingers at the ready," I said, marching up and down the deck. "Spears at the gunwales. Be ready to repel night haunts."

Most of the goblins listened, breaking out the weapon and armor stores on the airship and beginning to pass out arms and ammo. Someone handed me a plate carrier and I pulled it on. Other goblins ran to the sides, looking for any sign of the dreaded silhouettes of the natural goblin predators that prowled the Lanclovan nights. Over the sound of the engine puttering, I could barely make out the distant baying of cliffords in the forest below.

Armstrong stood next to me, leaning over the rail, fists tightened around his rifle as he scanned for threats.

"Anything?" I asked him.

The hobgoblin squinted. Now that it was getting toward sunset, he'd have much better eyes than the rest of the goblins. "Nuffink yet, boss."

<Your tribe has decreased to 342 members.>

I scanned as well. The sky was completely clear, but it shouldn't have been. "Can you see the other glider?" I asked. "Can *anyone* see the other glider?"

Nervous chitters went up and down the line. This was early in the evening, even for night haunts. The creatures relied on stealth and the cover of darkness to do their hunting. In the grand scheme of things, they weren't that tough—except compared to goblins. But the sky was still their domain, and we'd been pressuring them like they'd pressured us.

I heard a soft beating that at first I dismissed for the snap of wind against the canvas, but it stopped. "Steady!" I called. "Spread out, don't strain the rigging. Watch both sides. Eileen, lower the throttle."

My air delivery captain hauled back on the throttle and the engine dropped to a low rumble.

Luther approached from behind, wringing his hands. "King Apollo, should we not make all haste to the village before we're noticed?"

I shushed him. "You'll face worse than this on your mission," I said. "Besides, we've already been haunted."

The noblin canoneer gasped. "How do you know?"

"Because," I said, eyeing the numbers ticking down in a small System window, "we're losing altitude."

The night haunts, while not especially heavy, still weighed as much as a dozen goblins or more. That was apparently a few too many extra for Gertrude to hold aloft. We weren't in danger of crashing, but if we dropped four thousand feet, we'd still be in for a bad night.

I grabbed one of the goblins and pointed up the rigging. "Check up top," I whispered. "Be careful you don't damage the balloons."

He swallowed and moved to clamp his flint knife between his teeth. Once it was secure, he swung out on the webbing and began to scramble up the lines. I watched him disappear around the swell of the canvas as he scrabbled up to the top of the envelopes. All around me, goblins looked out, nervously clutching weapons. I steadied some of them, offering reassurances I only half believed myself. But I was their king, and I had to act the part.

Since the goblin on top of the airship didn't get immediately eaten, there was only one other option.

"It's on the bottom!" I called out. "Eyes over the side, it'll come from below!"

Goblins rushed to the sides again, angling spears and gun barrels down. A goblin next to me squawked and stabbed down, drawing my attention. But just as it did, the aircraft lurched hard to port, sending two goblins careening over the side and out into the air.

The night haunt clawed its way up, raking its talons against the bottom of the wooden craft for purchase. Its lantern-yellow eyes glared up and it snapped its jaws, biting off the front third of the spear of the goblin on that side.

"Hold fast!" I yelled. "Keep the ship balanced! Spears and rifles!"

Rockettes thundered behind me as goblins with rifles took aim and started to pepper the creatures with shots. Thick smoke began to choke the deck of the airship, but I saw the gunners score several hits. Still, night haunts were tough, and not prone to giving up easily. Rather than retreat, this one hissed in rage and went berserk, pulling itself through the hail of fire and sweeping several goblins aside to get at the gunners. I was surprised it knew what was hurting it, but then night haunts were unusually intelligent, even for Rava creatures.

Other goblins charged out in front with spears tipped with ceramic points or tesla wasps, giving the gunners a chance to reload as they thrust forward with weapons that the haunt couldn't simply ignore. Armstrong was in the middle of the line, deadly spear pushed up and blocking off a wide section of the ship. He stabbed his spear forward, shouting a battle cry. I hoped he would score a killing blow. Instead, the night haunt snapped his spear's haft, tackled the hobgoblin holding it, and drove its beak down into Armstrong's chest—only to recoil with a pained howl as the sharp beak cracked into a ceramic plate.

"Armstrong!" I yelled, pulling my new toy from my belt and rushing forward.

The hobgoblin gasped in pain, but the fact that he wasn't eviscerated thanks to his armored vest gave me hope. He raised his arms in defense as the night haunt started to rake with its claws. In such close quarters, the riflemen were hesitant to fire. Now that the creature was aboard and in the melee, they stood as much a chance of hitting their own friends as they did the raging beast attacking them. I raised the new prototype pistol Prometheus had given me and pulled back the hammer. Holding it in both hands, I centered the barrel on the bulk of the night haunt before it could drive down and hit Armstrong in the head.

I pulled the trigger, and the gun bucked in my hands. The night haunt jerked, whipped around, and smashed me with its tail. I went tumbling across the deck of the airship and nearly toppled over the side, but one of the scrappers managed to grab me and haul me back.

"Thanks!" I said.

"Don't mention it. We almost got 'im, boss!" said the scrapper, grinning.

The night haunt seemed to realize it was on the back foot. These weren't the same helpless goblins it had preyed on a month ago. We had armor, we had weapons, and we had a fighting spirit hot off victory against the piggies. Hurt, confused, and suddenly frightened for its life, the night haunt pivoted and leapt from the side of the airship, spreading its wings into a glide. Several of the goblins raced to the side in order to take shots at the fleeing creature.

I ran up to them, slapping the backs of their heads to get their attention. "No, no! The slingers! Tag it!"

Armstrong was the one to take up position at the heavy slinger and angle it down at the fleeing night haunt. He launched a dart with a smoldering pot of scat, and it managed to strike the night haunt on the flank with the glowing, smoking marker. It bucked in midair and flew harder.

"Eileen, full throttle!"

My pilot kicked the engine up to full power, and the airship shot forward. She heaved the rudder and turned us after the fleeing night haunt. The smoke from the smoldering tag gave us a trail to follow, even when the night haunt pulled away.

"Come on, come on," I said as we pushed the airship north after the creature. We followed it for twenty-five, maybe thirty minutes before I lost it among the crags northeast of Village Apollo.

"There!" said Armstrong, pointing at a bare cliffside.

Eileen followed his direction and dropped our altitude. I caught the hint of smoke coming out from a cave about two-thirds of the way up. Unless someone in there was cooking s'mores, this had to be our night haunt hideout.

"Not too close," I warned Eileen. I suspected the night haunts kept sizable communities, like bats. I'd seen them circling in numbers, after all. And occasionally they attacked the village in pairs. We'd fended off one, but two or three would overwhelm the airship's defenses, not to mention make it too heavy to maintain flight. Sure enough, I spotted two forms crawling on the rock face, and the flash of yellow eyes in the waning light. Neither was the one we'd fought.

"Alright, Eileen. Get us out of here," I said.

Armstrong leaned on the gunwale and looked at the hole in the side of the hill as the bulky airship turned. "What do you want to do, boss?"

"We've got bigger worries for now." I said. "Let them slink back home for now. But they've been harassing the village for ages. It won't be long before we're the ones paying them a call."

CHAPTER 17

FLAME OUT

<Your tribe has increased to 369 members.>
<They're still hungry.>

I didn't want to try attacking the night haunt lair without a more defendable airship and enough guns and flamethrowers to take them on. Ravan creatures seemed to sometimes have a much stronger alpha variant, and I'd bet money there was one in that cave. Fighting on top of the bluff where we could swarm them was an entirely different beast than going into their caves after them where *they* could swarm *us*, and we'd be limited in numbers and stumbling around in the dark.

Since I didn't have more airships in my back pocket, I added that to our long, *long* list of shortfalls that fell in the *materials* column. The biggest thing limiting our growth and expansion from Village Apollo was just a lack of pretty much *everything.* And the answer to solving it was, as ever, get more goblins to throw at the problem. But reproduction was feeling the squeeze with the food being tight, and more goblins would require more calories.

The pulp-slurp (what the hobbies had taken to calling the slightly alcoholic paper-pulp mash) helped as a stopgap, but it created the problem of putting food in direct competition with paper production and lumber for housing. Pulping the wood itself took time, resources, and labor, so it just wasn't efficient for it to drain down goblin gullets in the long term. Not with paper being so useful. Besides the comic books, gliders, and propellers, Buzz now had all the tools he needed to make windmills. And rather than making the bluff start to resemble a Dutch Impressionist painting, I had some wild conceptual designs perfect for the limited space.

I spent most of the next morning designing a clutch system with the help of Taquoho and Buzz while the construction team slathered paper sheets over helical windmill frames. Since almost all of our iron and engines were earmarked for aircraft and ground vehicles, except for the few that were powering lathes and other rotary tools for Sally, Buzz needed another source of mechanical power for his construction teams. Wind was the obvious answer, as there was no shortage of it at the top of the bluff. There was, however, a shortage of space—and water.

Currently we were bringing up water by hand and bucket, which was incredibly inefficient. But I'd devised a wooden trough aqueduct with a rotating screw—a design dating back to ancient Greece, really, but just as effective as a motor-driven pump at moving water uphill. It would also be good at pulling the oil out of the springs in the swamp, which would ensure we had a steady supply of kerosene out on the badlands to power our limited motorpool.

"What we need," I told Buzz, "are airborne windmills on kites or balloons."

"Lot of lines to get tangled," said Buzz. He slid a ceramic gear into place and closed up the gearbox. Working the clutch lever, he was able to marry up the drive gear of a new device with a test spire being manually spun by a handful of goblins. It made a protesting shriek for a moment as the teeth found each other, and then a *thunk* as it slid into place and the output shaft began to spin.

"This'un is ready," he said.

"Let's get the helix mounted." I raised my voice. "Clear the airspace, please!"

The windmill designs caught the attention of the Ifrit as well, and not just Taquoho. Those who had managed to make friends with igni hovered nearby on variations of Taquoho's coaxial copter, while others watched from a distance with their silent human guardians in tow. Only about half their number were still in their original proxy vessels. The other half had apparently gone somewhat native and were spending most of their time inhabiting various gadgets and devices around the bluff—including one that had taken a buggy for a driverless joy ride. A clear difference had begun to form between the two halves of the delegation, which included several splits and formations of new unions.

The more brass we used in our construction, the more likely the Ifrit were to hitch rides. Rather than being a nuisance, it was a boon. Engines carrying Ifrit ran more smoothly and were less prone to stalling. Gearing with an Ifrit was less likely to jam or break, and any moving parts were more resistant to wear or breakage when one of the fire spirits was on board. Gliders flew more accurately and more efficiently. The kilns even heated faster and used less fuel with an Ifrit relaxing in the oven, which I took to understand was something like a sauna for them. Across the board, the presence of the Ifrit had improved the goblin technology out of little more than curiosity and boredom on their part.

But it wasn't all sunshine and roses. Taquoho set his copter down nearby and watched as the paper-bladed helical wind turbine was fitted to the shaft. I glanced down at him.

"Your friends still planning on leaving?"

"*I hesitate to name them as such. But yes, Apollo, they are soon leaving.*"

"Can't say I'll miss 'em," I said, hauling back on the clutch so it didn't spin the output shaft as the helix started to rotate. The former de facto leader of the delegation (whose name I won't even try to pronounce) had kept his distance since I'd snubbed him in favor of promoting cultural crossover with his contemporaries—

an endeavor which had been quite successful. But the recalcitrant faction was preparing to return to the City of Brass with a shipment of ceramic parts. "Stuffy bunch. No offense."

"*This union will be going with them,*" said Taquoho.

I dropped the clutch lever in surprise, eliciting squawks as several goblins were smacked by the ensemble they were trying to assemble.

"What? Why? I thought you liked it here!"

"*Simplifying our feelings as 'like' is a crude and reductive description for a very complex platter of emotions that strike us, especially when faced with the prospect of departing both the village and your company,*" said Taquoho.

"I'll miss you too, buddy," I said. The pale flame flickered with surprise. "So, why leave?"

"*Tabun is certain Haut Voclai Behen Mira Do will report negatively about his time here, and how little we stand to gain from anything beyond a distant trade agreement. We must present the King of the Ifrit with an alternate perspective to extoll the virtues in continued . . . friendship. I do not know if we shall be allowed to return.*"

I could see that over-stoked Ifrit bad-mouthing (flaming?) us to their king. Beside me, a trickle of water began to fall into the waiting basin as the screw carried it up from a collector halfway down the bluff. We'd need another ensemble to reach from the staging point to the base of the bluff, but even eliminating the need for dedicated vertical transport would free up dozens of labor hours per day spent on goblins simply hauling water up the side of the cliff. Those were goblins Buzz could dedicate to making more windmills that ran things like lumber saws.

<Goblin Technology Unlocked: Screw pump'ems>
<Goblin Technology Unlocked: Parched pole pump'ems>
<Goblin Component Technology Unlocked: Aqua-move'ems>
<Goblin Component Technology Unlocked: Sticky-spinny press'em shafts>

Thanks, System.

Now that we were reaching the near-industrial phase of our society, the more tasks we could automate through captured power (be it steam, wind, or combustion), the faster we could expand. Instead of having twelve goblins hacking at a log, we could have six goblins feed it through a wind-powered saw. Instead of twenty working a gravity hammer and mixing sticks at the paper presses, we could have ten . . . you get the idea.

Taquoho's pale flame dimmed slightly. "*Quo would have liked to assist your infernal engines in traversing the badlands*," he said.

I leaned back and ran a hand under the outflow, bringing the water to my mouth. Establishing wind power was thirsty work. "Maybe you'll be able to come back. You're my unofficial ambassador, you know. Whoever was most senior in this delegation doesn't matter to me." I looked out over the edge of the cliff. "You crossed the desert and the badlands to get to us. What should I expect out there?"

"*Little that would think twice of making a meal of a goblin, I'm afraid. Predators, territorial beasts, great herds, furtive shaman, and even orcs have come deeper into Lanclova than ever before.*"

"How did you cross them?"

"*The Ifrit know many ways through the land. Some are safer than others. But we have the Paladin. And the orcs fear us as demons and spirits of their slain kin come to haunt them and play tricks. We go where beasts and orcs dare not.*"

I sighed. "Part of me wishes I could go with you. See the City of Brass."

"*It would be our honor if you were to do so.*"

I shook my head. "Can't leave the tribe. Armstrong would probably lock me in a box if I tried. And he'd be right to do so. If I got separated from the rest of the tribe, it would be easy to—"

"*To what?*"

"To get lost and not find my way back."

Taquoho flashed a myriad of colors, the living flame equivalent of a belly laugh. "*King Apollo, surely you must know we would provide a guide for your return.*"

I'd almost let slip the Head of the Snake skill. Even though I trusted Taquoho, the Ifrit as an organization was still an unknown agent in the grand scheme of things. While I'd grown incredibly close to the fire elemental union and was going to miss them dearly, no one outside the tribe needed to know that all they had to do to eliminate the entire tribe was stab me a couple hundred times. Hell, I didn't even like that *Ringo* knew about it. And he had the skill, too!

I straightened and whistled for a goblin runner, sending him with a quick order.

"If *I* can't go with you, maybe I can still at least send someone to speak for Tribe Apollo."

A few minutes later, Luther came waddling up with one of his fellow canoneers in tow.

"Just the noblin I wanted to see," I said.

"I wish to support my king's plans," said Luther. Both noblins made the sign of the moon over their chests.

I reciprocated, which seemed to make them happy. "Taquoho is leaving the bluff. I want one of the canoneers to be my voice in the City of Brass."

The canoneer in the rear began to speak up, but Luther smacked him with a meaty palm before turning back to me.

"Highness, this is a task I ought to handle myself. I shall bring the canon to the Ifrit *personally*."

"Uh-huh. And it has nothing to do with the fact that it means you won't have to ride the airship north to look for other potentially hostile tribes," I suggested.

The noblin chief sputtered. "Highness, there is no one in the tribe better with the pen than me. No one more versed with the histry of your—"

"Relax," I said, patting him on the side of the arm. "You've got the job."

I nodded down at the lazily spinning blades on Taquoho's vessel.

"Take care of Taquoho," I added softly. "I don't trust the other Ifrit."

Luther nodded. "I shall guard him with my life."

CHAPTER 18

DIVIDED IDEAS

<Your tribe has increased to 375 members.>
<Blue goblins need food badly.>

The day had finally come. Big Hoss Rig was ready in all her eight-wheeled glory.

Before we could put the pedal to the metal, I squared away the canoneer airship mission. All told, the expedition to the northern bluffs consisted of two canoneers, six scrappers to guard them, an ignis to keep the engine running, sixteen forest goblins, and Eileen.

"You're sure you want to do this?" I asked.

"Gotta see it done right, boss! Means *I* gotta see it," said Eileen.

Far from afraid, my intrepid air delivery chief was champing at the bit to take the aircraft to unknown reaches—farther than any Apollo goblin had ventured from the bluff on the back of a craft the likes of which this world had never conceived, at least not without the help of magic. I had to imagine there was some wizard out there on Rava somewhere with a floating ship, or, hell, maybe even a flying castle.

"I'm trusting you to get them there and back again," I told her, clapping her shoulder.

She grinned back. "And I'm trusting *you* on making certain something's here to eat what when we're home." She held up a hand to the side of her mouth. "*Elsewise, we're eatin' noblin.*"

I eyed one of the portly canoneers struggling aboard the airship with an armful of drawing supplies. He wiggled his chubby legs as he tried to navigate himself over the gunwale with his arms full. I got the impression Eileen was only half joking. Quarter joking, at worst.

I stepped back, and Armstrong swooped forward and scooped up the new captain of my airship into a hug. "Take care, little sis!" he said.

Eileen giggled and pushed his face away, kicking the scrapper until he dropped her on the ground, where she proceeded to sink her teeth into his leg. Armstrong howled and shook his leg until Eileen dislodged.

"Alright, alright. We've got somewhere to be, Armstrong," I reminded him.

The scrapper grinned and mocked spinning a steering wheel and stomping on a gas pedal. "*Vrumm vrumm*, boss! Let's get at it."

I left the airship dock with my bodyguards in tow and headed over to the motorpool, where something of a scene was occurring. Taquoho hovered near a fuming Promo, who was arguing with a flickering, flashing Ifrit that I soon made out to be the delegation's senior member. Two paladins were nearby, hands on sword hilts, which sent a chill down my little goblin spine.

"Hey, hey!" I said, jogging up. "What's the ruckus?"

"Finally!" said Promo, throwing up his hands. "Boss-man, yeh gotta tell 'im!"

"Tell him what?" I asked. I looked up at the hovering Ifrit. "Taquoho?"

Taquoho flitted nervously. "*Haut Voclai Behen Mira Do is insisting the rest of the Ifrit accompany him from the village. Many of the unions who move the landwalkers are refusing.*"

"What? Why? Where are they?"

Promo leveled his hammer at the motorpool. I looked closely, and began to see a host of pale colored flames glowing in engine air intakes and exhaust ports. And a lot of discarded brass bottles and slumped-over flying brass vessels nearby.

"Oh . . ." I said. "But we're leaving the bluff today. We're taking the fleet out into the badlands."

"*Yes. That is why they are wishing to stay.*"

Haut von *whatever* shifted hues and made a series of dissonant tones.

"*Haut Voclai Behen Mira Do demands that you force the recalcitrants from these ceramic and steel vessels so that they can perform their duties,*" Taquoho translated.

"I . . ." I cocked my head and looked over at my chief smith. "Promo?"

"What am I to do?!" he shouted. "I told this crawler I ain't exactly able to evict 'em. What should I do? Bang on the engines 'til they get headaches? They got no heads, boss!"

I ran a hand through my fur, groaning. "Is the senior delegation member planning on taking all of the landwalkers?"

"*All of the landwalkers, all of the Ifrit, and all of the paladin,*" said Taquoho.

Jesus. He was trying to pull everything and every*one* out of the partnership with Tribe Apollo. No more Ifrit, no more hybrid goblin tech, no more blows to his ego as he watched other Ifrit make friendships and gain flying bodies. No wonder his decision was unpopular. He'd lost a lot of clout. I knuckled my eyes and thought.

"We've been firing parts day and night, but you don't have enough ceramic parts to fill all the landwalkers," I said. "One or two at most. Does he have enough unions to support two landwalkers?"

"*He does,*" said Taquoho.

"How about this: Take the two landwalkers. When Rufus gets here we'll have enough parts for another shipment. We'll send them along with him."

I didn't need a translator to tell how well *that* suggestion went over.

Taquoho interpreted anyway. "*Haut Voclai Behen Mira Do says any Ifrit remaining here are removed from the protection of The City. He will not leave paladins here, and he will not be responsible for those who decide to stay.*"

"Well, they're grown Ifrit, and they can make their own decision," I said. I stopped short of adding that it was probably a coincidence I'd had Promo coat the throttle levers and steering columns in powdered zinc.

Haut von Behen smoldered. And let me tell you, no one smolders like a fire elemental. But eventually, he turned and stomped off on four ornate legs. I shook my head. "Taquoho, you sure you don't want to stay as well?"

"*Would that I were able,*" said the airborne Ifrit. "*In my absence, there is another union who has grown comfortable with the spoken mortal language. I believe he is in the three-wheeled infernal engine Prometheus test-drove late last night.*"

I shot my chief smith a dirty look. He avoided eye contact. "Just breakin' 'er in, boss. Trust."

"Uh-huh," I said, unimpressed. "Alright. So we're going to have Ifrit with us. Taquoho, I can't guarantee their safety, either. We're going out into the wilds and it's going to be dangerous."

"*My friend, they have watched the great inland sea dry and drain through cracks, leaving only brush, grass, and sharp stone behind. Countless blinks of Raphina's watchful eye. But in all that time, they have never crossed it at speed nor witnessed such artifice as your engines. They know the risks of which they assume—better than you, I dare suggest—and consider themselves the most fortunate of all Ifrit.*"

I huffed. "Hell of a speech. You come up with that on the spot?"

Taquoho's flame flickered. "*We may have bade our minds be elsewhere whilst Haut Voclai Behen Mira Do spoke at length. Alas, we must join him presently.*"

"Unfortunate. Stay safe," I said.

Taquoho dipped his props to me in acknowledgment and hovered away. "*Keep watch over my kin, please.*"

I watched the Ifrit go. Even if he didn't want to leave, I understood the sense of duty that compelled him southward. I couldn't imagine the king would be too happy about a mutiny among the manual laborers in his delegation, the porters and drivers meant to move freight and turn their eyes down. Well, Tribe Apollo wasn't exactly a bastion of workers' rights, but every goblin was equa—no, that wasn't true either. A caste hierarchy was practically a design feature of the goblin social structure. I just wanted to believe our way was better. And I'd only been doing it for weeks. The City of Brass had been kicking for what sounded like centuries, if not millennia.

You didn't get that kind of cultural longevity without being clever. How many countries on Earth could claim an uninterrupted heritage stretching back a thousand years? Egypt, maybe? I'm not an anthropologist and I'm no longer dating one, so I can't really answer that.

With daylight burning in the sky, and the sun still low enough for Raphina to at least give us a side-eyed glare, I headed into the motorpool to muster up some road warriors.

CHAPTER 19

MADNESS MAXIMUM

This may come as a shock, but supporting the troops was not my only reason for leading the badlands expedition.

Some might say I have an impulsive streak, or that I'm prone to unnecessary risks. I got a lot of flak whenever I rode motorcycles or flew planes, and more when I joined the NuEarth astronaut program. I think there's just a unique type of clarity only achieved with speed. A way the world seems smaller and more interconnected when you're cruising across it at 150 kph, through the air at 250 kph, or out of the atmosphere at fifteen miles per second. Ask anyone who does it, and they'll tell you.

Rava, above all else, seemed like a very large world. Vast distances separated even close points—at least to a tiny goblin. A distance traveled in an hour on a highway might be a week or more's journey through Lanclova. And that was discounting the myriad dangers you might encounter. Anything I could do to bring the points of the world a little closer together, I was going to do. And I was going to do it myself.

Plus, I loved me the heck out of speed freak movies. And I wasn't going to pass up the chance to cross the badlands as part of a motor-punk convoy of hooting, hollering, back-firing hooligans. Let's be real here. Going to space was living my dream. But tearing across the desert with the boys? That was living my *fantasy*. What's the point of living a second life if I didn't get to *live* it? Hide behind some wall like Ringo and I might as well still be dead.

But I was still taking a page out of Ringo's book. There were no less than 150 goblins in the motorcade, all of them carrying weapons, tools, armor, and whatever else they thought might be useful, from canoneer comics to spanners to baskets of spare rockettes. If goblins had moms, they would have packed them lunches. *Have fun storming the castle.*

As they say on Earth, the hype was very real. Neil, Chuck, and Prometheus were all there. And since Armstrong went where I went, that made four taskmasters *and* a king. The most tippest-toppest brass assigned to any one task, and it left only a handful of leaders actually *at* Village Apollo. This expedition was rolling deep, and we were coming back with enough to feed the tribe, or there was little point coming back at all.

I walked through the motorpool, looking at the assembled goblins, and noticed something of a trend. Some of them had plate carriers with the thin ceramic tiles. Others had on gear that offered less . . . coverage.

"Armstrong," I said. "Why do some of these goblins look like they're going to a bondage party?"

"Oh, that? That's just yer S&M Club, boss!"

My words caught in my throat. "The, uh, the *what?*"

"The Shafts and Motors club! Resident gearbox fanatics."

"I see. And the leather straps?"

Armstrong scratched his chin. "Less weight? Airy-dynamics?" He snapped his claws. "Airflow! It's hot down on the badlands."

"I see. Carry on."

The Shafts and Motors club hooted and cheered as wranglers started to mount up on the thirteen working vehicles we'd managed to cobble together. We had six buggies, two trikes, a trio of motorcycles, a single *mono*cycle (which is like a single big wheel that the driver sits in the center of), for some reason, and the Big Hoss Rig on eight wheels with Promo sitting at the sticks. The fleet *swarmed* with goblins. Each vehicle had been built to carry far more than its recommended amount might have been on Earth, and at least twelve goblins were on each buggy. Each motorcycle had goblins front and back, as well as a sidecar with a rifle mount, and the BHR alone carried almost thirty. The trikes carried a half-dozen goblins each, and the monocycle? I was surprised any of the goblins were brave enough to go near that thing, but a single member of the S&M hung from the ape grips.

"Ladies and gentlemen!" I yelled.

A resounding cheer drowned me out for a moment. I held my hands up for quiet. "I'm not one for speeches. So . . . *start . . . your . . . engines!*"

As one, the entire expedition started making *brrrrum-brrrrum* noises as the drivers fed rockettes into the starters and the fleet rumbled to life. The sound of all the rotary engines going was incredible. Visible flames shot out of many as drivers maxed out the RPMs, but the Ifrit stowaways kept them cycling smoothly. I could feel the thump of the fleet in my chest and vibrating through my blades, translating through the bluff like a living thing. I couldn't help but grin.

I made my way over to the buggy Taquoho had mentioned and climbed aboard. The hobgoblin in the driver's station scrambled out of the way, deferring pilotage of the craft to me and booting another goblin off the back to make room. Armstrong muscled his way into the sponson and checked the action of the rifle mounted there. I revved the engine, pressing a prosthetic down against the spring-loaded throttle pedal.

I raised my hands above my head and made the sign for the Church of the Right Angle.

"*Ad Luna!*"

Those capable of speech repeated the mantra. The rest just chittered and cheered. I kicked the trike into gear and pulled out of the motorpool, the convoy behind me. Chuck pulled up alongside, popping a wheelie on his motorcycle as his gunners held on for dear life. He saluted, grinning so wide I thought the top of his head would flop off. He slammed the front wheel back down and sped out ahead.

I leaned down. "Taquoho said you can speak," I shouted over the engine, "You with us? What's your union's name?"

"Please, O King, Tabun' Quo'Horal has acquainted us with the mortal custom of familiar brevity. It would honor us for you to call upon this union of Giral Mal Ksch as Girmaks, and we shall call you Ap. We have also made study of the practice of 'hunting' and wish for it to be successful, though we take no sustenance from the practice."

I laughed. "Apollo doesn't really need to be shortened, but if you like, I suppose Ap works. You going to earn your keep on this trip?"

"I shall endeavor to make this the best vehicle in the fleet," said Girmaks.

I slapped the top of the engine. "That's what I like to hear!"

"Would you like me to assume the steering and rotational combustion control?"

I didn't know what stars had aligned or when they'd give me an opportunity like this again. "No thanks, Girmaks, I'd like to keep it on manual for a little while."

"As you wish, King Ap!"

At some point I'd have to introduce the concept of theater to the tribe so I could teach them to re-create some of the movies I've seen. I pressed down on the throttle, feeling the RPMs surge in the rotary engine. Sure enough, the presence of the Ifrit made the engine transitions smoother, the steering tighter, and even the suspension less brutal on my backside.

At the south end of the bluff, we'd expanded the freight elevators to make a pair of extra-wide platforms. As much as I wanted to fit the whole fleet on one, a single platform simply wasn't strong enough. I watched as the first half of the vehicles went down, and then the platforms were hauled back up for the second set. More wranglers waited at the bottom with cliffords trained to run without riders.

By the time the process was complete, the departing Ifrit and the paladins were already descending the cliff face. I saw Taquoho hovering down alongside the brass vessels of the delegation members. Halfway down, they were joined by Luther and his retainers, who beat them to the bottom, shrieking as they fell.

I hopped off the trike and went over to help Luther back to his feet. He'd donned some robes that looked like they were made of leftover canvas scraps and shiny lizard frills, now hopelessly dusty. I took his hand and leaned back, hauling the portly noblin back to his feet.

"Thank you, O King. Truly, your magnanimous nature knows no limit."

"Anytime," I said. "We'll take the Ifrit to the border of the grasslands, then we're headed east. You'll have to take them from there."

Luther nodded and tried to beat the dust off his robes to what looked like no measurable effect beyond a small cloud that made nearby goblins cough. He made a quick circle over his heart and I left him to wait for the Ifrit.

Climbing back up onto the trike, I glanced over at Armstrong. "How do you think he'll do?" I asked.

"Yer too hard on 'im, boss. He's still a tasky and a noblin. He'll do us proud. Trust."

I curled my lip. "We'll see."

The Ifrit delegation joined us, and I revved the motor and started down the eclectic array of winding roads south that would lead us to the edge of the jungle and to the scraggly plain beyond. Trees rushed by as the faster of the vehicles shot ahead, trikes and bikes and ol' one-wheel all kicking up dust from iron-banded wheels. I pushed the RPMs up and shoved the buggy into high gear. With the Ifrit smoothing the gearbox transmission, I barely felt like the whole thing was going to explode underneath my seat. I whooped and hollered along with the rest of the tribe as the convoy of gas junkers thundered through the forest, eager members of the Shafts and Motors Club hanging off the sides with spears, cleavers, slingers, and the odd rifle.

The badlands weren't going to know what hit them.

CHAPTER 20

ON THE PROWL

After splitting from Taquoho's group with a final wave, we pulled out onto the open plain, farther than I'd ventured even by glider. We cruised across piebald grassland and bare, rocky turf while the sun beat down overhead. Armstrong was right about one thing: It was *hot* without the canopy cover of the forest. Of course, we were also riding unstable internal combustion motors burning explosively enhanced kerosene.

Not having to bear multiple riders, the cliffords were easily able to keep pace with the convoy, even ranging out ahead in some cases. They'd adapted well to the dense clutter of the jungle, but this was their natural habitat, and they dove through the grass stands like Olympic swimmers, barking their heads off and circling back for more. Wranglers rode bikes alongside to give them some semblance of order and direction.

We set a northeasterly course toward the rising sun, leaving a trail of dust behind us that climbed into the sky. I stood in the stirrups and leaned over the handlebars, enjoying the sense of speed as the terrain rushed by. The wind surged through my fur and the engine rumbled under my feet. This was almost as good as flying. *Almost.*

Speaking of flying, I spotted the flash of reflective lizard skin in the air, and Chuck pulled up alongside me.

"It's a glider," he said. "They've spotted something,"

"Let's check it out," I said. "Lead the way!"

Chuck took his bike ahead, raising his shock spear overhead and spinning it before pointing in the direction the glider was facing. The convoy whooped and cheered as they turned north-northeast, cutting across a small stream and bounding up the other side through a stand of scraggly trees. We rode for a couple of hours, keeping the circling glider in flight as it rode thermals and pointed the way to our destination.

The eclipse came and went. As it receded, I could see the flash of sunlight on water far in the distance. And near it, a small herd of white creatures with two legs and long tails. Pay dirt. I didn't know what they were, but I was sure they were delicious.

Chuck caught sight of them, too. And then the cliffords caught the scent. At the wrangler's whistle, they broke out to the right, bounding into the grass and vanishing from sight. One of the other bikes pulled up alongside.

"Pass word to Promo, take Big Hoss Rig and the fueler and set up near the water."

The bike dropped back to pass the word. Behind me on the trike, the goblins readied various weapons and tools, including lengths of rope with nets, slingers, tesla prods, and more than a couple of premature sets of eating utensils that they had to have filched from the paladins.

Armstrong opened up the magazine on his rifle and stuffed a handful of rockettes in, but I held out a hand to stop him. "Hold off if you can. We want herd animals if we can get them. Herds can be driven and bred. Carcasses have to be hauled and butchered."

"Aye, boss! Just in case, then, yeah?"

Sounded prudent. Herd animals suggested herbivores. Herbivores drew carnivores, and we didn't yet know what kinds of beasts stalked the plains. "Just in case," I agreed.

Rufus's bestiary had described large cats, bipedal lizards, diurnal birds at least as big as night haunts, and some manner of burrowing predator. But most of it was folklore, rumors, or just plain fabrication. The fact was, the interior of Lanclova was inhospitable to the "newcomers," as the Ifrit dubbed them. Which made any outside information about it based more on conjecture than experience.

I scanned the grassland for any sign of predators, but the trike was a little too low to penetrate the tall grass stands. Still, I didn't see any immediate threats. Behind me, one of the buggies was extending a line attached to a kite with a goblin strapped to it to get eyes in the air. That should give us vision for miles in every direction.

Unfortunately, the herd spotted the paper wings on the glider and decided they'd had enough to drink. The creatures, maybe thirty or forty strong, wheeled and started bounding in the opposite direction. All around me, engines roared as wranglers opened their throttles all the way up. Not one to be left in the dust, I did the same.

About that time, the cliffords broke out of the brush much farther up, startling the herd and forcing them to shift directions. No longer running directly away, they cut an angle that would let us close the distance. The goblins on the trike chittered and whooped as we neared, smacking the side of the vehicle with the butts of spears and the sides of cleavers as if to spur the iron steeds on.

As we got closer, I was able to make out more details of our prey. They reminded me of something between a kangaroo and a horned jackrabbit—with horns not all that dissimilar from the shape and sweep of my trike's handlebars. They were a little taller than a hobgoblin, with four eyes set wide, able to track us as we pursued, and long arms that they used for turning by slapping the ground. They also had thick haunches, and they moved in a bounding leap that carried them close to five or six meters per bounce as their long, floppy tails waved in the wind like streamers. Getting close enough to discern detail also started revealing their levels as between 6 and 10.

Strange creatures. But those haunches were thick, and one of these things could probably feed ten, maybe fifteen goblins for a day. My brain was vibrating too much to do the mental math, but if we got even a few of these creatures, it would be a huge boon for the village.

The creatures wheeled again, this time toward a grassy area where they must have hoped they could lose us. One by one, they started hopping through the wall of grass, vanishing as though they had turned into smoke. And it was true that these vehicles wouldn't do as well in thick grass as they would on bare dirt. But we weren't helpless, and we weren't afraid to get dirty.

The bikes split up and headed in either direction and I fell back behind a four-wheeled buggy with a wide ceramic cutter on the front.

"Armstrong, get 'em in line," I said, securing a scrap of canvas over my nose and mouth.

Armstrong stood up in his station and cupped his hands. "You lot, queue up! Single rank, onna double!" he shouted.

The vehicles pulled in, and then the front buggy hit the grass stand.

His cutter flayed the grass, sending clippings through the air as he carved a path ahead of himself. He necessarily slowed, and I eased off the throttle so as not to hit him from behind. The walls of grass rose on either side of it, taller even than the goblins atop the buggy who hadn't bothered to mask up and were currently coughing up and spitting out grass clippings.

One of the goblins on my trike got snagged by a scraggly branch from a tree in the grass field, and I heard his cry of *EEEEeee* as we kept moving, but I couldn't afford to stop. Hopefully he would find us before nightfall.

The front truck burst out the other side of the grass stand, back onto hard turf, and the driver opened its throttle back up. I pushed mine to the max as well and spotted the motorcycles on one flank, moving ahead to make sure the herd couldn't deviate again, while the cliffords sprinted up another.

The herd itself started to tire. Their breakneck pace slowly dropped, and individual animals began to lag behind. With the motorcycles and cliffords penning them in, the main convoy gained ground. The lead buggy drew close enough that the goblins on board started throwing nets and lassos—which immediately got tangled in the buggy's axle and caused it to spin out.

"Look out!" I shouted.

I jerked my steering to the right, aided by Girmaks, and narrowly dodged the grass-cleaving blade from making my leg remnants even shorter. Several of my passengers were not holding on especially tightly and flew off the sides of the buggy. The monocycle had been following me too close to react when I swerved, and they ramped off the front of the cleaving buggy, steel suspension acting like a springboard to launch the unfortunate, screaming pilot in his one-wheeled abomination at least thirty meters into the air. The accident caused a chain reaction behind me, as more vehicles were forced to slow or swerve to avoid wrecking against the buggy. Dust from all the wheels skidding across the ground rose up in a choking cloud that confused all four directions for a minute before the wind blew it clear.

We got it sorted, but the bulk of the herd used the distraction to build distance again. All that lagged behind were the old, the injured, and a few juveniles who couldn't keep up. I got us back on track and the trike began to catch up to the stragglers who fell behind the herd. Three vehicles, including the monocycle, the cleaver buggy, and one tipped-over trike did not rejoin the pursuit. We'd make do.

"No ropes!" I shouted over my shoulder. I didn't need a repeat of the buggy's blunder. I reached down to a holster by my knees and pulled out one of the tesla prods with a snapping, buzzing wasp pinched between its tines. As we drew even with one of the exhausted creatures, I thrust out my rod and was rewarded with the *snap* of electricity. The creature locked up mid-hop and toppled over. The goblins on the trike cheered, and I grinned myself.

I'd never been a hunter on Earth. My old man had told me only bakers and thieves woke up early enough for that sort of thing, and he didn't have the belly for an apron or the face for a mask. Just one of those weird things fathers say, I guess. But the point is that it didn't run in my family. Now I was riding the plain on a trike, zapping animals into submission with my tribe. And it felt *good,* to both the human and goblin sides of my brain. There was something primally satisfying to it.

We pulled farther ahead, and two of my gunners with reed dart guns shot another pair of wasps at another horn hopper. It bleated as the insects struck it, and it tumbled ass over teakettle with the angry bugs buzzing for freedom in its flank.

All around, vehicles veered off and chased down onesie-twosie hoppers as they broke and ran in different directions. But the main herd was still making its escape with renewed vigor.

"Armstrong, what's our fuel look like?

Armstrong opened up the brass tank. "Gettin' low, boss. Just below that line you scratched."

The bulk of the herd was still ahead. But we were also getting farther away from our support vehicles, and I didn't want to spend the evening trudging back to the lake we'd passed with bladders to fill and carry back just because I got greedy.

"Alright, load up the ones we stunned. Let's rendezvous with Promo and celebrate our first hunt with a proper fry-up."

That got the loudest cheer of the day.

CHAPTER 21

THE HARD THINGS

We drove slower back to the pond where Promo had set up the BHR. We took advantage of the stunned state of our newest livestock to feed iron pins through the septum of each animal and attach them to a line. Some of them surrendered to their fate as soon as they woke up, trotting alongside the convoy with heads lowered and tongues lolling. Others resisted, painfully, and the wranglers had to box a few snouts to bring them around. One of the motorcycles pulled up, and I looked over to see my wrangler boss handing off the controls before making the jump over to my buggy. The goblins on the bike squawked as their center of gravity shifted, falling back with a bad case of the wobbles.

"How'd we do, Chuck?"

"Way better'n on cliffords, boss. Seen these hoppers before but never caught the jump on 'em. Sixteen tied up. Ten of those can feed the hunt, and the rest we can send along tomorrow."

I nodded along. "Imagine if we'd gotten more of the herd. Our food problems would be sorted. We were *so close*."

"We'll get 'em, boss. We'll fuel up and track 'em again tomorrow."

I patted the engine beneath the trike. "You did great today, too. Nice job on keeping this engine running smooth."

"*Thank you, King Ap. This union experienced much excitement and thrill.*"

It took us about an hour to get back to the watering hole where we'd first spotted the herd. Promo had already unpacked the BHR, which was the next iteration of the portable goblin tower—on wheels, this time.

Since a forest canopy didn't exist out on the badland plains, we had the equivalent of a dump truck's rotating payload, only this one rotated a telescoping square tower onto the ground. Hollow inside except for a series of nets, it could sleep over a hundred goblins, with room for more at the top. Not as tall as the one we built in Huntsville, but hopefully just as secure. Especially with hobbies on bikes running night patrols. We detached it from the rig and staked it down.

Promo had two other igni and about twenty non-variant goblins with him, just there to back him up when setting up the rig and with whatever else Promo needed around the camp. More than a few of our rides were dinged up and needed maintenance. Luckily, he already had a forge fire *and* a cookfire going. They were, of course, the same fire.

I pulled the trike up near the tower and hopped down, shaking the dust from my fur. The wind sweeping across the badlands carried a lot of dust and debris. Promo eyed the hopping creatures we'd brought back, barely managing to keep his drool from dripping. "I, uh, see it was a success," he said.

"Not nearly successful enough," I said. "We've already had one total loss, and we'll need another vehicle tomorrow to take back whatever we don't eat tonight."

"We planned for attrition," said Promo. He rubbed his chin. "Want to start setting up here? Get a couple structures going, spare parts, some basic resources . . ."

I looked around. "It's got mud, grass, and fresh-ish water." I eyed the brackish, brown pond. "That's bricks and something to drink, at least. Be good to have a solid base of operations, and it's only a few hours southeast of Canaveral. Alright, let's do it."

Promo nodded and poked at his fire.

The goblins made quick work of the animals set aside for dinner. I didn't know if I'd ever get used to them tearing through prey like a school of land piranhas, but they had ten animals skinned and quartered as fast as you can blink, and the various bits were spitted and being turned over the coals by one group while another bunch went to work turning bones and gristle into tools. Soon the camp was settled into an evening of repairs and crackling fat starting to render. We kept the remaining hoppers in the lowest level of the BHR tower, which would hopefully keep them safe from predators. Or, failing that, alert the goblins sleeping above before the predators got *to us*.

Our first day on the plains had been fortunate in how few goblins we'd lost. I knew there were still a few stragglers out in the brush that might get picked off before finding their way to camp. But hopefully they'd find some way to survive the night on the ground.

Goblins weren't designed to be on the open plain. Maybe there was another variant suited to it already out here, like King Ringo's boglins. But without the trees and the bluffs, it seemed to me like isolated goblins were a snack waiting to happen. Still, in terms of our losses, we were doing well. Downed crewmembers were below my replacement reproduction projections for the sleeping arrangements in the tower, which were too large per-pile for optimal spawning efficiency but made good use of the available space inside.

I worked on the vehicles with Promo until dinner was ready. Lord knows I'd been elbow deep in an engine or two on Earth. Personally, I prefer rocket motors to Wankels, but I'd take what I could get on this new world. Finding problems with my designs wasn't hard from this perspective. The badlands weren't gentle on the primitive vehicles with their iron-banded wooden wheels. Replacement parts were the most jury-rigged contraptions this world had likely ever seen. By the time we were done with the repairs, I'd replaced the dust in my fur with grit and grime from the engines, and I smelled vaguely of the thinner lubricant oil from fish livers that we'd mixed in with the spring kerosene.

No one ever said this was going to be glamorous. But at least I was going to bed with a full belly for the first time in what felt like a week. And in the morning, I'd see to it that tomorrow was an even more successful day for the desert warriors of Tribe Apollo. I looked up at the stars above while I ate, and at the big shadow that was Raphina's closed eye marking a wide circle in the sky. It didn't have rings or a bullseye, but it was a target nonetheless.

We'd come so far in such a short time, but there were still so many steps along the way. Every thought I had, every decision I made, every goal I set; it was all meant to take us closer to Raphina. But none of it would matter if the tribe starved. And I didn't need to feed hundreds of goblins in order to reach the moon. I'd need to feed *thousands*, maybe *tens* of thousands of goblins by the time we were through. An entire nation working together toward a single challenge of space exploration. It was like JFK said:

We choose to do these things not because they are easy, but because they are hard.

I yawned, and the stars began to blur in my vision. I dropped the licked-clean bones I was holding and stumbled my way over to the BHR tower, climbing past the livestock into one of the nets stretched across the interior where several other goblins already lay snoring. I tossed myself on top of the nice, warm pile. And before long, I was out.

CHAPTER 22

ACCIDENTAL ANIMAL HUSBANDRY

<Your tribe is no longer starving. A spawning penalty has been rescinded.>

<Your tribe has increased to 401 members.>

<Congratulations! You have unlocked a new tribal benefit: Controlled Breeding. You may now prioritize the spawning of variants within the tribe. Would you like to view the sub-menu?>

I blearily selected yes. The new screen flashed in front of my eyes with a set of sliders underneath labels for all my unlocked variants. I played around for a minute, watching as dragging one slider up or down influenced the rest. Not all variants were equal, it seemed. The igni and the canoneers required more of the total variant capacity, while taskmasters required more still.

I dragged the slider for canoneers down to the lowest it would go, closed the window, and went back to sleep.

I woke up some time later, still sleepy and contented from the meal the night before. Starlight filled the opening in the top of the tower, with the barest glow of dawn gilding the eastern horizon. The tower swayed back and forth, pushed by the wind. I think the motion was what had woken me up. I wasn't worried about it tipping over, since we'd secured it with cords staked down at each of the four corners. I mumbled to myself and rolled over on the top of the pile. I could get at least another hour's worth of sleep in before we got the convoy on the move.

<Goblin Technology Unlocked: Thundercleave scratchy-post>

Wha . . . ?

A particularly stiff gust hit the side of the tower, and I heard the lines part with a *snap*. The whole thing tipped dangerously, becoming a tunnel of squawking, startled goblins as sleeping mounds all shifted to one side. That, of course, accelerated our rotation. I shouted in surprise as I went zero-g for half a heartbeat before the tower collapsed.

<Your tribe has decreased to 391 members.>

Panicked, screeching goblins worked to extricate themselves from the nets and iron and wood that had quickly turned from fortress to prison. I tried to free myself from the sleeping net and eventually resorted to simply biting through the cordage to get free from the tangle and out into the early morning light.

Goblins poured out of the collapsed BHR tower like ants scurrying out of a compromised hill, confused and disoriented in the dark. The hoppers we'd sequestered in the bottom of the tower all bolted, seeing their chance at freedom. They raced into the darkness, collectively shrieked in alarm, and then came racing back *through* the camp, knocking goblins aside as they decided we were better than whatever they'd found waiting.

Slowly, a lumbering shadow resolved, pawing at the downed tower. I squinted to get a closer look and then held my hands up against the sudden glare as an arc of electricity split the night between the two massive tusks of a white, shaggy creature. It was like someone had taken a mammoth, then taken away the trunk and squished it down shorter and wider and bleached its fur. It hunched down on wide paws with stubby toes.

It caught sight of us for the first time as well, flinching back in confusion. Numbers appeared over its head. *36.* The bioelectric arc cut off, and the creature faded back into shadow.

One of the goblins got ahold of a rifle, and I heard the *crack* of a shot splitting the early morning. The—what had the System called it, a *thundercleave*?—shied back, growling. Another crack followed, and the beast growled in response. A small silhouette ran out in front of the beast with its hand raised. It tossed what it held, and the flash of a popper exploded against the animal's tusk in a brief, bright flash.

The thundercleave took a half jump back, planted its feet, and lowered its head.

"Uh-oh," I said.

The bioelectricity snapped again, igniting an arc of what must have been extremely high voltage between the tips of the two tusks. Its front paws flexed, digging up earth, and its massive shoulders hauled the thing forward as it charged through the camp.

<Your tribe has decreased to 385 members.>

Most of the goblins got out of the way. The few that didn't scramble out of its path in time were caught in the bolt between its tusks. I saw a brief flash of big-headed skeletons, and then all that remained were rapidly expanding clouds of blue fur.

"Move, move!" I shouted.

The thundercleave tore past, swinging its head in a wide arc, and I managed to dive down and avoid being trampled under its wide front paws and rear hooves. I bounced on the ground with the impact of its massive footfalls, covering my head as it bounded over me.

Not interested in sticking around, apparently, the gigantic beast plowed through one of the trikes, smashing the vehicle into a cartwheel that shredded it from the force of the spin. The thundercleave shadow receded into the night as its footfalls continued to resonate through the hard-packed ground.

I climbed to my feet, knees shaking, and stared after the retreating shadow. I felt a pair of hands on my shoulders, steadying me.

"Boss! Boss, you alright?"

"Armstrong?" I asked, staring up at the hobgoblin. I shook my head to clear it, then shook his hands off my shoulders. "To the vehicles!" I shouted. "Everything we've got, move, move!"

The disoriented goblins snapped to attention like my voice had jolted them as bad as a tesla wasp. It was close enough to morning that we hadn't been put into a sleepless stupor, and they were *hungry*. The crowd of disheveled, rudely awakened goblins piled into the buggies, and the roar of engines started to split the night. I hauled myself up onto one of the four-wheeled buggies and looked around.

"Where are the wranglers?" I asked.

"No good to anyone, woken up like they was," said Armstrong, swinging into the driver's station. Much to my dismay, a canoneer seemed to have been born overnight before I could de-prioritize them, and he scrambled into the seat to my left with a handful of crumpled paper and a charcoal stick.

Armstrong dropped a rockette in the starter. "Lucky my boys went down early, so at least we got scrappers."

"It'll have to do," I said.

"You don't mean to chase that fing, do ya?" he shouted over the roar of the starter.

"Heck yeah, I do. The System let me see its level. Which means we should be able to take it down."

<That is a poor guiding metric.>

Armstrong threw the buggy in gear and we peeled out, chasing the receding shadow of the thundercleave. We may have lost the extra horn hoppers we'd kept in the base of the tower, but this thing was *big game.* I bet it could feed the whole tribe for a month. Maybe longer. Not to mention it had bioelectricity, like the wasps. Only this wasn't enough to just shock a goblin, it was enough to vaporize one. *Millions* of volts. Which meant that electricity had to be stored, channeled, insulated from the rest of the creature, and eventually released. That meant natural capacitors. And if I could figure out a way to release it gradually, instead of all at once? Well, that would make a fine battery.

The sun crept over the horizon ahead of us as we pursued the thundercleave. It looked back at the wedge of vehicles behind us and howled before lowering its head and charging away.

"Keep after it!" I shouted.

Armstrong floored the accelerator. Luckily we'd fueled up the vehicles the night before—the ones that didn't need critical fixing, at least. Surprisingly, the monocycle had survived its encounter with the bladed buggy, and rolled along right next to me, piloted by one of the leather-bound S&M Club goblins.

On my other side, a half-dozen bikes, trikes, and buggies made up the bulk of the fleet. Slowly, we started gaining on the thundercleave. It must have realized it wasn't going to outrun us, so it spun around, claws dragging deep furrows in the ground.

"Slingers ready!" I yelled. "Here it comes!"

I worked the crank on my own buggy's heavy slinger along with three other goblins, and we got the payload in place as the thundercleave dug its paws in and lurched toward us.

"On my signal!" I shouted as I cranked.

The other vehicles must have thought *that* was the signal, because most of them launched their payloads. Cast nets shot skyward from several vehicles, while others launched rocket-propelled poppers. Any goblin with a gun fired it, and even the monocycle goblin leaned out with a pistol and took a potshot.

Most of the nets fell short, but as the thundercleave began to charge, one managed to get tangled between its paw and right tusk, and it stumbled. Armstrong jerked his wheel to the side as the bulk of the thing tipped mid-charge and it rolled over, right where we'd have been in another second.

Three goblins shouted war cries and leapt from the buggy, catching the thundercleave by locks of its thick, shaggy fur. They climbed it, trying to keep their balance, and attacked it with spears, cleavers, and knives. Its fur was, unsurprisingly, an absolute deterrent to the close-quarters weaponry. We weren't going to take this thing down by stabbing it.

The thing pushed to its feet, shaking to try and dislodge the goblins on top. Two of them flew free, while the other managed to stick his spear deep enough to lodge it and held on for dear life as he whipped like a flag on a pole.

The thundercleave growled, and the lightning began to arc between its tusks again. It reared up on its back legs and then dropped into a charge at the circling vehicles.

The goblins in its path scattered in a dusty scramble as wheels spun out. One trike wasn't so lucky, and the 'cleave managed to plant a heavy paw on the back quarter as it ran past, flipping the trike and crushing a few of its riders.

<Your tribe has decreased to 387 members.>

The rest of the goblins bailed out as the thundercleave wheeled around, digging its tusks down and tossing the wreckage into the air, where it spun before crashing back down. All the while, gunfire rang and poppers popped against its hide, to little avail.

I cursed to myself. This thing was flesh and blood. We could kill it, but not with what we had here. We needed heavier weapons. Cannons might do the trick, maybe heavier rockets. But varmint rifle rounds? Might as well have been BB guns and slingshots.

"Pull back!" I said. "Make sure we get the Ifrit out of that wreck."

"Boss! Dust cloud! Something's coming!" shouted Armstrong as he swung us around close enough for the stunned fire spirit to jump from the destroyed truck into our own engine.

I stood up at the gunner's station, watching as a wedge of large, horned creatures barreled toward us on four hooves, with even larger creatures interspersed with the pack. They looked like muscular antelope. But that wasn't what worried me.

They had *riders*.

CHAPTER 23

HEALTHY COMPETITION

Regroup!" I said. "Keep distance!"

I didn't know what I was dealing with here, but we were not ready to be facing cavalry in the middle of a fight we were already losing. Armstrong pulled us out about the time the thundercleave noticed the new arrivals. It bellowed out a warning before turning and running again.

"Ready all guns and slingers!" I shouted as the badlands cavalry came on. But rather than angling for us, they shifted toward the thundercleave. As they did, I got a better look at the riders in profile. They weren't human, that I could tell. They were shorter—maybe halfway between a hobgoblin and a human. They were lean and lanky, with long arms, and they each wore wraps around their heads to keep out the dust. Their saddles were minimal on the antelope, but still ornate and worked with beads and charms. Their weapons, which sported black metal blades, were likewise decorated with feathers and beads.

One of the riders broke off, coming close enough to us to get a look of his own. I saw the puzzled tilt of a head. Clearly not sure what he'd found, he yanked his reins around and kicked the sides of his mount back to rejoin the chase. At least he wasn't immediately hostile.

"Who are they?" I shouted down.

"Dunno, boss. Wot we doing?" Armstrong called back.

I considered, watching them spread out to flank the thundercleave and keep it from heading for a thicket of tall grass. They clearly knew their way around the plains.

"Follow them," I said. "But keep your distance. Maybe we'll learn something. They obviously think they can take down the thundercleave."

Armstrong kicked the buggy back into gear and we shot off, with the other goblins following behind us. We maintained a respectful distance as the hunting troop ahead of us got riders out ahead of the beast, casting back some sort of dust that made the thundercleave flinch and break stride. It slowed enough for the larger of the hunting animals to draw close, and much to my surprise, hunters leapt from the tops of the bunkers onto the back of the thundercleave. These ones had thick, sharpened poles, and they wedged them down around the head and tusks of the beast to arrest its head movement.

The beast, caught, tried to work its head loose. But couldn't manage it. It tried to arc electricity between its tusks, but the poles must have had grounding wire, because the voltage just sparked off one tusk, and nothing else happened.

"Look at 'em go," said Armstrong, standing up in his station.

I climbed down closer to the engine. "Girmaks, you with us?"

"*Indeed we have that privilege.*"

"What are we looking at here? Elves?"

"*No, King Ap. These are orcs. It is rare to see them this deep in the interior.*"

Orcs. Rufus had all but warned me about them, with their name for Rava translating to something like "To be trampled beneath our feet."

Judging by how neatly they'd trussed up the thundercleave, I wondered if they might actually be capable of conquering anything they wanted.

"Based on what Rufus said, I'm surprised they didn't attack us," I thought aloud.

"*The orcs believe the Ifrit are spirits of their ancestors. They will not readily attack if they see subtle flame in your company.*"

I looked down at the pale glow. "Seriously? Do the Ifrit maintain this fiction?"

Girmaks flared with indignation. "*Of course not, King Ap. The Ifrit have told them many times this is not truthful. But they do not believe.*"

I looked out across the plain. The orcs had finished off the thundercleave and were beginning to process it. We held positions over the next hour as a large train of orcs on pack animals caught up with the hunting party and began to unload their gear. An impromptu camp was already starting to spring up around the carcass. Maybe they'd leave something for us—bone marrow or offal, or *something*. I wasn't above scavenging like hyenas if it meant keeping the tribe fed.

"Why don't the orcs believe you aren't orc ghosts?" I asked.

"*Orcs are cunning, and they believe the older the orc, the more cunning they become. Therefore, the spirits of elders must be the most cunning of all and would never admit to being who they were. Staunch refusals only stoke their conviction. A most vexing situation.*"

"It's a classic catch-twenty-two," I said, running a hand over the top of my fur. "So they won't attack us?"

"*Not readily*," said Girmaks. That wasn't an absolute negative. But we had guns and buggies and almost a hundred goblins. We might not have had the proper tools to take down a thundercleave, but we'd been fighting javeline, and I had to imagine weapons that had worked on the piggies would work well *enough* on an orc.

"Let's go meet the new neighbors," I said. "Maybe there's parts of the 'cleave they won't want."

Armstrong coughed. "Boss, is this one o' them times I ought warn you it's a bad idea?"

I looked up at the scrapper in charge of my Secretive Servants.

"We'll split if it turns ugly. But I want to know who we're sharing the plains with."

"I shall join you, if I may," said Girmaks. *"It may aid your entreaty to be perceived as under the demesne of a grandfather spirit."*

"I thought the Ifrit didn't play to superstitions," I said.

"They also did not fly or drive infernal engines. Yet here we are."

I got Girmaks's bottle out of the saddlebag and held it up so the Ifrit could move from the engine to the brass vessel. Armstrong and several scrapper bodyguards came along, as well as the new canoneer.

As we approached the orc camp being broken out, I noticed that the patrolling orcs regarded us not as threats, but as curiosities. They noted us, but didn't challenge us. This came as a welcome change compared to the reception we'd gotten from the javeline and the boglins. I also saw that they each had a band tied high on their right arm. Many wore yellow and blue, others had red on black, and a few had various other color combinations. I didn't know what it represented. Maybe rank or standing within the group? Many of them offered two fingers pressed to the side of their nose when they noticed the brass bottle. I took it to be a sign of respect.

"Strange they're just letting us walk in here," I said, looking around. The orcs had finished pulling freight down from the backs of their larger pack mounts and were now breaking out tents and tables. "Looks like they're staying a while."

"A night, at least, little brother!" said a surprisingly feminine voice behind me. It was so unexpected that it almost startled me, like turning on the TV and having the volume suddenly way too loud might do. I turned to the speaker, who had dropped her head wraps to reveal a slate-colored face with yellow war paint marked beneath bright copper eyes. A mane of jet-black hair covered her head. She had two spearmen behind her, both of whom had similar face paint. "Lura Sunskin, am I, hunt-chief of the Dawn's Light team. Be welcome to my table, little brothers, but touch not, take not. A thing curious, is a goblin on the plains. More still when he talks and carries an elder spirit."

"King Apollo. Charmed," I said. "Gracious of you to welcome us. I have to admit, I'm surprised you're so welcoming."

The orc huntress rolled her head back and laughed. "What threat pose you, to we who stride the world? A time for honor and rivalry, this. We may not have seen the thundercleave if you had not its ire roused by your strange artifice." She looked out toward the fleet of vehicles idling in the distance. "I know not what tricks our elders play, but they have conspired such that I owe you the scout's share. Come."

Lura turned and walked back into the camp. Tents and pavilions of hide or cloth were already being raised against the sun. With the heat of the day beginning to bear down, it offered the hunters some shade to work in as they processed the 'cleave. They were efficient in skinning and butchering the beast, with tanning frames ready and cookfires already starting to smolder. But the strangest thing, to me, was hearing them talk. From Rufus's description, and their toad-like faces, I would have expected guttural, gravelly voices and simple, brutish sentences capped with snarls. But Lura talked more like she was reading a classical play—or at least a high school drama club's interpretation of a classical play.

"Few songs sing yet of goblin kings, and deeds done by they," said Lura. "Tell me true, how many are you numbered?"

"We have over one hundred on the plains," I said, not wanting to give her an exact count. "And more in the jungle. But food is getting scarce. We came out here to hunt for livestock."

Lura rubbed her protruding chin. "You come at ill time, little brother."

"Why's that?" I asked.

"Because in the midst of the Stampede, are we. The great hunt. All beasts upon the plains of Lanclova are hunt-chief property claimed." She nodded to the brass bottle. "We compete for the right to hunt them the year round."

I bit my lip. "So you're saying we can't hunt the badlands because of this . . . *Stampede* event?"

"To do so, poaching it would be, little brother," said Lura. She looked back at the thundercleave being strung up to have the blood drained into barrels. "Be glad 'twas my team which prevailed and not your kin. For the punishment would make you envious of our departed quarry. I give you the scout's share in part so that you and I need not come to quarrel, for I do not wish the ire of the elder spirits, nor is there sport in the slaying of little brothers and sisters."

My heart dropped. "So what you're saying is, we're screwed," I said. "If we hunt while *you're* hunting, other orcs will attack us."

"Not all my kin are as magnanimous as I. Had it been the Sunless Shrine or the Hawk's Due, you might have found yourselves a cookpot lining, tiny king."

There was silence for a moment. If you were listening closely, I'm sure you could have heard my heart break to learn that any attempt to feed my tribe would be met with outright hostility.

"There's no way we could come to some agreement? Trade artifice for meat, maybe?" I asked.

The hunters with Lura laughed, but she merely shook her head. "You know not of orcs, I see. We do not *trade*. We take what we wish, have we the strength to do so. If your artifice we wanted, it would be ours."

"So there's nothing we can offer you?"

"As I said, you come at ill time."

We stood, looking at one another for several seconds as I racked my brain, looking for a solution. The orcs weren't hostile, but they would quickly turn so if we persisted in hunting the badlands.

Lura seemed about to leave when a small, brassy voice from between my hands split the silence.

"*King Ap wishes to join the Stampede.*"

CHAPTER 24

A HUNTER PAST PRIME

I looked down at the brass jar in my hands with the tiny blue flame licking out of the open throat. I liked to think I recovered quickly.

Lura pursed her lips. "Impossible. Goblins have no standing to join the Stampede."

"*It is my standing as a grandfather spirit which grants claim.*"

Lura Sunskin looked uncomfortable. "Elders are, of course, able to join the Stampede—but not so late in the season. The Keepers of the Stampede dictate the counting of the hunt-chiefs. They will not brook more—lest discord grow within the cadence of the spirits and the Stampede. Such a thing is taboo. You know this." She shook her head. "It is too late in the season for a new team to be founding."

"Is it his right or not?" I asked.

Lura chewed her lip. "It is," she admitted. "You carry the elders with you and honor the hunt—even if your methods of artifice are strange. Eligible, if ill-favored, this makes you. A conundrum." She considered, working through the idea in her head. "But another team so grows the competition, thus stacks my glory ever higher when I the victor am named. Perhaps there is yet another way. Come with me."

We followed Lura deeper into the camp. Most of the orcs weren't strong individually. Lura herself was only level 12, and most of the orcs ranged from 7 to 15. But they worked together with a level of coordination and diligence that put goblins to shame. It seemed they operated on pure muscle memory, as most of their time was spent in raucous laughter after telling one another jokes or anecdotes. Some worked with weapons or practiced riding in formation, and I could already make out the ring of a hammer on iron.

I also spotted several totems lining the camp, and stopped to examine one crested with the skull of a creature I didn't recognize.

System, can you tell me what this is?

<Masher Skull Totem: Orcs who appreciate this totem receive a buff to blunt weapon damage for a short time.>

Do the orcs have their own tech tree?

<Yes, but it is not as robust as the Goblin Tech Tree.>

Is it compatible with ours?

<There is some amount of overlap.>

Interesting.

"Dawdle not, Apollo," warned Lura.

I double-timed it to keep up. We crossed over to what seemed to be the workman's portion of the camp, already choked with coal-fire smoke and the smell of oils and lye. It was here I saw the metalworkers forging and mending equipment, as well as other artisans making arrows, saddles, clothing, dyes, and various other sundries.

Off in the corner, a shaded table sat beneath a stretched hide, where a half-dozen orcs hunched over mugs spread between them. Some of them had armbands of gray and white, others no armbands at all. Most had the lopsided build of smiths, clearly stronger on their hammer-hand side with corded muscle and faces framed by forge soot.

One of them, larger and higher leveled than the rest, looked up and scowled at Lura's approach, then looked at us and scowled. Then he looked back into his mug and scowled even deeper. One of his teeth was cracked and blackened, and his lips were drawn back over that side as though it pained him. His hair had gone mostly gray, with only a few black patches remaining in the bundle of locks bound behind his shoulders.

"Lo there, dawn huntress," said one of the other orcs, whose cheeks and nose had gone red. "This is a Flock table, and your own ought you find."

Lura leaned in. "And gone ought you get, little Wormwood spawn, for Sourtooth's ears my words are. Difficult you'll find it to jest through tusks clipped and nose awry."

I grinned. An orc argument was like Shakespeare in the Park with more threats of bodily harm.

"Be off with you, Lura," said the older orc, hunching lower over his cup. "Poor enough the season cut short, without your come to gloat of fresh killing."

"Sour words from a sour orc spill forth, proven lies before reaching the ground. These little brothers wish to join the Flock—unless a stubborn old orc prefers continuing to turn out nails, rings, and oryx shodding to the wind through his locks."

The orcs leered over the table at us, as though noticing us for the first time. Then they all burst into laughter. The only one not laughing was Sourtooth as he glared daggers up at the huntress. Lura waited for them to finish.

The old orc reached under the low table and dragged out his stump of a leg, thumping the remnant—and a crude peg prosthetic—on the top of the table, overturning two drinks in the process. "It seems the morning star of the dawn hunt has forgotten. Numbered are my hunting days. One who cannot ride, cannot run, and cannot leap? Cannot stride the world, he. And now *goblins*, you bring to replace my hunters lost? This jest is salt rubbed deep in fresh wounds, Lura, and insult so easily offered may not be as easy forgiven."

I looked at the remnant of his leg, severed raggedly just above the ankle. His peg leg wasn't much better. It was poorly balanced, and slightly too short for him. Likely he'd walked with a terrible limp ever since he'd gotten it, which based on the bruising under the strap, had been fairly recently.

Of my own initiative, I bounded up onto the table, knocking a few more drinks over and putting my own prosthetic blades on full display.

A couple of the orcs shied back, startled. But Sourtooth stared. Even without lower legs, I'd jumped up to the field table—fully half my own height—and landed without a stumble.

"I'll have you know," I said, "that missing both legs, I still run, jump, and ride wherever I please,"

Sourtooth stared at me for a moment. "Clear off, lads," he finally said. He scowled at Lura. "And back to your skinners, you. Think you not that I see your ambitions?"

Lura Sunskin bowed out with a grin. "My work here is done, then. I shall set eyes on you afield, elder."

The old orc waved her off and then craned his neck to make sure she'd gone before gesturing me closer.

"Far too clever, she, for an orc so young." He leaned in and squinted at my prosthetics. "This is no orc artifice," he said, peering at the spring-steel blades. "From where came these feet of steel?"

"My igni made them," I said. "And I can make you one as well."

Sourtooth massaged his thigh, digging long, lean fingers deep into the knobby muscle. "Would be a waste of fine steel to do so. But *igni* . . . and scrappers aside, unless my mark be untrue. And . . ." He narrowed his eyes at the canoneer. "Whatever that one be. Your tribe numbers higher than the gaggle of hellions what suns south of the Stampede."

"Yes," I said. "And they're hungry. They're hunting and fishing, but they haven't taken to farming. I need to hunt the plains, and I can't hunt the plains because I'm not part of your Stampede. If you quit because of your injury . . ."

Sourtooth huffed. "Not the injury you can *see,* little brother. I retired when the whistler that took my leg cleft the souls from the bodies of near three dozen oryx. To the spirits gone, and half again as many riders. 'Tis a hollow shell, now, of a once-proud team."

"Rough accident," I said.

"Twern't such." The orc spat on the ground. "Braced between the hammer and Lura's hunters, my team under foot was forced."

"Ah," I said. "That'll do it." Explained why the orc hated Lura, at least. I had to imagine orc hunters were a bit like corporate lawyers—cutthroat and quick to blame the victims of their cruelty.

"I don't expect a goblin to understand loss."

I thought of my fellow astronauts Dave Sanders and Sandy Davis. I thought of my dad, who never got to see me be an astronaut (though maybe it's best he didn't see his son explode). I thought of coming home from Cape Canaveral after the motorcycle accident, when people I'd long thought were my friends never even tried to reach me in the hospital, or in physical therapy. And I thought of how my dreams had been dashed until NuEarth headhunters came along.

"I understand it," I said. "I can't give you back everything you've lost. But I've got a hundred hungry goblins atop self-propelled chariots and they all want to eat. And I can give you a new leg. Like mine. We can scout, we can chase, we can even fly."

Sourtooth shrugged.

"Plus, with my craftsmen and your forges, I can build you a motorcycle," I said.

"What's that?"

I revved my hands. "It's got two wheels, it's loud, and it's fast."

"Is it safe?"

"Absolutely not," I said. "You're likely to kill yourself learning to ride it. But . . ." I pointed to his peg leg, "You'll only need one foot."

"Welcome to the Flock," said Sourtooth. He looked up into the air. "Grandfather spirit?"

<Goblin Technology Unlocked: Orcxiliaries>

<By partnering with the Flock, you can share certain tribal benefits from both groups—including temporary access to the Goblin Tech Tree. Note that auxiliary races may not be able to create or properly operate many advanced goblin devices.>

"Advanced" goblin devices. There was an oxymoron.

<Congratulations! You have joined the Stampede! This orc festival of big game hunters establishes hunting rights for the coming season.>
<Congratulations! You have joined the Flock team of the Stampede. Your tribe's hunters have been granted all bonuses.>

My tribemates behind me slipped into a stupor for a moment as their little goblin brains absorbed the new changes.

Sourtooth shuddered and pushed himself to stand. "Always sends my flesh a shiver to see that happen—the goblin king skill transfer."

I looked at the old orc. "You've seen goblin kings before?" I asked.

"Of course. The humans and elves as a nuisance see your kind, to be stamped out on sight. But our homeland, Kelem, has many goblin tribes, and on occasion does a king emerge from within their ranks. Of course, we do the sensible thing and kill them 'fore they get strong enough to threaten." He slapped me on the shoulder and grinned, broken tooth looming in his smile. "Fortune favors you, we are not *in* Kelem, little brother."

I swallowed.

I suddenly didn't feel very fortunate.

CHAPTER 25

THE FLOCK

Unbelievably, we had the run of the place. Once the armbands (somewhat bloodstained) were passed out, the orcs seemed to take it completely in stride that there were goblins tearing around their camp. If Sourtooth was to be believed, goblin tribes coexisted alongside orcs in their homeland—though not allowed to grow beyond measure. Goblin kings were killed on sight for the threat they represented—which meant their entire tribe was wiped out, too. Apparently all bets were off in Lanclova, though.

I sent two of the bikes back to link up with Promo at the Big Hoss Rig and have them bring the camp to meet up with the Stampede. Now that we had access to the Flock's forges and resources, Prometheus was going to have a field day. Metal was in no short supply to the orcs, and they had some idea of the basics of material science, so I made a note to secure sulfur and charcoal from their stores, as well as iron bar stock and even rubber.

Sourtooth accompanied us to the vehicles so that he could see for himself the artifice that his temporary access to the Goblin Tech Tree had given him.

"I believe it not," he said, clambering awkwardly aboard one of the buggies. "The grandfather spirits must be playing some great jest. They are the true source of this contraption's power, yes?"

"It's actually a liquid that burns and creates torque," I said. "The Ifrit were just as surprised as you are that it works."

"They would tell you to say that," he said. He settled in on one of the stations, if a bit tightly. He was thicker and taller than a hobgoblin, and the seat hadn't been designed with his stature in mind. We brought the vehicles into the Flock's dismal corner of the camp, where I saw several riderless mounts tied off near pack animals that hadn't yet been *un*packed. I surmised most of them belonged to Sourtooth's decimated hunting team. I directed my goblins to help get supplies and provisions down.

It was close to nightfall when the Big Hoss Rig approached the Stampede camp and set up in the forge yard with the new vehicles that had come from Apollo. I'm sure that's where Promo found himself most at home, among the smog of coal smoke and the ring of hammers. By the time the sun went down, the temporary tower was erected and the thundercleave had been seared.

The "scout's share" turned out to be about two hundred chooms of offal and gristle, which was fine by my tribe. It disappeared down the goblins' throats almost as fast as the cooks could flip it onto wooden platters. Even then, we still had plenty left over. If we'd brought down the 'cleave ourselves? Well . . . we'd probably have been killed for poaching. But now that we were part of a hunting team, we *could* bring one down. With my tinkering and Sourtooth's experience, there was no way we could lose.

"We're definitely going to lose," Sourtooth said over his 'cleave burger. The orcs had apparently mastered the arts of ground meat, bread-making, and cheese. Despite the surreal sight of an orc chowing down on what was effectively a cheeseburger, my mouth watered so badly watching him eat that I had to ask him to repeat himself.

"The season has seen the Flock idle for weeks, after more beast bitten than we could chew. Trailing the pack, we. There are few prizes yet unclaimed, and none would see us sit at the winner's table," he continued. I noticed that he chewed entirely on one side of his mouth, avoiding the inflamed tooth. "But hunting rights require not a place of glory, only one of standing. If to feed your tribe you seek, then we yet have merit. But we must focus efforts on prey not easily conquered. What is the greatest beast you've bested? A level thirty? Thirty-five?"

If I had a collar, I'd have been tugging it. "We killed a stone-sloth alpha and a croc-knocker in their twenties. Oh, but we defeated an entire javeline army."

"Mention of the porkbellies makes a rumble in my stomach to rival a giant's tracks. Hunting big game is like fighting a war not at all, little brother."

"Well," I said. "I'm hoping my technology ideas will help close the gap, some. Tomorrow, we'll get to work getting the Flock back in the game."

<Your tribe has decreased to 374 members.>
<Your tribe has increased to 406 members.>

The orcs were slow to wake, and in fact it wasn't until mid-morning that a growing buzz overhead finally drew their attention.

<Goblin Technology Unlocked: Infernal combust'em bi-gliders>

Huh. Sally was still hard at work on the home front, I guessed.

I shaded my eyes and scanned the horizon until I saw a dot that started to grow larger. The pilot banked, and I could make out the profile of a pusher-prop biplane soaring under power. The pilot made a circuit of the orc camp as the Stampede shook off hangovers or dragged blankets over their heads against the noise.

Finding a flat enough stretch, the plane bled off altitude and leveled out, flaring off for a landing on what appeared to be a set of two-wheeled landing gear—one at the front and one at the back, like a motorcycle. I briefly wondered how they would keep the paper wings from being shredded on landing until a pair of goblins scrambled out and hung beneath the wings, pumping their legs as if they were running through the air. The rear wheel touched down and the craft lurched, but the goblins' feet touched the ground and the aircraft trundled about as the pace goblins struggled to keep up. The whole ensemble finally came to a stop and a handful more goblins piled out of the vehicle, including Sally, who immediately began fussing over the aircraft and squawking at the wrangler climbing down from the control station.

I approached, looking at our first powered airplane. Sally had built a leather fuselage over a frame of wood and bone, with paper-covered wings and a multi-rotor engine at the back. The wings, stacked as they were, were each of slightly differing lengths, but it didn't seem to affect the performance much.

Armstrong ran past me and plucked my lead engineer right off the side of the plane to wrap her in a bear hug until she squawked and bit him, at which point he dropped her on her head. She responded by clamping her jaws around his ankle, and he shook his leg frantically trying to dislodge her. I caught up a few moments later, after I finished laughing, and took some time to admire the quick work she'd made of rigging up the aircraft and applying composite technological theories. But I was a little concerned. Sally was simply much too valuable to be risking out in the field. Of course, she was a free goblin and I couldn't keep her cooped up on a bluff—even if it was where she chose to spend most of her time anyway.

Maybe she'd just missed Armstrong.

Armstrong finally managed to shift my lead engineer off long enough to give a report. "Food situation eased up some, what with us out 'ere keeping our own bellies full. But still more out than in—or maybe in than out, innit?"

"We're still running a deficit, is what you're trying to say," I said.

"Yeah, that. Anyway, Sal' figured you'd want to peep the latest in airy-knotics. Din' even crash it once!"

"That's a good start," I said.

Armstrong leaned down for Sally to whisper in his ear. He nodded. "Two more buggies and a trike headed our way," he said. "Another ignis, s'well."

I rubbed the top of my head. "Good. We'll need all the smiths we can get if we're riding for Sourtooth and what's left of the Flock."

Speaking of the foul old orc, the leader of the Flock himself was stumbling out of the camp with a blanket clutched tight around his waist, staring at the biplane.

"Goblins on wings! Tremble the skies, once free from shackle. In all the tribes in mine eyes seen, I knew not that little brothers could make such . . . racket! Damned if the cry of its coming didn't echo a thousand-fold in my head."

I grinned up at the hungover old orc. "Still think we've got no shot?"

Sourtooth slumped down to his haunches, and his eyes took on a glazed-over look as they scanned back and forth. I realized he was reading through System menus. "No simple spears and stubby legs, this. How came you by such discoveries? I have knowledge passing of the goblin artifice but have never seen one progressed in this manner. Nearly half the tree, you've jumped, and rarely from such narrow path tread. *Infernal combust'em*? *Rock'ems*? I know not these artifice, but I know well enough the path from whence they spring. What need have you of such singular purpose?"

I slapped the orc on the shoulder. The leader of the Flock might have been gnarled and withered as an old root, but it still felt like slapping a slab of granite. "It's a long story, Sourtooth. And a long road ahead to get where I'm going."

"What, prithee, are *boom tubes*?"

I whistled and sent one of my bodyguards to bring over his rifle and a handful of rockettes. I worked the action and loaded in a few shells. "Well, they're not going to help your hangover any. But I still think you'll like them."

CHAPTER 26

FORGING FRIENDS

"Make hot the coals and put backs to bellows, my lads!" shouted Sourtooth. The old orc had swapped his blanket for a thick leather apron and a pair of hide gloves. "These metals mine must be shaped with haste, should we wish to be ready whence the Stampede begins to march."

The old orc strutted through the forge yard, still a bit uncertain on his new spring-steel prosthetic—a larger mirror to my own. But beneath the hangover, he'd found his fire. His renewed zeal had trickled down to his smiths. All across the yard, bar stock and billets were heating up, and goblins were beginning to assemble bricks for kilns to tap the clay supplies of the Flock. Not only that, but heated vats belched forth black, acrid fumes. The orcs had *rubber* from trees in the badlands. We were going to have actual tires for the second-generation orc buggies.

All throughout the yard, Promo worked with his smiths, blending the principles of orc and goblin technology to make our buggies larger and tougher, adding panels and platforms for the orcs. Our canoneer scrambled back and forth, transcribing sanctified engineering diagrams onto paper.

As for me? Well, I couldn't lose sight of my end goal of securing hunting rights. Simple small-caliber guns weren't going to cut the mustard when it came to big game. With access to the orcs' ample stores, I was going to make something that a thundercleave couldn't shrug off. The orcs had sulfur and charcoal, of course. But they also had impure bauxite powder, magnesium, grain alcohol, and plenty of old iron parts, rusted beyond use. Stolen loot to them, with limited use because they didn't have an Earth scientist's understanding of how to properly combine them into something amazing. Since Sally had come in person, I co-opted her and the canoneer in order to codify a new set of devices into the Church of the Right Angle, in hopes that would tighten tolerances enough for the igni to produce working designs.

I began sketching out plans for armaments on the new buggies. By the time the wranglers and scrappers started waking up, I had the basic schematics figured out. I found Sourtooth once I was ready to start forging components and showed him what I was working on, then explained how it would work. Then I pantomimed it while several of his hunters watched the confusion and laughed. When he still didn't understand, I appealed to System.

<Try the hand thing again.>

Very funny. But I got the message: It was something we'd have to unlock in order for the tree to translate it to orcish tech through the auxiliary system.

Sourtooth just shrugged. "What more have I to lose? To the forgemasters, get ye."

"That's the spirit," I said.

I made my way over to Promo, who was working at the forges with the orc smiths and the Ifrit. An ignis was a new novelty for the orcs of the Flock, and his cooking had ingratiated him with our new hunting team. It didn't hurt that the orc smiths got a bonus to heat-based crafting through the auxiliary system when he was around, and our fire elementals made furnaces more efficient.

<You're welcome.>

I ignored System and presented the designs for the new parts to my forgemaster. "You think we can rig these up?"

He took the vellum (the orcs had no shortage of hides) and turned the drawing about, taking in the drawing. "This will kill goblins."

"Only if they don't let go. Think I'll have a shortage of volunteers?"

Promo emphatically shook his head. "The S&M Club'll be over the moon. Like to try one myself, truth told. How big we talking at this end, boss?"

I made a circle with my finger and thumb. Promo grinned. "No problem. The orc iron isn't as good as our boom furnace steel, but it will do in a pinch."

I reached up and slapped him on the side of the arm.

We worked well into the evening, the entire contingent of goblins that I'd brought with me into the desert, as well as Sally and the small flight crew she'd brought. I sent her home after lunch, watching as the strange pusher-plane took off in much the same way it had landed.

I had intended to keep working until nightfall, but three horn blasts sounded, interrupting our progress. I looked up from my work as the Stampede camp suddenly buzzed with frenetic activity. Orcs ran this way and that, carrying equipment or bundling up supplies.

"Sourtooth?"

He limped by, stuffing effects into a bag. "The Dawn just signaled their intent to put hoof to turf and the hunt resume."

I chased after him. "You said the party from a thundercleave would last three days."

"*Could* last, little brother. Advanced the game, has Lura. She presses us and answer we must this challenge given."

"But they're not ready! We haven't even tested the new modifications!"

He shaded his eyes against the sun. "Time not to dally and dither upon doubts. We must beseech Grandfather Spirit for his blessing, and hope to find his mood not coy. You have until the sun dips a hand's span from the horizon. As much as I can offer, this."

"Your hand or mine?"

The sour old orc glared down at me.

"Right. Stop wasting time. We're going to wing it," I translated. At the end of the day, this was still Sourtooth's show, his culture, his traditions, and his rules that we had to follow if we wanted to participate in the Stampede and feed the tribe. Hunting rights were on the line.

Prototype, test, rapid iteration. Combining quick and dirty engineering with monstrous beasts capable of killing dozens of goblins? What could ever go wrong?

I delivered the news to Promo, who offered much the same complaint I did, before supervising the teardown of the forges and the BHR.

Once things were packed up, I climbed up onto my newly enhanced buggy and dropped a rockette into the starter slot. I pulled out the bestiary as the engine warmed up, trying to get a clue as to what we might be in for. I thumbed through the pages of the plains beasts, but the weight shifted as Sourtooth pulled himself up to the rear position. He eased down into the seat and dropped his bag of forge tools by his feet. He looked over my shoulder.

"What have you there?" he demanded.

I handed the bestiary back, and he flipped through it, scowling. He tossed it over his shoulder in contempt.

"Hey!" I said. "Why did you do that?"

"I can't read," he said. "But a book which with four spines a rockscraper presents is worth not the vellum of its pages." He tapped the side of his head. "Trust that I know the beasts of all lands, little brother." He reached down and rubbed the connection with his new prosthetic. "All too well, some."

He slapped the side of the buggy.

The gears shifted under my hand and the throttle pedal pulled away from my foot as Girmaks revved up the engine. The buggy lurched forward, churning turf on its new rubber tires. While not exactly performance rallycross tires, the hard rubber was still leaps and bounds better than the metal-banded wheels as they bit into the badlands ground. Engines across the forge yard roared as the rest of the Flock scrambled to find places on vehicles of their own as my goblins hooted and hollered and waved spears and guns.

I couldn't help but grin. I lifted my feet entirely and left the controls to the Ifrit, who pulled us out into the mass of orc hunting teams scrambling to quit the camp. The Stampede had sounded like a rolling thunderstorm when we'd been watching from the outside. But now, in its midst? The cacophony of hundreds of mounted orcs pounding across the badlands riding baying beasts of a dozen different sizes was intense. It was infectious. The orcs were trampling, and we were trampling *with* them. We were part of this dangerous, deadly festival of speed and skill. Maybe it's the competitor in me talking, but aside from launching the first glider, this was the most excited I'd been since coming to Rava. And I wasn't the only one.

I felt another subtle pressure mounting, the telltale weight of the System's increased attention on me. Well, we'd give it a show.

I stood up in my chair and looked back at the dozen goblin vehicles arrayed behind me, with goblins in questionable leather garments hanging on by their dozens. Scrappers had their rifles in the air, while wranglers at the controls of the buggies and bikes expertly maneuvered the vehicles. Even the canoneer was furiously scribbling on a piece of paper that flapped so hard in the wind I was surprised the fibers didn't come apart.

I put my fingers at the corners of my mouth and whistled. The trill rose above the clamor of the Stampede, soon joined by other goblins who had mastered the trick of whistling. Those who hadn't simply screamed, and then the orcs of the Flock joined in, and I even caught a half-smile creeping onto Sourtooth's twisted face. That clarion pierced the wall of sound that was the Stampede, and I saw other hunting teams looking over at us.

I raised my hands above my head, making the circle in the air.

"*Ad Luna!*" I shouted.

The tribe cheered, mirroring the sign.

"Maybe we won't all die!" Sourtooth shouted over the cheering. "Who's Adluna?"

CHAPTER 27

PERSUASIVE UNIT CONVERSION

We rode for an hour before Sourtooth whistled and pointed north. Girmaks pulled the buggy left, leading the convoy away from the main pack of the Stampede. I stood up in my seat and looked out at the main body of orcs as we distanced ourselves from them. The thunder of hooves fell away, leaving only the sound of rough-burning engines on bare rock and scrub.

"We're not joining them?"

Sourtooth held his hand up to the sun. "We need not follow the Dawn for we aim not to unseat them. Lura possesses skill unmatched, and many would claim glory by knocking down her standing at the fore. We seek only to *place*. Leave glory to youth, little brother."

A smaller pack of riders also broke off from the main group, keeping their distance but also clearly following in our trail.

I turned to face the old orc. "We've got company,"

He nodded. "Aye, the Blood Gorgers, should my eyes favor me. A complicated dance is the Stampede, with steps aplenty. They will interfere, should it look as though we may bring down a halting totem. Make no mistake, there will be blood on the steppe."

Yikes. "Is that what happened to you?"

"Aye. Drove my hunters down the gullet of the Whistler. Was ruled fair by the keepers, though just. And if tides favor, they may lend aid, instead."

I wished I had a pair of binoculars so I could get a better look at our pursuers. "Orc games sure are cutthroat," I said. "What are keepers?"

Sourtooth pointed a couple of vehicles back, to where a hooded orc crouched atop a buggy, working beads between her fingers. I hadn't noticed before that she didn't have an armband to link her with the Flock. Instead, she had coal-black markings around her eyes and nose and under her cheeks, giving her a bit of a skull-like appearance. Her closed eyes only added to the effect.

"The keeper job lets they who have it speak to each other through the elder spirits. They see the Stampede and make rulings, and call halts when confirmed is a kill." The old orc held up three fingers. "But they also tell us the progress of the other teams. There are twenty-one foes chosen. The festival will end when the greatest totem beasts are killed—monsters of scale and fang, legend they. With the thundercleave claimed, a third their number go to Lura's spears, and some fewer to our other rivals. But numbers matter little, as weighted points are applied—by level, rarity, ferocity, and size factored. All you need know is that should one more kill the dawn huntress claim, no one may overtake her. Should it look as though she'll claim it with haste, our company may lend aid to clip her wings and force a stop."

"I see." I said, thoroughly confused by the internal orc tournament politics. "So, three unique monsters left. I take it one of them is that whistler thing?"

"Aye. But, too strong for we. A dartwing, I think, we should pursue—a day east of us, its hunting grounds. With these mounts of iron and flame, she could outrun us not long, and she is much less a foe than a whistler if we need only place."

"Why doesn't Lura just kill an easy one to end the Stampede right away?"

Sourtooth laughed. "Glory, little brother. The reason of her sending you to my side. Points awarded come from rivals conquered and the strength of a totem both. She seeks to break a score long-held by my grandfather in points. And she may well do." Sourtooth spat off the side of the buggy. "Curse his spirit, the foul old orc."

A bit ironic, coming from him, I thought.

"Asides, 'tis not a thing so simply done," said Sourtooth. "Finding the beast is part of the challenge and so is safeguarding it. Lura's Dawn Light are numbered only second to the Blood Gorgers, who will at nothing stop to claim her kills. They follow her just as they stalk our footprints."

We came across a herd of the hoppers, and Sourtooth sent two of our bikes and one trike to wrangle them while we continued on. We rode until the sun slipped behind the horizon and then made camp.

The Flock had animals of their own that needed to be fed and watered as we topped off fuel bladders for buggies and bikes. I took a walk around the perimeter of the camp with Armstrong.

<Your tribe has decreased to 397 members.>
<Your tribe has decreased to 393 members.>

Huh? I shared a glance with Armstrong.

<Your tribe has assimilated 25 new members.>
<Your tribe has increased to 418 members.>
<Congratulations! Assimilating new tribe members through persuasive religious conversion for the first time has unlocked an optional job for non-variant goblins! You may choose between Goblin Zealots or Goblin Templar.>

"Nice!" said Armstrong. "Eileen musta got 'em to a new village."

I narrowed my eyes. *How exactly is this "persuasive conversion" performed?*

<Typically by removing elements who are not persuaded from the target audience.>

Great. There was only one thing this could be: Luther's canoneer aboard Gerty had reached another bluff and spread the doctrine of the Church of the Right Angle, resulting in a significant scuffle. The scuffle couldn't have lasted long against even superior numbers, due to our technology, which I had to assume was more advanced than any other local tribe's.

Did the assimilated tribe even have any variants?

<The tribe had unlocked Goblin Flatulators, but they are quite volatile and were all killed during the persuasion, and thus were not assimilated with the remainder of the tribe.>

Volatile goblin flatulators . . . that sounded like a mixed blessing, if I was being honest.

Tell me about zealots and templar.

<Goblin Zealots are especially zealous goblins. They receive bonus combat skills and crafting speed when assigned to a Noblin Canoneer, and additional bonuses when fighting or working alongside other zealots and canoneers through the Fervor skill. They will also never break morale in combat. Non-variant goblins may occasionally become Zealots.>

<Goblin Templar are defensive goblins capable of absorbing one lethal blow without dying, even if the templar was not the intended target of the attack. This is particularly useful to safeguard rare or important variant goblins through the use of the Ward skill. They will also never break morale in combat. Non-variant goblins may occasionally become Templar.>

Alright, let me think.

As much as I liked the idea of extra-life goblins, zealots seemed to have a lot of upsides as well. Receiving a bonus for fighting and crafting with other zealots nearby had the potential for limitless scaling. The only problem was, I didn't know if this bonus scaled with the number of zealots or if it was a binary thing.

<Additional variant information available upon selection.>

Yeah, that's why I didn't ask. I sighed, already wondering if I was going to regret this. *Give me the zealots.*

<Goblin Zealots will now spawn in your tribe. Would you like to automatically assign zealots to canoneers based on spawn location?>

Yes, please.

<12 of the newly acquired tribe members have converted to Goblin Zealots.>
<66 other goblins in your tribe have converted to Goblin Zealots.>

Woah, woah! That's nearly a fifth of the non-variants! You said occasionally!

<Occasionally they will. Now they have.>

I ground my teeth. Friggen' System. *Give me the deets on the Fervor skill.*

<Fervor: Goblin Zealots gain a moderate bonus to tasks directed by a Noblin Canoneer, and a small bonus for all other Goblin Zealots assigned to the same task.>

I breathed a sigh of relief. It was cumulative scaling, not binary. Instead of the bonus simply being applied or not, it would stack the more zealots were near one another. With some reluctance, I opened up the spawning menu and increased the canoneer priority. *Slightly*. Confident I'd chosen the right variant, I turned and headed back to camp.

Already, several of the non-variant goblins had switched jobs to zealots, and they had removed their skull masks in order to carve or draw various religious iconography onto the dry bones. I saw sketches of eccentric shafts, propellers, kilns, starter pistols, *regular* pistols, and a variety of other technologies we'd canonized as part of the Church of the Right Angle. The most common was simply the circle of Raphina on the forehead. Because festooning one's self with arcane symbols was a sign of a stable, rational adherent of science. But at least it was a religious devotion to progress and the scientific process, and not to an invisible man in the sky.

<Ahem.>

No offense to present company.

<None taken.>

Sourtooth limped up, watching the goblins who had so suddenly abandoned their tasks. "I know not what my eyes do see," he said.

"Ah," I said. "My tribe just unlocked another variant," I said. "Zealots."

"And what are they?"

I tilted my head. "Goblins, except even more manic than usual."

Sourtooth shook his head. "This truly is a land of madness, to have you visited upon its shores."

"Not going to cull us like you would in Kelem, are you?" I asked cautiously.

"We are on Kelem not, little brother," said Sourtooth. He glanced at the vehicles and the Ifrit flitting about the camp in their personal vessels. The old orc rubbed at the white stubble on his chin. "The elder spirits are playing at some mischief, mark me. I know not where their twisted plan ends, but be it not upon my spear, little brother. Not when life breathed once more into the Flock." He looked back down at me. "Tarry not long. There is work to be done before the fall of night. And we rise with the dawn. Tomorrow we will find a dartwing, and we will drive it to the ground before Lura takes her next kill, or your people will starve."

I waved as the old orc trotted off, starting to get the hang of his new prosthetic. There was indeed work to be done. The S&M Club had taken to hammering and wrenching on the vehicles to keep them in good working order, so I continued modifying the buggies with Promo until dinner.

As the sun dropped and the day cooled, I munched on a hot hopper burger and thought about what Sourtooth said. *We are on Kelem not.*

Lanclova was a land of monsters and goblins, fire spirits, and more. The rest, the orcs and humans and elves, were strangers to these lands. I was technically the native, even if I'd come from Earth. Like it or not, I was responsible for what happened here, and I was making big waves.

I just hoped they didn't end up drowning me.

CHAPTER 28

SCALING NEW HEIGHTS

<Your tribe has increased to 431 members.>

I have something for you, Sourtooth," I said.

The old orc followed me to the temporary motorpool, where we had our newest functioning vehicle—mostly cobbled together from the remains of vehicles that had met their untimely end.

As the sun crept over the horizon, the red rays lit the long, high ape handlebars of a brand new chopper-style bike, built with the lanky proportions of an orc in mind. Sourtooth circled the machine, eyeing it suspiciously before climbing up into the seat and wrapping his hairy knuckles around the grips.

"What is the purpose of having so far extended these?" he asked.

"Style, comfort," I said. I pointed to one of the wrangler bikes, where one of my Secretive Servants hobbies was hunched over. "See how he has to lean forward? Yours is designed to let you lean back instead. Kick that first pedal."

Sourtooth obliged, and the engine rumbled to life. Being much stronger than a goblin, it seemed an orc would have no need for the starter rockettes in order to get a goblin engine to turn over. Figured. Sourtooth's back straightened as the vibration mounted below him. "Little brother . . ."

Other orcs took notice of Sourtooth on his new chopper and wandered over, talking amongst themselves and pointing. One came forward with a brace of spears and stuck them into the open holders on the side, then hopped up on the back of the bike, ready to ride.

"Kick that second pedal," I said.

Sourtooth obliged, and the bike started forward. Unfortunately, I couldn't do a grip throttle without hydraulic oils, but the leader of the Flock figured things out quickly enough, making a circuit of the camp. As he came back, I began to worry, assuming the orc was in some sort of pain—until I realized the withered expression on his face was probably the closest he ever got to a smile.

"Truly the elders have outdone their artifice. Much more practical, these, than brass bodies that walk on points."

Other than supplying some brass and zinc parts, the Ifrit had very little to do with the creation of the vehicles—that was Earth know-how and Goblin Tech Tree chicanery. But I didn't see the benefit in revealing that fact to Sourtooth.

"So, we should find that dartwing today, right?"

"If luck rides with us, yes, little brother. Tell me truth, have flying beasts you fought before?"

I nodded. "Night haunts, er, *skyenas,* I think they're actually called. They try and steal goblins at night on the regular." I spread my arms wide. "Leathery wings, beaks, claws. We're getting pretty good at it."

Sourtooth rolled his head back and laughed. "I said *beasts,* not *pests.* 'Tis like boasting of skill in killing rats, little brother."

I'm sure under the blue fuzz on my cheeks, I was blushing furiously. Sure, the night haunts might not be much of an obstacle for a party of leveled-up orc hunters, but the memory of being a tribe only a tenth the size was still fresh in my mind, and I didn't know if I'd ever forget the terror of seeing one for the first time. Still, we'd managed that with little more than sharp sticks and flint cleavers.

And since then, we'd only gotten stronger. Sourtooth claimed the dartwing was easier than a whistler or a thundercleave. In fact, we were going after it specifically because it was weak. How difficult could it be?

The orcs began to ride out, and we followed on our buggies with our lone monocycle rider weaving dangerously between. Once we got up to speed, I ordered the kites deployed, and goblins on tethered gliders caught the wind and ascended to altitude for scouting. Behind us, the band of rival hunters keeping tabs on our progress mobilized as well. I could see the dust trails rising in the air.

The riding oryx our pursuing orcs favored were strong, sturdy animals with good endurance and long legs. They had no trouble keeping pace with us as we rode for several hours. When the rest of the wranglers and scrappers began to wake up from where they dozed in the back of the BHR, we drove close enough for Chuck to climb over. He took my spot at the controls—not that we needed a driver, as Girmaks was proving to be more than deft as a pilot. The Ifrit seemed to have very little learning curve when it came to transitioning from the multi-legged clockwork proxies to internal combustion-driven vehicles with wheels. The buggies had become extensions of their fiery bodies.

The kite goblins began to squawk a short while after that, and following their direction, we changed course and came up on a dead creature lying on the gravel flat. Sourtooth hopped down from his chopper and probed the beast. I climbed down with Chuck and Armstrong and took a look as well.

The creature on the ground was pretty big—at least twice the size of a stone-sloth. It had been disemboweled so that whatever killed it could get at the soft innards, but there were curious yellow spikes sticking out of it. I waved away the cloud of flies and took hold of a spike. It took both hands to yank it out. It looked like a crossbow bolt, but close inspection revealed it was a feather—albeit one with a barbed quill and symmetrical fringe. I handed it up to Chuck.

He grunted. "Well, they are called *dartwings*."

"I thought that just meant they were fast," I said. "Make sure everyone's wearing armor before we start up again, yeah?"

"Good as done," said Chuck. He left to wrangle the rest of the goblins to start putting on their vests.

Sourtooth examined the carcass. "Definitely our girl," he said. "Good color to these quills, and no maggots. The guts still hold heat. Not yet an hour's past this feast. Sluggish and heavy, she. Headed to the deep desert to sleep off her dinner. We yet stand to catch her before she makes the dunes."

Armstrong tapped me on the shoulder and pointed at the carcass.

"Yes?" I asked.

"Lotta good eating on there still," he said.

Admittedly, I was trying to ignore my own mouth watering at the smell of the kill. Funny how quickly I was leaving the old trappings of humanity behind and looking at fly-covered roadkill with hungry eyes now. As a human, the sight would have turned my stomach. I glanced at Sourtooth.

He shrugged. "Haste behooves a hunter, tarry not long."

I turned back to Armstrong. "Not so much that they get lethargic."

Armstrong grinned and whistled, and a collective cheer rose from the convoy. The goblins swarmed the remains, and after a few minutes of what sounded like electric saws whining, they were loading cleaned bones onto the back of the buggies for later use.

Sourtooth, again, shook his head.

We got on the move again, but this time I climbed up onto the buggy with the Stampede rule-keeper and sat in front of the orc, facing backward. If Sourtooth was old, this orc was *ancient*, looking more like a gnarled old willow trunk than a hunter. She had heavily lined folds of skin on her face, with closed eyes that sat deep under a ridged brow, which itself rested in the shadows of a hooded robe.

She'd shrunk in age, little bigger than a hobgoblin now that I got close. As she sat cross-legged on the top of the buggy, she worked several sets of beads in her hands made from bones, stones, colored clay, carved wood, and twists of leather and string.

"I'm Apollo," I said.

"Is that so?" she asked. "Strange thing, a goblin named. A king of the little brothers yet more. Why the elders have blessed you, I know not."

I waited to see if the orc would say more, but she didn't. I bit my lip in consternation. "What's your name?" I asked.

"Keepers have no names in the Stampede, little brother. To remain neutral, we call upon each of us as such, and by nothing other."

"Alright, Keeper. So, you're in contact with all the other keepers, right? Is it a type of magic?"

"A simple spell," said Keeper. She held up the beads. "Each of these twinned, responds in kind."

For the first time I noticed several of the beads on the string were spinning on their own. I reached out to touch the beads, but Keeper slapped my hand away. There was no malice in it, and she didn't even scold me, just kept the same impassive, closed-eyed expression.

"Sorry," I said, shaking the sting out of my fingers. "Other than the Ifrit, I haven't seen anything especially magical. I'm just curious. Is this communication spell instant? Or does it have some sort of delay, like a radio transmission? Not that you'd know what that is, I suppose." I scratched my head. "For that matter, does it go through rock or water as easily as air? If I had a radio tuner, do you think I could somehow tap into it?" What was the bit-rate of information sent through the beads, and could it be optimized with a compression algorithm?

Keeper opened one eye and regarded me, then closed it again without response.

"Fine," I said, annoyed. "How are the other teams doing?"

"The Dawn Light have caught the trail of a Spinesnake and pursue it with all haste. The Blood Gorger scouts have just located the same creature from a different angle. Talon's Talons have just lost the trail of a Gaiwyrm and must circle back. The Hallowed Spears have just been rebuffed by a Vindleclaw and are licking their wounds before a second attempt they make."

"Got all that just from twirling some beads?" I asked.

Keeper sighed deeply. I decided to leave well enough alone—and none too soon, as one of the glider goblins raised the alarm, and I shaded my eyes in order to spot a black splotch surging up into the sky.

We'd found the dartwing, and we were gaining on it.

CHAPTER 29

DARTWING

<*Your tribe has decreased to 428 members.*>

The dartwing must have spotted us as well, because it suddenly cut at a right angle, heading south. Far in the distance, I could see heat shimmering off great dunes that our buggies would never be able to handle. The dartwing's enormous, bat-like wings cast a silhouette against the sky as it turned, and its long body undulated like a sky banner. Sourtooth was right; this wouldn't be like trapping night haunts. This thing was *massive.* Maybe not as heavy as the thundercleave, but long and sinuous. Despite the presence of feathers, it looked more like a winged serpent than a bird. I started to wonder if the 'dart' in its name referred more to the shape of its body than its weaponized quills.

Maybe it was both. I cast a look over at the sour old orc. Between their name for the world ("to be trampled beneath our feet"), the names they had for creatures, and the name of our team captain in his esteemed self, I got the feeling that orcs were very literal namers.

Sourtooth leaned his bike into a turn to match the dartwing's new trajectory and the rest of our convoy followed him.

I did a check around the buggy to make sure all the goblins had their armor on. I wasn't sure if one of those quills could pierce the bone of a skull-mask, but I'd issued all the drivers ceramic versions. The goblins hooted and hollered as we began to close the distance.

The dartwing didn't flap its wings as it flew. Rather, it used them to glide and then dive down to the ground in a huge plume of dust before somehow shooting back up into the sky to glide again.

I directed our Girmaks to pull the buggy close to Sourtooth's bike. "That's *sluggish*?" I demanded.

The orc looked over. "Oh, aye. Heavy of wing and scale with her belly full, she. Hungry, we'd never catch her, nor likely, the coming of her see!"

"Splendid," I yelled over the motors. Behind us, the Blood Gorgers had closed the distance some, ready to interfere with the chase on their oryx. They leaned far forward in their saddles, and I saw them using a horn on the side of their mount to draw and nock crossbows with one hand while they gripped the manes of their mounts in their other fist. Well, we'd see how their crossbows fared against our rifles.

I raised my hands above my head in the circle and whistled for attention. All the goblins turned my way and echoed the hand signal as they cheered, including ones that ought to have been driving—nearly causing two trikes to collide and the monocycle to wobble alarmingly. I held out my hands and mimed working the action of a lever-gun, complete with *chck-chck* sound effects. My tribe echoed the onomatopoeia and then followed it with the real thing. The mechanical slam of dozens of rifle actions dropping into place filled me with an electric anticipation.

Less than a kilometer ahead now, the dartwing slammed into the ground in a plume of dust and folded its wings. Through the haze, I could see the form coiling like a spring and then launching itself into the air before unfolding those wings again. Dust cascaded off the trailing edges. Its feathered head twisted back and hissed at us, and I could see its distended belly dragging against the wind and slowing it down.

A creature like that could feed a tribe twice our size for a week. More, even. And I could make a half-dozen prop planes from the membrane of its wings. Maybe a larger airship. There was only one problem: the large *XX* superimposed over its head where its level should have been. I gritted my teeth. No choice. All hope now lay in trusting that Sourtooth knew his business.

"Ready the launchers!" I called.

Across the convoy, bits of canvas and leather dustcovers came off the new additions to our buggies—courtesy of material from the Flock's stockpiles. Armstrong climbed up to the gunner's mount and pulled the cover from a hollow metal tube. I joined him and slid open the action on my newest rendition of Earth's ballistics science converted to Rava goblin blastics.

The black iron shells for these looked like up-sized rockettes, but they weren't *rockets* per se. Though, looking at the long, hollow tube of the launcher, you might think that. I slid the cover back into place and latched it while Armstrong got his shoulder under the controls and locked the firing mechanism back. He pressed his eye to the targeting ring and started to angle the muzzle up, waiting for us to get in range.

The dartwing, however, must have realized it wasn't going to outrun us. It wheeled with frightening speed, twisting back on itself and folding its massive wings tight against its body. The shriek from the wind through its quills reached us, sounding like a diving Stuka siren from a WWII flick. The dartwing crashed a couple hundred meters ahead of us, shaking the ground with its impact as a wave of dust erupted.

A low whistling was my only warning to throw myself to the floor of the buggy before a staccato of dull thuds peppered the front of the vehicle. The other goblins onboard squawked, and at least one fell off the back.

<Your tribe has decreased to 423 members.>

A blue flame tendril emerged from the gearbox underneath me. "*King Ap! The Dawi appears to have impressive defensive capabilities at distance*," said Girmaks.

Something Rufus had said came back to me. *You could take a thousand goblins into the desert and you'd lose a thousand goblins.*

"No kidding," I muttered, lifting my head. Several quills had buried themselves in the sloping front side of the buggy and were blowing in the wind. If this was the type of creature that existed in the deep dunes of the desert, the interior of Lanclova never being settled or conquered made a lot of sense. I looked back. Armstrong had two quills standing out of the front of his armor but was otherwise fine. He yanked them out of the plate carrier and threw them behind him.

"*How exciting! I am certain we can defeat the Dawi!*"

Right. Exciting. *Dawi*, huh? Even monsters weren't spared Girmaks's unique brand of familiar brevity.

Ahead, one of the trikes surged forward, occupants cheering. I spotted the canoneer on the back, and a bunch of goblins who had supplemented their skimpy leather with religious iconography. The driver opened the throttle so wide the trike bucked up on its rear wheels, surging forward. So many zealots had crammed on board that the spears made the vehicle look a bit like a wedge-shaped hedgehog.

Armstrong reached down and pulled me back to my feet. "C'mon, boss! Can't let the nutters 'ave all the fun!" He stomped on the deck, and the engine began to roar as Girmaks opened the throttle up all the way to match the zealots.

A massive shadow slithered in the dust cloud, coiling in layers like a set of gears. It stilled and compressed for a moment before the body of the thing shot from the cloud directly above us. The massive head twisted down and hissed as it flew over, its mane of feathers rattling. Its head was big enough to swallow a goblin whole. Its wings spread and cast a shadow over the entire group.

Girmaks swerved to the right to avoid the drooping tail that dragged a rake of spikes across the badlands terrain. As I held on, I could hear the screech of crude rubber tires, and then the *crunch* of at least one vehicle that hadn't managed to get out of the way in time and the collective squawks as a dozen goblins were sent flying.

<Your tribe has decreased to 422 members.>

"Bring us around qui—*woooah!*" I shouted. We might not have had brakes on the vehicles, but that apparently didn't matter to an Ifrit who could simply jam the gearbox. The buggy slid sideways, and the engine screamed. We bucked forward.

<Goblin Technology Unlocked: Extra-lock braking>

The zealots who had been leading the pack were now bringing up the rear, which they were not fans of, from their angry shouting. Their vehicle ramped up on two wheels as it pivoted nearly in place. Goblins swung from the frame like pennants, doing whatever they could to hold on.

"Nice going, Girmaks!" I shouted. Then, back to Armstrong, "Ready!"

"Ready, boss!"

I glanced over at Sourtooth, who had brought his bike around and had his pistol raised straight up in the air. "*On my order!*" he shouted.

"Prepare to fire!" I called out.

In our path, the Blood Gorger detachment was now directly in the path of the dartwing, which they seemed to notice only just before the big snake folded its wings and that air-raid alarm noise grew. A wave of dust and quills spread out from the impact, peppering more of the colorful feathers against the front of our buggy. One of them hit me in the chest hard enough to knock the wind out of me, but Armstrong caught me before I could tumble off the back of the buggy.

One of the Blood Gorger mounts stumbled, sending a pair of riders flying, but the rest managed to dodge the worst of it. I looked down to see Sourtooth pluck one quill from the meat of his shoulder with his teeth and spit it out behind him. He held his pistol up.

Once more, the dartwing rocketed into the air. But as it spread its wings to catch the air, Sourtooth fired one of our new signal guns, sending a rockette with a colorful trail through the air where it burst in a puff of green smoke.

As one, the gunners on the buggies fired.

CHAPTER 30

RECKLESS RIFLES

<Goblin Technology Unlocked: Reckless rifles>
<Goblin Technology Unlocked: Buster-busters>
<Goblin Technology Unlocked: Drogue slow'ems>

S*woosh-whump!*

A shell went flying out the front of Armstrong's cannon as a blast of exhaust sprayed out behind. Fire rippled up and down the line of buggies, and only one of them burst into flame. I'd consider that a huge success for untested designs. Most of the shells went wide, bursting harmlessly in the air. A few struck home in the leathery wings of our target, and their chutes deployed.

The weapons we'd mounted to the buggies were an old anti-tank technology that I'd co-opted for big game hunting. Recoilless rifles look and function a lot like rocket launchers—a big shell comes out the front and a jet of exhaust comes out the port in the back. But, as their name would suggest, they have more in common with traditional firearms. In this case, the payload wasn't a rocket, but a self-contained iron shell with a hook in the front and a secondary charge in the back that deployed a small braking parachute. Individually they wouldn't slow the dartwing much. But as they started to increase in number . . .

I heaved open the action on the recoilless rifle and pulled out the steaming expended primer case before dropping another one in place. Additional shots *whooshed* out from other buggies as well. Armstrong adjusted his aim and fired again, this time striking home. The dartwing's glide began to falter with the additional drag pulling at its lithe, otherwise aerodynamic body.

"We're in it now, boss!" shouted Armstrong. "Get after 'er!"

The dartwing hissed back at us, now flapping its wings in frustration to maintain altitude instead of gliding. It reared back and ripped two of the chutes out, snapping the lines. But for each one it pulled, two more goblins landed hits. The beast began to lose lift and entered its dive. The chutes worked to blunt its impact, and the wave of dust and quills was noticeably lessened.

<Your tribe has decreased to 422 members.>

Not entirely, of course.

<Your tribe has decreased to 420 members.>

The bark of lever guns sounded somewhere to my left, and a crossbow bolt whistled in front of my face. I looked over to see the Blood Gorgers closing in on our flank.

"Sourtooth!" I shouted.

The old orc glanced over and his face twisted into a laugh. He yanked his handlebars and moved to intercept, and two buggies with his orcs aboard followed suit.

"They move to intercede! The Gorgers must draw close to their own kill. They fear we might actually have a chance this beast to bring down first! At them!"

Girmaks swerved us left to avoid the dust cloud and brought us over to shore up the flank. I shouted over at Neil, who was commanding a special new vehicle not unlike the Big Hoss Rig in size but of very different purpose.

"Keep the rig safe, Neil! And keep hitting the dartwing!" I shouted before Girmaks carried us into the melee.

The orcs had reached our line on the left, close enough to see their face paint. The Blood Gorgers all had a red splatter painted across the lower half of their faces, with blood-red stained cloths tied around their arms. One of them threw a spear at Sourtooth, but the old orc steered back away and returned fire with his new rockette pistol. The shell took the Gorger in the shoulder and knocked him out of his saddle. He rolled through the dirt before coming to a stop and beginning to laugh. But there were more ready to replace him.

Armstrong picked up his double-barreled lever gun, detached from the original stone-sloth mount we'd ridden against the javeline. He fired on the orcs as they closed in. The first of the orcs began to leap atop the buggies. Guns were dropped in favor of cleavers and spears, but the orcs were terrific infighters, nimble, coordinated, and quick. They struck with daggers in close while those still riding oryx probed with spears from the backs of their mounts.

<Your tribe has decreased to 416 members.>

The buggy shifted, and I whipped my head around to find that one of the Blood Gorgers had managed to get onto our ride. He kicked the rear gunner off the back of the buggy and pulled a dagger out from between his teeth.

I had expected him to snarl in rage, but instead, his eyes lit upon me and he grinned. "Ah, little brother king! How find you the Stampede? A lark most bracing, yes?"

I was so stumped for words that I just looked at the orc. Behind us, I heard the *whump* of the dartwing attacking again somewhere in front of the buggy, and then three feather quills appeared in the Blood Gorger's chest. He looked down at them curiously, ran his fingers over the fletching, and then tipped off the back of the buggy. But more were charging in on oryx, ready to board for close combat—until the zealots hit them.

And when I say hit them, I mean *hit* them. The buggy plowed into the line of oryx, engine and occupants screaming. What goblins didn't go flying into the desert were quick to swarm onto the backs of the oryx, weapons raised as the cumulative combat bonus from their Fervor skill let them fight toe-to-toe with the much stronger orcs—at least with a significant numbers advantage. Armstrong fired his rifle, and I threw several of the poppers we had onboard. It sounded like being caught in the middle of a Midwest thunderstorm.

<Your tribe has decreased to 412 members.>

I spotted one of their members farther back, speaking to a keeper on the back of an oryx. That orc raised a horn to his lips and blew a low blast. The Blood Gorgers, whose main goal had been to distract and delay, withdrew from the melee. But was that because they were badly outnumbered? Or because their own team elsewhere was close to securing their own quarry?

Sourtooth seemed to share my concerns. He pulled back to speak with our own keeper and then moved up to the side of my buggy. "'Tis now or never at all, little brother mine. When it launches again, we strike!"

"Right," I said. I whistled to get Neil's attention. My taskmaster looked over at me from the back of his vehicle and nodded. His driver came close enough for me to make the transition. Ideally we'd have slowed the dartwing with more of the small chutes, but the Blood Gorgers simply didn't give us the opportunity. Together, Neil and I pulled the dustcover off the second part of the plan.

The weapon on the back of the buggy crewed by Neil's most fanatical hunters wasn't a recoilless rifle. We finished removing the dustcover and threw it into the wind to reveal a rack of two large rockets with a terrifying new addition: *cockpits*. While I hadn't expected a shortage of volunteers, neither had I expected a practical civil war to erupt over who got to be the ones to strap in. The S&M Club smacked and bit and pulled at one another until two goblins finally managed to get to the top of the pile and tumbled into the small seats, laughing maniacally.

I locked eyes with Neil. "No time for speeches," I said. "They know what's to be done?"

Neil grinned wickedly and opened a small tinderbox to reveal two glowing coals. I reached in and grabbed one, thankful for the heavy hide gloves I'd donned to act as loader for Armstrong's recoilless rifle. The material hissed and I could feel the heat through it. I moved back to the rear of the rockets as the hunters made a hole to admit me. Neil and I nodded to each other, and we touched the coals to the igniters at the back of the rockets. They fizzled for a moment, and for a few terrifying seconds, I worried that I'd gotten the liquid mixtures wrong.

<Goblin Technology Unlocked: Liquid rock'em fuel>
<Goblin Technology Unlocked: Single-crude rock'ems>
<Goblin Technology Unlocked: Composite goblin rock'ems>

The sputtering sparks turned into a roaring jet of flame. I held a hand against the heat, and the two rockets and their cheering pilots shot off the racks and toward the dartwing, just as it launched back into the air.

The goblins still aboard the buggy all held their hands above their heads, whistling and making the sign of the moon.

This was it.

CHAPTER 31

STAGE 2

The plan to bring down the dartwing wasn't the only thing with two stages. As the rockets climbed up toward the flying serpent, they carried with them two lines on reels locked to the front of the rig. I could just make out the tiny figures in the cockpits maneuvering the missiles as best they could, considering the circumstances. The liquid fuel began to sputter out, and then the back half of the missiles fell away.

<Goblin Technology Unlocked: Drop-away rock'ems>

With the first stage successfully separated, the second-stage motors kicked on, and the icky-putty power pumped the smaller delivery vehicles with the energy needed to climb up above the dartwing's altitude. The serpent hissed, eyes up, tracking the new threat. It wheeled to the left, trying to evade, but the drogue chutes slowed it down, and one of the two rocket pilots course-corrected. The other struggled to bring his craft in line.

"Come on, come on!" I shouted. The reels on the rig shrieked as they played out the cord. Overhead, the two rockets caught up with the dartwing. The first pilot bailed out, deploying a personal glider that carried him up and away from the rocket just before its payload exploded. A wide net spread out, courtesy of the Flock, and just missed the dartwing. It dropped, and Neil slashed the line coming out of the reel that had been connected to it before it could tangle in the vehicle's axles.

The second rocketeer got his craft back on track—but didn't bail out. He screamed toward the dartwing on a column of sickly brown exhaust smoke. The two converged in the air, and then another explosion . . . and no glider.

<Your tribe has decreased to 409 members.>

The dartwing flailed in the air as the second net wrapped about its wings, tangling and driving the creature to the ground. This time it fell, rather than diving. It hissed and shrieked as it came down, twisting in the air, until it landed on the badlands with a *whump.* By this time, the goblins had learned to duck, and we didn't lose any more to the quill barrage.

"Let's go!" I shouted, pointing at the downed creature. "Finish it!" It was down, but not out. My mouth was already salivating at the thought of how much meat was on that thing. We're talking snake filets, we're talking wing meat, we're talking shoulder roasts.

A horn blast sounded from one of the vehicles at the back of the convoy. I looked back, and the blood drained out of me as I saw the orc keeper with a ram's horn in one hand and her beads raised high in the other. Sourtooth brought his bike nearby, and I didn't need to hear the words that passed between them to know we were too late. Sourtooth's dark glower said it all.

The Blood Gorgers' interference had delayed us just long enough from bringing the dartwing down, and someone else had managed their kill first. If it was Lura, then that would mean the Stampede was effectively over, as she'd have more points than anyone would be capable of overtaking. Unbelievably, I had to root for the jerks who had just attacked us.

I had Neil drop our buggy back alongside the orc leader.

"Sourtooth, who got it? Are we still in this thing?"

The old orc looked at me. “The Blood Gorgers claimed a kill. Onward the Stampede marches, little brother.”

I breathed a sigh of relief, then glanced at the dust plume from where the dartwing had fallen. “At least my tribe won’t go hungry for a while,” I muttered.

“We must free her of those binding ropes,” said Sourtooth.

I snapped my head around. “What?! But we have her!”

Sourtooth shook his head. “Forbidden to claim a totem outside given time. To do so is to rob another team of hunting. This law is ironclad, and violated would see us thrust from the Stampede.”

I threw my hands in the air. “So all that work, the goblins I lost, and the resources we spent, and it’s all for nothing?”

“’Tis the way of things, little brother. The strong prevail and whine not. Come, we must free her and join the slayers’ camp.”

The rest of the Blood Gorgers were already headed south. I had the convoy stage up while a few of us went on to where the dartwing had landed. Trapped on the ground, coiled and caught, it didn’t look like such a monstrous threat. System had let me see its level, finally, and a luminous *43* hovered over it. This was one of the winged creatures the bestiary had only alluded to, and there were much stronger threats farther into the desert. But it was the toughest thing we’d brought down to date, and we weren’t even going to get to eat it.

It glared at us even as we cut the binding lines off the nets and allowed it to slither free, though it didn’t attack us as we did so. Some part of it must have known that we no longer intended to kill it. With a final hiss and ruffling of feathers, it sprung back into the air and headed toward the dunes on the horizon.

Sourtooth sighed, shaking his head. “There’s no catching her in the desert on these chariots, little brother. We must regroup and plan anew. Come. We shall see if the Gorgers’ quarry is of their name worthy.”

It was with some reluctance that I piled on the scattered bits of the vehicles we’d lost onto the backs of the buggies and headed south after the detachment of Blood Gorgers. It wasn't until the sun had dropped nearly to the horizon that we came in sight of the Stampede camp, centered around a massive carcass. The celebration was already in full swing, with the red-faced Blood Gorgers getting a head start on the merriment. I left Chuck in charge of getting our corner of the camp set up and followed Sourtooth into the encampment.

"Little brothers!" I heard one of them shout, and the rest pointed and cheered. One of them sauntered over, grinning. I recognized him as the leader of the detachment that had hounded us. "Well fought, 'neath the spreading of the dartwing's shadow. Had we dallied but a few heartbeats more, we might have been feasting on snake tonight, instead! Taste in our victory."

He handed down a pile of dripping meat wrapped in a flatbread like a gyro, the smell of which made my mouth fill with saliva. I reached out, half expecting him to rip it away in a cruel jest. But I took it, glancing at Sourtooth, who already had one of his own, which he chewed on the good side of his mouth. The Gorgers had more ready for my Secretive Servants that accompanied us, and even a platter to bring back to the rest of the goblins.

The sandwich itself was fresh and hot and greasy, packed with seasoned meat that reminded me of a kebab joint near my university. The orcs liked things spicy, and my eyes began to water along with my mouth as I dug in. The Gorgers moved on, clearly half-drunk already and shooting for full.

Once they left, I shook my head. "I don't understand orc customs," I admitted to Sourtooth. "They refuse to trade, but Lura and the Gorgers both offered us food from their kill."

Sourtooth stuffed the last of his gyro into his mouth and swallowed it. "For a goblin, you think oddly like a *human*, little brother."

The accusation made me stiffen. On one hand, retaining my humanity shouldn't be a bad thing. On the other, humans weren't exactly popular in the Lanclova interior. I had to be mindful of who I was talking to, and what I let slip.

Sourtooth continued. "I know not from where this backward reason comes. Men and elves show wealth by hoarding it, by wearing trinkets of soft, useless metals and building stone houses to anchor them. But an orc's wealth, only by what they can spare is it displayed. All can see the quality of a feast spread amongst respected rivals and know an orc to also be of quality. That is the way of things."

I pressed my hands to my forehead, trying to understand. "So, you take what you want, because the strong taking from the weak is the way of things. But you share as much as possible with anyone who doesn't have as much, because that shows off how rich you are?"

Sourtooth clapped a hand on my back. "Now you're getting it!"

I really didn't. It was some weird inverse Robin Hood custom. Steal from the poor and give to the poor. It was as backward as their high school drama club speech. But if it resulted in gracious winners and me not going hungry tonight, who was I to judge?

CHAPTER 32

VERTICAL THINKING

<Your tribe has increased to 465 members.>

Finding out we had to let the dartwing go had dampened some spirits, but finding out we got to eat anyway lifted most of the goblins' moods back up again. Still, I had a taste for competition, and I wanted to get the Flock a placement that would see hunting rights secured for my tribe.

Since the Blood Gorgers had secured the latest totem beast, that meant they were the ones who decided when the Stampede would resume. And they weren't in quite as great a hurry as the upstart Lura. Which suited me, since it gave me a full two days to do some much-needed repairs and modifications using Sourtooth's stockpile of supplies as we regrouped and planned. Chuck helped me out when he wasn't busy with the dogs and the captured herd stock, and I couldn't help noticing the resident canoneers eyeing us closely as we worked on engines together.

"With the dartwing out, what's our next best option?" I asked Sourtooth. I hammered at an engine that had developed a warp, trying to get it back to spec—er, *goblin* spec, at any rate. Reinforcements from Village Apollo had brought more vehicles, including one small biplane with a crew of only three goblins.

Fortunately, the orcs found flying goblins to be more of a novelty than a threat—and they still attributed the artifice to the Ifrit. The only ones who knew it was actually goblin tech were members of the Flock.

"We find ourselves trapped twixt anvil and hammer, little brother," said Sourtooth. He rested, crouched, on a flat rock in the middle of the forge yard. "What totems remain play cruel tricks upon us, either elusive or deadly."

"And the dartwing wasn't?"

Sourtooth ignored the jab and sucked at his namesake a moment as he thought. "The Dawn will seek the red trapper totem, having been denied the rasker by the Blood Gorgers. Lura gained insight fair on the location of one. Never beat her to it, we. The Blood Gorger's kill brings them in striking distance of the Dawn's Light. Either can take the winning totem now, and the Gorgers will seek to end it quickly while Lura draws the game out to stack her glory. We ought hunt a lesser drake perhaps, should one hunger enough to leave the mountains—alas, likely not this time of year. A long shot. A vine-grabber perhaps. How fare your artifice in swamps?"

"Not well," I admitted. "But we've got boats and cliffords—er, the red badlands dogs."

Sourtooth shook his head. "They would cower and flee before the thing."

I pursed my furry lips. "What about trying to muscle out one of the smaller teams? You've seen what our guns and rockets can do. We defeated the javeline with them and have only gotten stronger since."

The old orc huffed a laugh. "Brag at bagging bacon, you. Orcs are no rutter mob. Keen hunters, we, even of temper and steady of hand on spear and pommel. Prone to anger not, and not so easily goaded as a pork-brained buffoon. No, the weakest of the teams would make easy sport of you. Skirmishes are good diversion, but best not raise their ire, for a team moved to bloodlust is not easily sated and clever goblins would run and hide, not stand and fight."

I put down my hammer and examined my handiwork. With an arm in front of my face in case the ensemble exploded, I dropped a starter rockette into the chute and let the engine turn over. It rumbled to life, rattling, shaking, and generally raising an unholy ruckus. In other words, perfect working order for GTT tech.

I cocked my head. "What about . . . the *whistler*? Is that what you called it?"

Sourtooth stilled. This was a very touchy subject for him, I expected. I pressed on with caution.

"It had to be released, right? Since Lura beat you to a kill? That means it's still out there."

"You'd feed it my spare leg, little brother," growled Sourtooth. "Your tribe's not ready for a beast of that caliber."

"But you know where it is?"

Sourtooth held still a moment. "Aye. It's gone to ground in the canyons to lick the wounds given by the Flock, grandfather spirits rest them."

I cut the throttle on the engine and leaned against the crankcase. "And no one else has it in their sights?"

Sourtooth straightened. "No other team is damn fool enough to follow it into its lair where it may weave and charge as it likes."

<Your tribe has decreased to 459 members.>
<Your tribe has decreased to 457 members.>
<Your tribe has increased to 482 members.>
<12 of your tribe members have assumed the zealot job.>

Eileen and the canoneers must have converted another village. That was the third so far.

No new variants?

<The tribe had only one variant: Hobgoblin Scrappers.>

I tsked. Bad luck. I'd hoped each tribe would introduce a new needed skill or specialization into the tribe. So far, we'd narrowly missed something called *flatulators* and gotten a duplicate variant.

I turned back to the problem at hand. "We won't have room to maneuver in a canyon. Maybe we could build a big missile and launch it into the area? We've got two-stage guided rockets. We just need one with a big enough warhead to send this whistler to the next simulation."

But even as I spoke it, I knew it wasn't feasible yet. Guided rockets with enough payload to function as long-range artillery were going to take time and trials to develop, and even entirely mechanical inertial guidance systems required precise instrumentation like gyroscopes. We'd gotten lucky with the net missiles working as planned, but precision short-range ballistic missiles were another beast altogether. We weren't exactly working with advanced guidance systems here.

Still. We had manpower, we had materials. That meant this was an engineering problem. A canyon might not have enough space to maneuver on the ground, but they had plenty of verticality. Maybe we needed to attack this problem from a different direction. Literally.

"Let's go talk to Promo. I have an idea."

I choked out the engine and wandered over to the forge yard. Several of the Blood Gorgers were still sleeping off hangovers, dozing in the heat given off by the forges. The ringing of hammers on anvils seemed to bother them not at all, and I had to step over one of them in order to reach the head of my smiths.

"How long would it take to dismount the engines from, let's say, half the buggies?" I asked.

Promo cocked his head at me. "Rest o' the day, reckon. What you gettin' at, boss?"

I nodded to the Ifrit floating around the camp in their coaxial vessels. One of them passed by a pair of orcs, who offered the two-fingers-to-the-nose gesture I had learned was a sign of respect/warding to/from ancestors. I turned back to Promo.

"We can't get at this next monster from the ground. The next option is the air. Do you understand the principles of those flying Ifrit vessels enough to make a version capable of carrying a crew?"

Promo scratched at his jowls and a glaze passed over his eyes, typical of a Ravan looking at System menus. A grin spread across his face. "Reckon I can at that, boss. Why only half the buggies?"

I huffed. "Because the abomination unto aerodynamics that are helicopters are very fuel-inefficient. We're going to drive them to the canyon and launch them from there to maximize flight time."

Sourtooth grunted. "I've seen your skyborne artifice, little brother. If you hold notion that I'll ride the winds on a wreck in the making, absolve yourself of it. For my lads that goes as well. We tolerated your wheeled contraptions, but good faith and daring takes an orc only so far. An oryx twixt our legs is the only sure thing in terrain like that."

I shrugged. "You'd be too heavy anyway. We need to minimize weight. Besides, someone's going to have to be the bait."

"The *what*?" asked Sourtooth, having very clearly heard me. "I know the rate at which goblins breed, but an orc life is not easily cast before the charge."

"Figured you'd want to be as close as possible when you get your revenge. The canyons might not have the terrain for buggies to maneuver, but what if I could make you a shield capable of taking a hit from the whistler?"

Sourtooth closed his eyes and muttered something under his breath. I caught *Lura*, *blight*, and *womb*, and a few other terms best not repeated in polite company. And of course it wasn't Lura he was upset with. It was me.

"Alright, little brother mine," said Sourtooth. "But once we commit, there will be no turning back. The whistler will not keen be to grant us a third audience. It is like a meteor made flesh, and it will finish what I started."

"The whistler, then."

Sourtooth absently rubbed the remnant of the leg he'd lost to the beast. "The whistler. More than those peashooters, we'll need. What more artifice have you a will to forge?"

I thought about the advancements we'd made so far. I hadn't followed the linear path of human technological development. I'd skipped around, cut corners, jumped entire fields of research by already knowing the termini those innovative-yet-obsolete stepping stones had led to. We had internal combustion engines and I hadn't even gotten around to making a steam engine, a light bulb, or a transistor yet. In some regards, we were up to the early 1900s. Hell, we were getting ready to make helicopters. But in many other regards, we were still in the BC era. We didn't have running water or sewage, our government was a pure monarchy—or rather, some sort of gestalt colony with a king at its heart. We didn't even have agriculture, despite my best efforts. On the other hand, we had heavier-than-air flight, we had rifles with internal magazines, and we had multi-stage rockets. Military technology was certainly progressing. But, then, a large amount of innovation and development had been spurred on by conflict on Earth. Well, if we were doing it by hunting wild animals instead of killing humans, I certainly didn't have a problem with it. Bonus points if it kept my tribe sufficiently fed.

But they also needed to be protected. Sourtooth didn't think the buggies would cut it, and I had a feeling the oryx weren't going to get the job done, either. The majority of our military technology was about at a pre–WWI level. Well, the First World War introduced more than just dogfights and trenches. There was one area of technology that we were still behind on.

"Promo. Bring the rocket rig around. We've got work to do."

CHAPTER 33

KEEPER SECRETS

<Your tribe has increased to 561 members.>

The morning of the third day, the Blood Gorgers finally signaled their intent to continue the hunt. And believe me when I say we didn't waste a single minute. We wasted many, many minutes. Goblins aren't exactly the most attentive of workers, prone to getting distracted if there's not a taskmaster hovering over them—and even then, the taskmasters were prone to get curious about whatever shiny object had gotten the original goblins' attention. So when we rolled out behind our scout biplane, we didn't have as many vehicles as ready to go as I'd hoped.

But we had more than I'd expected.

We had more company than I'd expected, too. Word from the Blood Gorgers must have gotten around that we weren't just a gaggle of hopeless goblins, but a competent team capable of bringing down totem beasts. It wasn't just a contingent of Blood Gorger scouts that set off after us. A party with black-and-white bands followed us, as did one wearing viridian green, and even a set of Lura's colors was present. Like the Gorgers, I was sure they would try to interfere if it looked as though we would claim another totem.

What surprised me most was our keeper climbing up on the lead vehicle and leaning down to our engine to give the sign of respect to elders.

"Elder, you honor us," she said before settling back to ply her beads.

I glanced at the engine that glowed with a soft blue, distinctively *Ifrit* flame, and then at the elder orc. I couldn't help it. I sidled back.

"If orc grandfather spirits are so cunning and devious, why would they help us?" I asked.

"I'm sure they have their reasons," said Keeper. "Perhaps you should ask *them*."

"But the Ifrit deny that they are orcs," I said.

"So . . . ?"

"So . . . they couldn't possibly answer the question."

"How convenient." Keeper tapped the side of her nose with her finger. It was such an Earth gesture that it made me miss my old life, which made me realize how little time I'd spent missing my old life since coming to Rava. Was that a biological aspect of my new body? Goblins didn't tend to show regret for the past or any sense of loss, even after an action that resulted in the deaths of other goblins. Brushes with their own mortality deterred goblins only momentarily. On more than one occasion, I'd witnessed a goblin choke on a bone only to cough it up and try to eat it again.

A series of beads spun in Keeper's hand, and I eyed them, considering.

"I think I've figured those out," I said, pointing to the beads.

Keeper raised a solitary eyebrow.

"At first, I thought it was like a serial connection. Some beads for sending, others for receiving. Certain faces of certain beads represent syllables to exchange messages. I figured there must have been some central keeper operating a switchboard to keep message traffic flowing. I had thought I could optimize the whole system with a few days to iron out inefficiencies. Pass more data with less fluff, you know?"

"Clearly you no longer believe this to be the case."

Around us, the vehicles had begun to start up.

"I think all the teams are represented on each string," I said. "That's why we couldn't join late as a new team. Each one of those multicolor beads represents one of the team's colors, and the beads that follow give very basic information on direction, intent, proximity, and status. The rest you infer and pass it off as having more knowledge than you actually do."

The corner of the hooded orc's mouth twitched upward.

"I bet I could still improve it for you—by *making* it what I originally thought it was. Bidirectional communication based on simple syllabic syntax and short phrases, maybe encoded in hexadecimal with a central operator sending mass notifications. One side of the beads would be *out* and one side would be *in*. I'd be happy to help you figure out a basic communications manual." I rubbed my hands together. "If I could get a couple sets of those beads for my tribe."

Keeper considered for a moment and then reached out and offered the beads to me. I grinned and reached out, wrapping my fist around the links.

As soon as my skin touched them, my vision flashed white and a lance of pain shot through my temples.

In my head I heard a cacophony of voices, some shouting, some whispering, but all trying to burrow into the folds of my brain.

Dawntreadersfifteenmilessouthof PIN VALE headingeast

Flatbottoms HUNT by dust storm sullied—

—FRIGHTENED bycarelessscouttingcost

finding tracks led to carcass killed by GARGA—

returningtoStAgInGcampWeStNoRtHwEsTofrookery

"Jesus!" I let go of the bracelet as if I'd been stung—and it felt like I had. My fingers steamed, and I shook them out and put them in my mouth to soothe them. My hair stood on end, something the other buggy occupants were more than happy to point and laugh at.

"*Yer culda trld me thr were just margic warlky-trlkys,*" I muttered around my fingers.

"And dash hopes of yours for stunted syntax and short phrases?" Keeper leaned over, a sly smile spreading under her hood. "I may not yet a grandfather spirit be, little brother. But I am a stranger not to mischief."

"Clearly," I said.

Boy, orcs must pull some serious pranks on one another. So. Orc magic. The first I'd seen of magic, really, outside of the Ifrit—though they were beings *of* magic, apparently, they didn't practice sorcery. I had so many questions. Unfortunately, I didn't think I was going to get them out of the recalcitrant keeper.

I had Girmaks take us alongside Sourtooth's bike and made the transition over. As a human, I never would have considered jumping from a moving buggy onto a moving motorcycle, but as a goblin it was as easy as walking down the sidewalk. I'd made a gunner's mount on the back of the motorcycle, and I busied myself doing a quick once-over until Sourtooth stopped glaring at me.

"You been to a lot of places on Rava doing these Stampedes?" I asked.

"Across the burning sands and the shimmering salt, amid trees both tall and twisted. 'Neath sun and moon in years remembered only by song," said Sourtooth.

"Ah, so yes . . . I think. Who's the toughest? After the orcs, of course."

Sourtooth laughed. "Pad the ego not, little brother. Flattery gains not amongst my kind." He scratched at his chin. "The Noll are the best fighters, man-to-man. Strong and swift, fierce and cunning. They melt into the forest as though wrought from a subtle breeze. When the Stampede reached their shores, a wide berth we offered their fortress monasteries—and a Noll team was offered a place at the hunting table. However, they eat but fish and greens."

"How about Habberport?"

"A splinter of the Duchy of Habb. Sealed within their loathsome walls, they, when my kin come to hunt. If strayed a totem to the coast, we would chase it through their gardens with not a fear. Yet given time and space to muster legions from the Duchy, they are not easily turned."

"Their prince wanted to capture me. Sent the javeline to do it."

Sourtooth barked a laugh. "He will stop not, then. Men of the Duchy know well the sting of a goblin king grown strong. Long have they coveted this land, and long has it rebuffed them. But never has it *threatened* them as you do."

"What about the strongest magic practitioners?" I asked.

Again, Sourtooth considered. "Elves are quite skilled in natural magics, but physically not so imposing. Outside of the elves, perhaps the Midnight Queendom. They read fortunes in the stars. They are impossible to ambush, on land or at sea, and through trade they have amassed great riches. They can see your movements and intents reflected in the night sky."

"Astrology?" I scoffed. "Fortunes are best left in cookies where they belong."

"Mock them at your peril, little brother. They have swept greater foes than you aside as you might brush dirt from your tunic." He pursed his lips. "Greater foes than I as well. Numbers amount to naught, for they count them. Plans count for not, for they see them. There is only one thing that blinds their eyes and one place they dare not tread."

"What's that?" I asked, admittedly now a little worried. On Earth, astrology was junk mysticism. But I had to lend credence to the idea that maybe in this world, it might be a job that came with serious skills of tactical and strategic benefit. I needed more information about everything outside of my local sphere.

Sourtooth pointed up at the moon, nearing its eclipse. "Raphina shadows this land from the stars. It is the one place the queen is blind."

CHAPTER 34

CANYON MODEL

<Your tribe has increased to 583 members.>

The number of goblins we'd amassed in the convoy of gear-headed speed freaks had grown noticeably. Even though we'd added new vehicles, the fact that the convoy was self-sustaining in terms of food meant that there was more food to go around back at the villages, and the spawning penalties had been rescinded as a result—at least for the time being. One extra benefit I found from the spawning sub-menu was that I could restrict new goblin births if I so needed, to maintain the tribe at a certain level with only enough growth to account for daily attrition, which had been markedly higher after inventing multi-stage missiles and internal combustion engines.

Our fleet was now over twenty strong, with each new replacement vehicle hauling bladders of fuel pumped from the swamps of Huntsville and framed from the steel refined from its iron. Damaged vehicles were sent back to Village Apollo with captured herd animals, scrap parts, and cast-off materials from the orcs. And that figure was after accounting for the biplane that was attacked by a four-winged bird and the bike that was taken by a dire trapdoor spider creature while we were setting up camp for the night—taking six goblins with it.

But having split the fleet into a mix of ground vehicles and choppers made it slow going as the buggies struggled to haul their heavy loads across the badlands. Our rival teams kept pace easily and also stopped whenever we camped for the night. Spirits in the tribe were high, but Sourtooth kept mostly to himself the closer we got to the beast's lair. The terrain grew rockier and more mountainous, turning into sharp stone and pink gravel that crunched underfoot.

At a maintenance stop, a glint caught my eye, and I reached down and picked up a piece of the gravel, turning it in the sun. It shone with a grayish luster in a couple of spots, and I held it up to my eye. I could see metallic flecks in it. Some sort of surface ore. Worth collecting, maybe. Studying it would have to wait. For now, we were on a time crunch to make sure we hit that whistler before Lura tracked down her own quarry. I returned to the convoy, where the igni were overseeing the unloading and reassembly of the new aircraft.

When I say aircraft, I mean it in the barest sense of the word. Helicopters are aerodynamic freaks of nature, flying primarily by rattling and shaking so hard that the ground rejects them. In fact, I wouldn't even have to dumb them down or make them more dangerous for them to fit in the Goblin Tech Tree. If a Blackhawk had followed me to Rava, it would have immediately triggered a GTT unlock prompt.

Still, it was another step toward the terminus of orbital space travel and landing a spacecraft on the surface of Raphina, whose watchful eye hung fat and heavy in the sky above. It must have been getting close to summer on this continent as well, because the days were getting hot, and I was grateful for the shade that offered a brief reprieve from the rays baking the dusty hardpack. I'd been to the salt flats in Utah on a few different occasions to watch races and a rocket test-fire, but I hadn't been blue and furry at the time. It wasn't quite to the point where I considered the limited coverage favored by the Shafts and Motors Club. But it wasn't far off, either.

Clutching the gravel in my tiny fist, I stashed it in a pack I kept on the back of the buggy and then helped Promo get one of the choppers sorted. None of them had a standardized layout—having been cobbled from disparate parts meant they had unusual setups in terms of number of rotor blades, tail configurations, and payloads. Each one would fly completely differently from the next, so the canoneers had their work cut out for them trying to canonize them. Hell, it'd be a miracle if the pilots didn't crash them on takeoff, even with the Ifrit smoothing out controls and flight. So far, we'd only tested them with tethers, and never multiple together. It was time to change that.

"Fuel 'em up!" I called. "We're going on a dry run." The tribe cheered and ran to the back of the new and improved Big Hoss Rig for bladders of kerosene to power the choppers. The wranglers, meanwhile, were fighting with the goblins possessing abnormally high mechanical aptitude for who would get to be at the controls, and it somehow managed to work out that every wrangler pilot seemed to be squeezed into a craft built for a nonvariant, while each of Eileen's air deliverymen were stuck between reaching the foot pedals and the flight stick (called a "cyclic" on helicopters).

As for me, I had my vehicle already marked out, and Armstrong was already in the gunner's station waiting for me.

"Ready, boss!" he said, offering a salute. His skull mask had been painted with ash-gray streaks—matching the gray and white of the Flock's colors. I climbed into the pilot's station above and behind Armstrong while a half-dozen other goblins clambered onto the various stations, or just kind of held on to the bare-bones frame. Even with them aboard, the heaviest weight by far was the engine and fuel bladders. But around the engine, I could see Girmaks's pale blue shimmer. I dropped a charge in the engine compartment and started it up.

The engine roared to life, and I cranked the clutch belt to engage the main rotor as it warmed up. Overhead, the coaxial blades started to turn, but I kept the pitch flat while the rest of the fleet got their vehicles up and running. In total, we had eight choppers of various sizes. Three of them didn't have controls at all, being piloted entirely via Ifrit while the goblins aboard were simply along for the ride—a fact that dissuaded them not at all.

The thing about helicopters is that they're *loud*. Not only is there the engine noise, but the noise of the main rotors and tail rotors cutting through the air essentially produces sound at three different frequencies that drowns out nearly everything. Voice communication is basically impossible over the racket, and goblin helicopter blades had none of the modern aerodynamic creature comforts that reduced the sound profile of Earth helicopters from *deafening* all the way to *nearly deafening*. Necessity being the mother of invention, and being a fantastic engineer myself with 2,500 hours in the cockpit, I had foreseen this—and built the tribe's first electrical device: a simple sound-powered intercom.

It was a crucial first step on the way to radios, I slipped a pair of leather ear-cups over my head and pulled a handset closer to my mouth.

"Check, check,"

Inside the handset, my voice caused a diaphragm to vibrate, inducing a charge across a pair of lodestones connected to a wire in what amounted to the world's dirtiest transducer, and the Goblin Tech Tree did the rest of the heavy lifting. In my ear-cups, the process reversed, and the faint electrical signal repeated my own voice, sounding hollow and tinny—but understandable.

<Goblin Technology Unlocked: Zap-talkies>
<Goblin Component Technology Unlocked: Transduce'ems>
<Goblin Component Technology Unlocked: Wire-talkies>
<Goblin Component Technology Unlocked: Induced zaps>

"*HEY BOSS, IT WORKS!*" shouted Armstrong. I pulled one of the ear-cups away from my head, wincing. The scrapper tossed me a grin and a thumbs-up over his shoulder.

"*NOT SO LOUD!*" I yelled back. He flinched in his seat.

Tribe Apollo had the means to build one of these ever since Rufus's second visit to the bluff, but they hadn't ever been a priority, what with the tribe suffering crisis after crisis. Electrical devices had simply fallen to the wayside in favor of weapons and vehicles to hunt with. But now that we were starting to unite the tribes of the region and working out a way to keep them fed, we were going to need communication more reliable than glider messengers. Sound-powered phones were a step on the road to radio—and the jump wasn't as big as you might think. A power source, a modulator, an amplifier, an antenna, and a receiver to demodulate and reverse the process. Hell, there were radios even simpler than that, ones that just worked on induced AC current across a coil. But that would still take time and focus to develop the electrical components, so right now comms were limited to per-aircraft, while red-tinted smoke swirling from two flares at the back of our craft let the other pilots know to follow our lead.

I twisted the throttle and checked the response on the anti-torque pedals before lifting the collective pitch control lever. The chopper started getting light on its wheels, and I tilted the cyclic control forward.

Our engines still weren't amazing. Don't get me wrong, it was amazing that they worked *at all*. But they were heavy, being made primarily from cast iron, steel, or ceramic, which meant a strength-to-weight ratio less than ideal for heavier-than-air flight. Combined with the inbuilt inefficiencies in the aerodynamics of helicopters, we had a fleet of whales that struggled to get off the ground with a full belly. Luckily, helicopters become more efficient as you build airspeed and escape your own vortices. I pressed forward, letting our ground speed climb, and I felt the aircraft shudder as we passed through that boundary into clean, efficient air. I hauled back on the cyclic, and we lifted into the air to cheers and the loss of one goblin who got so excited she forgot she still had to hang on.

I craned my neck to see that most of the rest of the fleet had gotten off the ground, with the exception of one aircraft that tilted too far back, shearing off its own tail in the process. I winced as the crew bailed out before the still-spinning main rotor could turn them into furry blue clouds.

Flying the choppers was strange, being used to fixed-wing aircraft as I was—and yet again, I felt the telltale pressure of System's increased attention on me, as I often did when I was flying. I focused on maintaining the controls and checking the simple gauges I'd built to monitor the remaining fuel weight and rotor RPMs. It all seemed to be working as I climbed. The whole aircraft vibrated, but the feeling of peace that flying always gave me still settled into my core. Every problem I've ever had was on the ground—and lifting off left them all behind. I was part of the sky while I was in the cockpit.

I banked to the right, toward a formation of stone pillars that created a small channel. With the whistler licking its wounds in a canyon, tight and rocky terrain was going to be our battlefield. Dumping collective, I brought us low and then flared back. I lined up on a spindle formation down the center of the lane. Geological forces had conspired to give the formation an hourglass shape, heavy on top and bottom with a narrow bit in the middle.

"Armstrong, hit the skinny part."

My scrapper lined up the two recoilless rifles built into the nose of the chopper and let 'em rip. Acrid, smoky back-blast blew through the open cockpit, stinging my eyes. But through the haze, two small explosions burst against the pillar, near the narrow section. Around us, a half-dozen other sets of rifles fired, and contrails raced ahead. Some of them missed, but most of them hit. A handful of cheers came over the sound-powered headset from the goblins on board. I tilted us to the right and traversed us while endeavoring to keep the nose pointed at the spindle. It wasn't easy. I wasn't used to flying sideways. But several goblins took the opportunity to fire rifles and pistols at the stone pillar.

I straightened us back out and circled behind our target pillar, weaving through the forest of stone formations. The engine and the main rotor thumped, stressed by the hard maneuvers. I pulled the stick back and raised the collective to bring the chopper up and slow us before banking around for another pass.

I grabbed the sound-powered handset. "*Tally ho!*"

One of the goblins squawked and climbed down to the compartment underneath the cockpit. Once we were lined up, I cranked hard on a plunger built into the front dash, and I felt a mechanical *clunk* from underneath. The chopper got significantly lighter as our primary payload dropped away. I banked us and looked below, where a rocket had detached with a single goblin holding on. The rocket motor kicked on, and I swear I could hear the *EEEEeeeee* as it sped toward the spindle on a plume of dirty smoke. To my left and right, two other teams released their payloads as well, goblin guidance systems steering the rockets to the pillar.

Just before impact, three gliders unfurled and the goblins detached from their rockets, turning velocity into altitude as they caught the air and soared high above the choppers. They'd find their way back to the convoy, having completed their task. Below them, a trio of explosions kicked up a cloud of dust and smoke against the spindle. A thunderous *CRACK* echoed throughout the confines of the canyon.

Uh-oh.

<Goblin Technology Unlocked: Excavation blast'ems>

CHAPTER 35

TURNABOUT

The top of the massive rock formation shifted, dust and debris falling off it. Then it tilted. *Toward us.* My mind raced. This wasn't part of plan A, B, C, *or* D. No time to climb, no space to turn. There was only one thing to do.

"*King Ap, we appear to be in some danger!*" shouted Girmaks from the engine.

"Hold on!" I shouted as I dumped the collective and jammed the cyclic stick forward.

"*I have no arms with which to hold!*"

A feeling of weightlessness overcame the craft, and I could feel myself floating up against the simple restraints as we fell. We tilted forward just as the spindle began to topple at the narrowest point. With our altitude dropping fast, I yanked up on the collective. It didn't do much for our descent rate, but it pulled us forward, underneath the toppling rock formation. Rubble fell around us, and a shadow not unlike the eclipse enveloped us as the bulk of the formation passed overhead.

"Wooooooo!" shouted Armstrong from the gunner's seat. He had both his arms raised high in the air as if he were on the world's best roller coaster. The other goblins just hung on for dear life and squealed.

Shadow turned into sunlight as we shot out from under the collapsing spire, and I craned my neck around to see that most of the formation had followed my maneuver—albeit two a touch too late. A falling boulder smashed through the main rotor of one chopper, pulverizing the aircraft in an instant. The fuel caught, and the whole ensemble exploded.

<Your tribe has decreased to 577 members.>

The occupants of the other remaining aircraft saw what had happened. To a goblin, they all bailed out, some unfurling personal gliders, others just tumbling through the air, screaming at the top of their lungs. I saw one of them holding onto a small brass jar that glinted in the sun, which hopefully meant the Ifrit had bailed out as well. The now unmanned chopper spun out of control, spiraling in place until the bulk of the spire hit the abandoned aircraft and it disappeared from view. The pillar crashed down with the noise of an entire thunderstorm compressed into a few seconds, and I watched, awestruck, as the whole thing collapsed into a billion pieces.

I brought the chopper around, lowering us down. A layer of dust had risen, but I still spotted the wreckage from the first chopper. Hauling back on the cyclic, I slowed us up and dipped us down, low enough to make sure that there was no Ifrit still in the wreckage.

Another chopper followed and picked up the goblins who had bailed out. Several crews had dismounted to run and kick the rocks broken off the main pillar and cheer at our victory. I even spotted a canoneer scribbling furiously to document the event. Even though, effectively, *we'd shot a rock.*

Still. Who was I to rain on their parade? Truth be told, I was feeling pretty euphoric myself. The tribe was beginning to master powered flight. How long before we had turbine engines? Scramjets? Reusable rocket boosters? *Space shuttles*?

I climbed atop my chopper and whistled for their attention and formed a circle over my head with my thumbs and forefingers. A cheer swept through the assembled air crews, and I raised my voice to be heard over the clamor.

"Target practice is over! Time for the real thing!"

The goblins scrambled to get back to their vehicles, and the whine of engines rose again. The aircraft, having burned up fuel and shot ammunition, were now light enough to take off in a hover. The birds rose unsteadily into the air and waited for me to climb back into the cockpit of my own.

"*We going after the whistler now, boss?*" asked Armstrong.

"*Not exactly,*" I said. I hauled up on the collective and took my place at the front of the formation. The remaining aircraft fell in behind me, some smoking from the stress they'd put on their engines or malfunctioning recoilless rifles. "*We've still got some unwanted company. Time to show them the door.*"

I tilted the stick back and began to climb out of the valley, cresting the ridge of the spire field and angling back toward the camps. The goblins with Sourtooth and the rest of our convoy were watching and cheering, having seen the spire collapse. But they weren't the only ones observing the spectacle.

Four orc tribes had set out from the Blood Gorger kill camp in order to keep an eye on us, and most of them had already started to set up camp while some watched our antics. A few of them waved and whistled when we emerged from the valley. This was all fun and games and glory, for them.

Well, for me, it was survival. If we were to have any chance at actually killing the whistler, I couldn't have four separate tribes harrying our flanks. They'd already cost us the dartwing. I angled the column of aircraft toward the orc camps. The orcs on the ground ran along with our circuit, pointing and laughing amongst themselves. I made a full circle, making a note of the layout of the camps.

"Armstrong, you loaded up?"

"*Loaded 'n ready, boss!*"

I dipped the cyclic forward and hauled up on the collective, dropping our altitude but increasing our speed as I spun the nose toward the orc camp. The engine whined at the extra strain, but Girmaks kept it running smooth-*ish* as I drew more power.

<I see where this is going.>

I grinned. *Any tech tree unlock for a coordinated strafing run?*

Instead of responding, *music* started to play in my ear, and everyone else's, judging by the goblins looking around confused—a perfect rendition of Wagner's "Flight of the Valkyries."

I laughed. *Excellent choice, System.*

The orcs faltered, unsure of what was happening. They saw the choppers coming, of course. But in their heads, we were still *just goblins.* You could see the cognitive dissonance on their faces as their eyes saw harmless pests, but something in the back of their brains screamed *this isn't right.*

"Hit their mounts," I said.

The recoilless rifle belched out black smoke, and down in the camp, the hitching post securing the oryx and pack hogs for the Blood Gorgers exploded into splinters, freeing and startling all of the Blood Gorger mounts and beasts of burden. They shrieked and scattered, bolting in every direction—including *through* the camp, shaking off harness, tack, and supplies as they trampled tents. The other choppers opened up as well, hitting their foodstuffs, tents, water barrels, and other prime targets. I didn't want to kill the orcs, but I did want to force them to return to their main camps.

<Goblin Technology Unlocked: Air super-ornery>

We had more than just the explosive launchers. The individual goblins aboard the craft hauled back and hurled poppers by the bushel at the orcs below, as well as taking potshots with rifles and pistols as we passed. Small explosions began to pepper the ground between the orc hunters, who ducked or ran for cover, having been caught completely flat-footed. A few flinched as they were hit by stray shots or shrapnel, but it was impossible to tell at this speed how badly we were actually hurting them. The orcs were tough as old leather, and I expected the ordnance would sting their pride more than cause them real harm. But I couldn't afford them interfering with my hunt again. They had cost us the dartwing. They *wouldn't* cost us the whistler. The whistler was the linchpin of keeping the tribe fed and growing, and we couldn't get to the moon without a large enough tribe to support the industry required to manufacture space-capable rockets.

In just a few seconds, we were clear of their camp, and I angled toward the next one as the goblin loader slammed new rounds home in Armstrong's guns. These ones sported green-and-black armbands and had seen what had happened to the Blood Gorgers. Several hunters were already at their hitching post trying to untangle mounts now scared and skittish from the sounds of chaos in the first camp. Others had gone for weapons of their own. Crossbow bolts began whistling past us, taking at least one of my goblins right off the aircraft. I kept us low and fast to minimize our exposure. Several of them thumped against the underside, and a couple clanged off the back of the engine as we passed the perimeter of the camp.

Armstrong angled his recoilless rifles down and smashed the second camp's hitching post, sending orcs diving to the ground. More explosions popped off in the orc camp from the column, but the orcs were fighting back. A spear sailed past us, and several thick arrows punched up through the hide and thin wood planking. I almost jumped out of my seat when one arrowhead jutted up through the floor right between my knees. But a few seconds later, we were done with the second camp.

The third had managed to get a few of their mounts free and were riding them away from the unexpected attack. The goblin choppers weren't exactly fast, but they were faster than a buggy and could keep pace with an oryx. I got us lined up with their retreat path, swooping down. Crossbow bolts thudded into the pole on my left side, and one bounced off my chest plate. It felt like getting hit by a hammer, and it knocked the wind out of me. But Armstrong responded with the launchers and it blew the oryx right out from under the orcs. We sailed past the scattered pursuers, banking to the right. I leveled us out to gain altitude, but the engine draw seemed sluggish.

"Come on, *come on!*" I called, glancing back. My heart dropped when I saw a feathered shaft sticking out of my fuel bladder, and a decent amount of the liquid dribbling out around it while the engine belched out black smoke. The goblins on board noticed it too, and one squawked, panicking, and started climbing toward it.

"Stop!" I shouted, but it was too late. The goblin plucked the crossbow shaft out and held it triumphantly above his head right before a deluge of kerosene blasted him full in the face from the now unplugged hole in the bladder. I built what altitude I could, but it wasn't long before the engine sputtered and died completely.

An odd quiet enveloped the aircraft in the wake of losing the engine. All I could hear was the *swoosh* of the coaxial rotors as air started to rush up through them. System's helpful altitude reading began to drop again.

Most people think a helicopter without power glides about as well as a paperweight, but they're actually just *almost* as bad as a paperweight. I'd never performed an autorotation, but I had heard of them and understood the principle. I dropped the collective all the way to the deck and watched as the main rotors began to spin faster and faster, whistling as the air passing through sped them up. We dropped even faster, but we were going to need rotor RPMs to get through this, and that was the only way to get them. The spinning blades still gave us some lift and pulled us closer to the improvised landing zone.

<Interesting.>

In the meantime, I angled us back toward the goblin camp, where the goblins had already seen me start to fall and were now shouting and panicking.

As we dropped closer to the ground, I hauled back on the stick and lifted the collective just a little. The whistle in the rotors became a strained creak and the whole aircraft shuddered. I heard the *snap* and *pop* of fasteners bursting. But our downward velocity halted and we shot ahead, trading those rotor rpms for a little altitude control. We actually climbed maybe a dozen meters, which I hadn't intended, and I lowered the stick again. The ground shot up to meet us, and at the last second I hauled up as hard as I could on the collective to soften our impact.

The chopper hit the ground like a sack of dirt, bouncing and rolling on its gear as the main rotor blades overhead spun out the last of their energy. We rolled to a stop.

<Goblin Component Technology Unlocked: Oddy-rotation>

I shrugged out of the restraints and jumped out of the smoking chopper to assess the damage. It looked . . . well, it had looked battered and barely functional to begin with. Now it looked to be in very much the same state, just with dents, crossbow bolts, and a few less goblins aboard.

"Promo!" I shouted, looking for my chief engineer. The noblin waddled up, hammer at the ready. Sourtooth wasn't far behind.

"Emergency repairs. Let's get these patched up and get on the move."

"We can fix some of 'em *on* the move," he said.

"Even better. Sourtooth, your plan worked. But I didn't see Lura's Dawn hunters."

The gnarled old orc spat on the ground. "Aye, too clever by half, she, for one so few of years. Broke camp as soon as flight yon *choppers* took, lest she be caught flat of foot like the others. Still, a good showing. Sent afield the Gorgers and the others."

I helped a handful of goblins shift the chopper onto the back of one of the buggies we'd converted to flatbeds in order to transport the aircraft. The rest of the choppers who hadn't had punctured fuel tanks were already landing. "Will it be enough time to take down the whistler?"

"Supposing we *can* take the whistler . . ." Sourtooth rubbed his scarred chin. "Perhaps."

Perhaps was better than *no chance*. But if Lura decided to interfere, those odds would not be in our favor. We needed insurance.

I left the chopper and went looking for Keeper. The hooded figure was working her beads, getting and giving updates—no doubt informing the rest of the Stampede about our little maneuver and our new toys.

"Keeper, can I send a message through those?" I asked, pointing.

"A message, I believe you have just sent, little brother."

I huffed a laugh. That was true. But it wasn't all I had in mind. "How are the Dawn hunters and the Blood Gorgers doing?"

"Both close in on quarry. Both are confident they can stave off challengers, but neither are sure which of them will be first to bring low their beast."

"I'm confident," I said. "Because I'm sending three choppers to the Blood Gorgers."

Keeper raised an eyebrow. "You think to succeed in thwarting them where others dare not?" he asked.

"Bad enemies to make, the Blood Gorgers," warned Sourtooth.

"On the contrary," I said. "I'm going to *help* them take down their monster. And I want Lura to know that if she does anything to prevent us from taking down the whistler, she can kiss her glory goodbye."

Keeper spun her beads. "Unorthodox, is this. It strides gray trail in the spirit of the Stampede . . . yet breaks no covenant. Very well.

Relayed to both chiefs, your words have been. The Gorgers welcome your aid."

"Thanks, Keeper," I said.

Most of the choppers had been loaded up. I climbed aboard our buggy, followed by Armstrong. Sourtooth strode up as well. "Bold plan, little brother. But what should happen, should your ruse she see through?"

"It's not a ruse," I said. "I'm sending Chuck with two choppers to help the Gorgers. Armstrong, see to it."

"Aye, boss!"

Sourtooth sputtered as he watched the hobgoblin dash off. "What?! Not a—we need every chopper we have! And likely a few more, in order to take down that whistler. We can't spare any to help the Blood Gorgers. Need remind you, I, that the Blood Gorgers themselves are but a totem away from claiming the mantle of champions, just as the Dawn is?"

I nodded. "Like I said, it's not a bluff. It's an extortion. Lura knows I'm desperate to get the Flock a kill. She also knows that set in motion, whatever arrangement might be made, my chopper pilots will never hear of it because they won't ever be given access to the Gorgers' keeper. It's in her best interest now for us to take down the whistler before the Blood Gorgers take down their totem with our help."

A voice piped up from the engine. "*I believe this plan will work.*"

Sourtooth grumbled. "A devious plan. Very orcish, little brother. But it rides the knife's edge. Gamble your tribe's empty bellies on out-priding a very prideful woman."

It was a gamble. I was gambling with the lives of the entire tribe. But attempts to introduce agriculture weren't working, with goblins eating all the roots and seeds except for the ones they forgot where they planted. Farming would never keep up with the pace at which the tribe expanded—it'd help, but by the time crops grew, there'd be twice as many goblins to feed. I doubted anyone would be willing to send shipments of food or grain deep into the Lanclovan interior, either, so trade was out. The orcs were the only ones who didn't hate us, but their version of trade was more along the lines of, *If you have something I want, I'll trade it for you keeping your life.*

Livestock and big game were the only calorie-dense foods capable of supporting us until I got the tribe big enough to take a shot at the moon. And Lura had to know why I was forcing her hand.

CHAPTER 36

AIR RAID

"Where's Lura?" I asked Keeper.

She spun her beads before answering. "She has left her hunt to her lieutenant. With all speed, she makes her way to the narrows to find us."

I gritted my teeth. "Very well."

I looked over at the ramshackle choppers being pulled down off the backs of the buggies and fueled up. "With Chuck already on his way to the Gorgers, I don't think we have time to wait for her."

"And at whose feet lay that fault, little brother?" scoffed Sourtooth. "Never mind. The tinder is set ablaze, and we must outpace its flame or be scorched upon it."

The old orc certainly had a way with words. With a final hock of phlegm on the gravely floor of the canyon floor, he reached up and dropped the lid on the reworked missile buggy. The heavy vehicle rumbled to life, spitting black smog from a pair of smokestacks at the back. Promo stuck his head out the side as it trundled past, giving me a salute and the sign of the Right Angle. "Don't worry, boss! We'll do you proud!"

I waved him off as he and the other buggies, along with the half-dozen orc hunters still aboard Flock oryx and a gaggle of yapping cliffords, set off into the narrows to poke the bear.

Sourtooth had told me he wouldn't face the whistler in a light buggy. So I'd built him something new. I'd wanted a tank, but tanks require things like treads and drive sprockets and tensioners—things we simply didn't have time to fabricate during the hunt. So Big Hoss Rig had been turned into something closer to an early armored car, six-wheeled and up-armored, with a turret and sally ports for the goblins within to fire from behind steel plates. Two separate engines kept the whole thing running. And I was reasonably sure it could survive a hit from what we were about to throw it against.

Meanwhile, we'd fixed the choppers that had failed to take off during the test flight and built another besides. The Flock's supplies of raw materials on hand were dwindling, but the daily resupplies from Village Apollo helped keep us afloat.

"Ready, Armstrong?" I asked.

"Always, boss!" he said, pulling down his skull mask and swinging into the gunner's station. A half-dozen other goblins climbed aboard, including our semaphore signaler zealot, who strapped himself in at the rear. Over the past day, I'd canonized a set of signal flags, and our signalman relished his role with religious dedication.

I patted the engine block. "Girmaks?"

"*With you, King Ap. I will keep this vessel running smoothly.*"

"That's what I like to hear," I said with more confidence than I felt. By sending my best pilot to help our rivals, I'd put a guillotine hanging over our own heads. I had to make sure we were out from under it before it fell. We'd come so far and, simulation or not, I didn't want it to end here. A couple of months ago we'd struggled to fight a low-level stone-sloth using a dozen goblins with makeshift spears. Now we were mounting up in attack helicopters and taking on kaiju. Well, *small* kaiju. The very monsters that kept most nations on Rava out of the Lanclovan interior (but apparently drew the orcs like a magnet), and we were butting heads with them. And even though the vast majority of our goblins were still stuck at level 1, we were venturing forth in the hundreds. Once I established food security, we would be in the *thousands*. And the orcs, the Prince of Habberport, the Ifrit, and the other races? They could keep the ground. I was claiming the sky.

Okay, confidence restored. I dropped a rockette into the starter slot and cranked the engine, bringing the aircraft to life. My chopper started to rumble, and around us, the rest of the fleet started to spin up. The rest of the goblins began to climb aboard, armed with poppers, slingers, pistols, and boundless enthusiasm. To my right, I spotted a portly canoneer tumbling into a gunship scrawled with designs of gears, crankcases, and tools. The zealots piled in with him, and the aircraft almost drowned out their fanatical screams. On my left was Neil, with his favored hunters—looking primed and ready for big game. How he managed to work the throttle and collective with his hook hand, I couldn't say. But he'd proven just as deft a pilot as any of the wranglers who helmed the other craft.

"Light the flares," I shouted.

At the aft of our aircraft, a pair of smoldering scat flares was lit by our semaphore goblin, hopefully giving the rest of the fleet some semblance of a way to keep in formation and coordinate our fire.

I pulled pitch and turned us on the ground, lining up with a flat stretch for a rolling takeoff before opening the throttle. We bumped and ground down the gravel stretch, building speed, and then with a shudder, bounced into the air. I looked over my shoulder at the rest of the fleet, who were all lifting off one by one in their loose, meandering formation.

I spotted the dust trail of the buggies and BHR on the ground and angled toward them. They were heading into a narrow canyon with dozens of slender spire formations dotting the floor. Sparkling water coursed through in a selection of narrow streams, glinting in the sunlight. Long ago, a wide river must have carved these arches and pillars, but now it was little more than a trickle. To the west, the shadow of the eclipse marched toward the hunting ground. Sourtooth had mentioned that the whistler was like the pale lizards, most active and dangerous during the eclipse—but most vulnerable an hour before it woke.

"*Seems quiet down there, boss,*" said Armstrong. He leaned forward over the nose of the aircraft, far enough that I had to tilt the controls back to counteract the shift in the aircraft's CG. "*Feels weird, gettin' the drop in broad daylight.*"

I could understand that. But if this thing could sleep through the racket of a dozen buggies and choppers besides coming into its den, it probably needed a bomb to wake it up anyway. I craned my neck, though Sourtooth had been cagey when I'd asked for details on the beast. *You'll know it when you see it. Stay clear of its path*, was all he said.

I banked us around for a better look, avoiding the spires that crowded the airspace.

The ground itself looked . . . fairly clear. I didn't spot anything huge and horned, though a few small herd animals scattered before the buggies. Scrub brush dotted the gravel near the streams and along the walls of the canyons. I banked again, angling us through the maze of spires and dropping us low enough to clear a natural bridge connecting two adjacent columns, curious at the spiral ridge on the closest spire. Sourtooth had arrayed the buggies in a wide wedge formation, and his turret was raised and turned toward us.

"*Wot's he watchin' us for?*" asked Armstrong. "*He should be lookin' for 'is whistler.*"

Despite the heat of the day and the boiling engine block behind my seat, a cold feeling crept down my spine. A shadow passed over us, and I looked up at the underside of the rock bridge spanning the two spires on either side of us. Dozens of dangling vines waved in the breeze.

Not vines. *Legs*. Dozens of *legs*. I caught movement out of the corner of my eye. The ridges spiraling the spires to the left and right were undulating, curling themselves around the rock formations. They weren't rock as I'd first thought, but bone, lined with thousands of small holes. The whistler was apparently a giant segmented insect—like a millipede. *Gross*. I've never liked creepy-crawlies.

Especially the ones with too many legs. I swallowed my disgust and pressed on.

I pushed the nose down and got clear, looking around frantically for the head. A dozen of the pillars were now alive and undulating, and several of what I'd taken for natural arches and land bridges were actually parts of the monster spanning the gaps.

"*Where's the front?*" asked Armstrong. "*What am I s'posed to—*"

His sentence was cut off by a noise like a freight train's steam whistle passing directly in front of us in a blur of clacking jaw parts and milling legs. The noise was immense, and the rush of the thing blasted us with a concussive force that knocked us completely off course. I struggled to control the chopper, maneuvering it away from the new airborne obstacle.

The head of the creature reached another pillar and started to spiral down before doubling back and launching itself across the gap at yet another column. The noise was incredible, all the little holes on its carapace made for a natural whistle as it passed through the air.

On the ground, the BHR fired up at the whistler. An explosion struck it on the side. It immediately changed course, jumping toward a low pillar near the canyon floor, but its tail still hadn't cleared the pillars in front of the fleet. This thing had to be hundreds of meters long!

Armstrong leveled the front guns and put two recoilless rifle rounds into its carapace, as did several other choppers. The explosions rippled across its hide, drowned out completely by the shrieking of its natural airhorns. I spotted a few cracks in the bony plate as it blurred by, but nothing substantial. This was a tough nut to crack, and we could hammer it until we were empty on ammo and blue in the face (well, blue-er), and not make a scratch.

"Follow the head!" I shouted. Not that any of the other choppers could hear me. But they could follow our flares just fine. I dipped the stick and dropped collective, chasing after the head as it zigzagged across the canyon toward the Big Hoss Rig. The whistler was faster than the choppers, but it seemed like it needed to rebound off pillars for sharp turns. Of course, the more it doubled back on itself, the more obstacles in our flight path. It reminded me of playing *Snake* on my old man's cell phone back when I was a kid, the way you had to dodge your own tail as it kept getting longer and longer. Only this wasn't a game.

The whistler doubled back again, cutting directly in front of my flight path, and I yanked us over almost ninety degrees to avoid getting chomped. One of the choppers with us was not so lucky, and it caught the bony ridges and flew apart as though it had been hit by a full-speed train.

"*It's really got it out for us, boss!*" shouted Armstrong.

"No kidding!"

<Your tribe has decreased to 569 members.>

Still, I could see the head as it spiraled down the pillar, and I got us lined up. Armstrong had managed to catch his loader and keep the goblin from being flung out of the aircraft by my maneuver. He yanked the goblin back in place and the two started hammering rounds home as fast as the tiny hands could open the hatch and slam fresh rounds in and Armstrong could get the barrels lined up.

Bursts of flame and dust erupted on the face of the pillar, and the whistler roared, even louder than its natural shriek. It hit the canyon floor, zigzagging toward the BHR, and I led the choppers in close behind it. Now that I'd identified it, System helpfully stuck an *XX* over its head. And, of course, we all know what that meant it thought our odds of success were. Maybe System was right. But maybe we were going to kick this thing's carapace-covered butt.

CHAPTER 37

PAIN TRAIN

On the ground, the whistler barreled its way across the floor of the canyon, churning gravel and dust underneath hundreds of legs. Directly in its path, the Big Hoss Rig stopped, and its wheels started to spin backward. The turret on top swung, tracking the head of the whistler, and fired. It had the biggest gun we'd built yet, and I could feel the explosion as it kicked up dirt and debris in advance of the whistler's rush.

The monster flinched to the side but kept on coming. The Flock hunters still on oryx bounded out of its way, hurling spears and firing crossbows at its eyes—and there were a lot of them on the thing's face. At least twenty eyes covered the front of its face below an armor mantle. While the majority of them were fixed on the BHR, others scanned in every direction. There was no sneaking up on this thing while it was awake.

Another shot from the BHR exploded against the whistler's back, twisting the creature just enough that it only caught the front corner of the BHR on its attack run. The armored rig spun out, tires shrieking almost as loudly as the whistler's natural airhorns. Almost immediately, the head diverted right, spiraling up and around a pillar before shooting the gap to another—directly at us.

My eyes went wide, and I hauled back on the controls and yanked up on the collective. The maneuver shot us almost straight up, though I could hear the main rotors shuddering as the engine struggled to put out enough power to meet the demands of the steep climb. I fully believe that the engine would have exploded then and there without Girmaks inside it. If this little chopper had a safety envelope, I was flying well outside it. And worse yet, through the flicker of the rotor disc, I could see an arch directly overhead. I slammed the stick full forward, and we lurched ahead, tail over teakettle with our semaphore signaler squawking and waving his flags helplessly in the air.

Some of our choppers followed high, a couple followed low, but at least one of them failed to maneuver in time and I felt the heat of the explosion on the back of my neck.

"King Ap, I must advise against pulling such a maneuver again."

"It might not be up to me!" I shouted back.

<Your tribe has decreased to 562 members.>

With our increased altitude, I spotted a glint of metal in the sunlight at the top of the canyon's ridge. Spearpoints from Lura's Hunters, if my mark was right. But they were just waiting and watching. Why? They had to know the Gorgers were closing in on their own kill. Still, they did nothing.

The whistler shot the gap again, again aiming straight for us. I was treated to a close-up of its gaping mouth and dozens of eyes all fixed on my aircraft before the whistle of a rocket-motor and an explosion knocked its head off course. The head narrowly missed me, and I hauled on the collective. The passing of the creature created a low-pressure zone that threatened to suck us right into it, where we'd be ground to fine powder against its carapace. I just managed to get us free and climb up.

The whistler changed targets again, spiraling down a pillar and snaking across the ground to snap at the oryx riders who dared leave the shadow of the pillars and cross the open ground.

I tried to calm my heart. The whistler kept prioritizing my chopper. Did it know I was the leader? Why was it focused so heavily on my aircraft? I didn't know what would happen if I was swallowed whole. Would the tribe simply count down while I slowly dissolved in the dark? Would the whole of us croak at once? Could I somehow escape, given enough goblins dying in my place?

Looking down at the massive creature, I could see the telltale damage we'd inflicted in the form of shattered shell and pock-marked carapace. Even a pair of direct hits from the BHR had only served to break its armor—and the thing seemed to be *mostly* armor. It was like fighting a cast iron freight train with an appetite and a grudge. Nothing this big had a right to move so quickly and change direction on a dime. But then, it didn't exactly act like a single cohesive creature. Segments followed other segments, and no brain or nerve system in the universe could control that many independent limbs in a creature of such scale. It was Rava's greatest game of follow-the-leader, no different from the goblins in choppers following my flares and signal flags.

I could exploit that, somehow. But I couldn't do it alone. Even with rockets and recoilless rifles, we just didn't have the firepower to strike a decisive blow against this thing. On the ground, two buggies tried to hit it with a net launcher, and the whistler tore the net to shreds without even noticing the effort. Maybe if we had some mines we could set underneath it, they might flip the beast and expose its weaker underbelly. But against an outer hide that seemed to be, at least in part, metal plating? I hadn't designed any kind of munition to get through that. What would it take, a steel dart? Tungsten? Once again, I'd come to a fight unprepared and found myself in an untenable position.

I grabbed the handset. "Signal the squadron to continue the fight," I barked. I looked over my shoulder as the semaphore zealot clasped a hand to his ear-cups and then gave me a salute. His flags began to work, and I peeled out of the formation toward the ridge line to find the Dawn Light chieftess, Lura Sunskin. As I climbed, my stomach just about jumped into my throat. Keeper had said she'd left the hunt to her lieutenant. What she hadn't said was that Lura had taken the vast majority of hunters south with her. Hundreds of orcs on boars and oryx and even a pair of thundercleaves spread out across the top of the ridge, all waiting and watching, unafraid, as I approached. This wasn't a force meant to hunt a whistler. It was a force meant to finish off what was left of the *Flock*. The threat was immediate and obvious.

Well, I'd certainly caught her attention. The fact that she hadn't wiped us out already told me there was still a way out of this. I wheeled the chopper around and brought us down on a clear patch near the head of the column where Lura waited, cross-legged atop her oryx with a small ladder and a highchair with a goblin-sized seat. It was obvious who that was for.

Armstrong hopped out of the chopper with me, as though he could protect us from fifty times our number in orc hunters. But I was grateful for his company. I moved over to Lura and scrabbled my way up the ladder. The Dawn's Light huntress looked at me with a mix of emotions—anger, barely concealed, but also curiosity and no shortage of chagrin.

"I have naught other than my pride, for blame, I suppose," she said. "Pressed to my throat, is this dagger, yet its blade would cut us both—and it will slide 'cross skin at any moment with the aid you lent the Gorgers, unless I aid your elsewise lost cause. Your intent, 'tis clear."

"Where I'm from, we call it a sword of Damocles," I said.

Lura grinned. "It's become all too clear, O little brother king, that where you're from is not the Land of Shaded Skies." She gestured with an open palm to the roughshod chopper behind me. "And despite your artifice so clever, you will break upon the whistler without my aid."

<Your tribe has decreased to 554 members.>

"That's true," I said. "And without your aid, the Blood Gorgers win the Stampede. So, will you help me?"

The sound of another explosion reached us, and Lura made a show of cupping a hand to her ear and waiting until the last echoes had died off. Every moment she dallied cost the Flock.

"There is a price, little brother. I know now why the grandfather spirits led you to my doorstep."

"What is it?"

Lura grinned a wicked little smile. "I'll tell you not, lest you balk and query further, and we've time for neither. I want your word as king of goblins that this pact you'll honor."

"And if I don't want to give it to you?" I asked.

Lura Sunskin laughed. "Then we watch you crash upon the beast, and we crush what's left. This dagger may against both our throats press, yet it's still I who directs its course. Shall it cut us both?"

I opened my mouth to respond, but Lura cut me off.

"Before you answer, know that should your words you renege upon, I will carve your tribe from the jungle and the name *Apollo* will become a word meaning only *death* upon the plains and forests and sands of Lanclova. Choose quickly, little brother."

"You've got me between a rock and a hard place here," I said. I raised two fingers. "There're two things I won't do: I won't wage war on another sentient species for you, and I won't betray the Ifrit."

"Neither is my desire. An accord, have we?"

"You have my word."

Lura laughed and raised her spear. As one, the troop surged forward, hooves pounding as the orcs streamed to either side of us, disappearing over the ridge and dropping into the valley.

Lura angled her spear down at me as she heeled her mount to action. "A whistler is meteor given flesh, little brother. It cannot be slowed. But when it grows as this one has, its own length can be used against it. Take heart and take aim. Do not miss."

CHAPTER 38

A METEOR MADE FLESH

I ran back to the chopper with its engine still hot and running.

"*What did she demand?*" asked Girmaks.

"She wouldn't say," I said. As soon as all the goblins were aboard, I pulled us into a rolling takeoff. We still had our trump card: the two-stage rocket mounted in the belly compartment. I'd already seen the whistler take a direct hit on the armor from one of them and keep trucking. A headshot would probably do for it, but with the erratic way it moved, we'd never nail its head with a rocket—even if the goblin guidance pilot rode the warhead all the way in.

I lifted us up off the deck and soared over the ranks of Dawn's Light hunters on their oryx, spilling over the side of the canyon and bounding down its walls on the sure-footed beasts toward the battle below.

"How did you know she would demand something?" I asked.

"*She is an orc. She is devious and exacting—always ulterior motives and plans within plans. But I believe I know her mind. I believe I know, King Ap, what she will ask.*"

"Care to enlighten me?"

"*It is not my scheme to expose. To do so would be—*"

"Crude and reductive?" I guessed.

"*—dishonoring her culture.*"

Considering her culture was currently, in large part, the extortion of Tribe Apollo, I couldn't find myself to be too sympathetic. But we had bigger fish to fry and a freight-train millipede monster that sounded like it was tearing through the Flock. I angled down into the valley, flying almost low enough to brush the tops of the Dawn hunter spears as I built speed. Ahead, I could see the wreckage of another chopper and at least two buggies on the floor of the canyon. The narrow spires were crisscrossed with the body of the whistler. It continued making passes at the fleet of choppers and ground vehicles.

The first wave of the Dawn's Light hunters hit the canyon floor and thundered toward the whistler. Before they reached it, they split into several groups and circled, shouting and waving spears. The whistler, which had been making another run at the BHR, shifted course. Its eyes tracked the bright light reflecting off the spears, and it zigzagged toward the closest contingent of Lura's hunters.

I tilted my stick to the side, following along as the orcs wrapped around the back of a pillar, then changed direction abruptly. The whistler rammed through dirt and gravel where they would have been and kicked up a gale with its passing.

I pulled up, watching as another group of hunters angled small, polished shields to catch the sun's light and reflect it into the whistler's eyes. It diverted toward them, mouth open wide. Not all of them were fast enough to get out of its way, and an orc and mount both disappeared down its gullet without it slowing.

What were they doing? Not striking any decisive blows, that was for sure. Hell, they hadn't even attacked it at all. I climbed in altitude for a better view but had to angle quickly out of the crisscrossed segments of the whistler. Again, I marveled at its length, easily hundreds of meters of stampeding legs headed by what looked like a cast iron dome of a skull plate that could crush through a bunker door. And even as I watched, it smashed a boulder to gravel with barely any notice.

Again, a group of Lura's hunters flashed light into its eyes and distracted it once more. It split from the group it chased in favor of, quite literally, the new shiny thing. This time it had to maneuver over one of its own segments in order to reach the target. The thing was so damn big it was doubling back over itself and . . .

Oh.

Oh . . .

Lura was a devious one. She'd seen what these aircraft could do and put it together even better than I had. She wasn't going to make things *easy* for me, because it suited her pride to rub my little goblin nose in it that I'd bought into a bargain I hadn't even needed. Damned orc. *Use its length against it.* And she knew we could do it because *I'd already shown* her. I looked back at the smoldering sunbursts at the stern of my chopper. The whole time, I'd wondered why it was so focused on us. I grabbed the handset. "*Flares!*" I barked. "Pass the word! Every chopper, scatter and ignite flares!"

"*I believe I understand what she is trying to show us, King Ap.*"

"Way ahead of you, Girmaks!" I shouted.

My little semaphore zealot worked his flags while another of our crewmen ignited another smoldering torch and slotted it into the back of the chopper. None too soon, as Raphina's shadow passed over us and the Dawn hunters lost their method of distracting the beast. That's why it was more dangerous during the eclipse, because it was easier to distract the whistler with bright, shiny things. Now the only sources of light were the flares igniting on the backs of the choppers.

I wasn't low enough to see its eyes fix on us, but I did see it suddenly snake toward the nearest pillar, spiraling up.

Wait for it . . .

It lunged, gaping maw coming within a few lengths of our aircraft as I dumped us into a temporary autorotation. I quickly maneuvered behind its skull plate, and it fixated on another chopper's glowing flare. It hit another pillar, swung around it, and shot right back. Unfortunately, this chopper pilot wasn't as quick on the sticks as me and barely had time to bail out along with most of his crew as the hardened skull of the whistler obliterated the aircraft.

<Your tribe has decreased to 554 members.>

"Ready the missile!" I shouted into my handset, looking at the central spire the creature had wrapped around several times. The crew of my ship squawked and fought to be the first down into the belly compartment. One of them got situated, and I brought the craft around.

The rest of the fleet, cast out of formation, was now flying as erratically as any goblins—which was perfect. The whistler simply had too many bright lights to chase. It had doubled back on itself so many times that it had coiled around the same pillar in three different places. For the first time since we'd stirred the beast, I actually saw the end of its tail snaking toward the spire.

I pointed the nose of the chopper between two of the sets of coils, at what looked like the narrowest part of the spindle formation. "There!" I shouted. "At the skinny part, just like the practice run! Tally ho!"

I yanked down on the plunger and felt the mechanism beneath me give way. The squawk of the goblin riding the missile fell away, and a moment later I heard the rocket motor ignite. Our payload shot out, erratic and barely under control. But its pilot managed to get it on track. Even the whistler took notice, and it screamed after the rocket, mouth open and ready for the kill. The goblin pilot bailed out at the last second, and the warhead hit the pillar and exploded. The *crack* echoed off the canyon walls, but it was nothing compared to the *thump* of the whistler skull-bashing the impact site. A spiderweb of cracks spread out from the hit, and I could *feel* the impact in the air. It quickly reeled back and circled the spire, shooting off in another direction. But when the dust cleared, I could see a fissure had been opened in the rock face. What's more, so could the rest of the fleet, and the BHR on the ground. Two more chopper missiles followed, and then the cannon of the new and improved Big Hoss Rig. And it had a secret of its own.

The back of the armored vehicle split open, and a pair of the largest rockets we'd made yet rose up on geared platforms. Cased in steel and tipped with several chooms of explosives, these were multi-stage monsters built with a single purpose: to kill a whistler.

The two motors ignited on the platform, and even in the chopper I could hear the distant rumble over the shriek of the whistler's perforated carapace. I held a hand up to the glare of their ignition as they roared to life. The two rockets shot off their launcher—one of which immediately exploded, knocking three buggies *and* the BHR completely over.

<Your tribe has decreased to 550 members.>

The second rocket struggled to right itself, pilot desperately wrestling with the controls. But the first stage fell away, the booster kicked on, and the second stage shot up toward the gap, the sun-bright flame of the burning accelerant illuminating the eclipsed canyon.

"Come on, baby!" I shouted, pumping my fist in the air. Armstrong was leaning so far forward watching that I thought he would tip right out of his seat.

"*Woooo!*"

The goblins on board were all cheering and whooping at the sight of the full-fire rocket riding a plume of blazing flame. But a sound was mounting over both their shouts and the sound of the rocket: the shrill freight-train horn of the whistler. Its iron-plated head shot up into the sky, mouth wide, every eye fixed on the brightest source of light in the canyon.

And it swallowed the rocket whole, rider and all.

The noise of the rocket motor cut off with the clamp of powerful iron jaws, and my own mouth dropped open. The goblins on the chopper froze mid-cheer, and the whistler barreled right past us, deafeningly loud.

<Your tribe has decreased to 549 members.>

"*Boss?*" asked Armstrong, looking back at me.

"*Did . . . did that really just happen?*" I asked.

BOOM!

A wave of hot air and steaming viscera splattered us from behind. Some of it hit the rotor, which showered us even further with finely mulched whistler meat. I had to fight to keep control as the shockwave threatened to slam us against the standing spindles of rock in the canyon. Several of our crew were thrown completely free of the craft. Finally, I got the aircraft under control and leveled out and looped us around a pillar as I wiped whistler innards off my face.

The enormous millipede monster, now headless, slumped to the canyon floor. The weight of its body hitting the ground made the whole canyon quake, and for a moment I thought the damaged spire *would* come down. But it held, and I brought the chopper in for a landing near the capsized Big Hoss Rig. I jumped out and ran to the tank, and over the ringing in my ears I could hear a clanging from inside.

The side hatch on the rig opened, and a very discombobulated Sourtooth pulled his wiry frame on top of the wreck. He looked around, finally seeing the decapitated whistler. He looked at me, looked at the whistler, looked back at me.

"Pray tell, O King," he roared, pointing at the decapitated beast. "Why was *this* not our *opening* gambit?!"

CHAPTER 39

FINISH LINE

Perhaps not the path I laid before you, yet a king haunts not the steps of those who walk before," said Lura. She climbed down from her oryx and surveyed the carnage. "Still, a bargain struck, honored it must be. Will you keep faith?"

I looked up at the huntress. "I'm a goblin of my word. Now, what's this favor you want?"

Lura looked southeast toward the high desert. "This land has a great creature that devours magic. A sky devil of unimaginable power. But it never touches the ground, except to feed—so no orc could hunt it. Not even with a shaman of immense skill and cunning or with beasts of magic flight. But you fly without magics. This, you will give to me, that we may hunt the greatest of quarry."

Sourtooth's sharp intake of breath quickly turned into a cough. Clearly this creature had some major significance.

"I . . ." I considered. The bestiary had mentioned a creature from the desert that was at least in the 90s level range, well above anything we'd fought before. Even the whistler now had a *52* superimposed over its head. "You're asking me to build you a fleet of aircraft to hunt a magic-eating dragon."

"It is strong and swift, and these ramshackle vessels will avail us not. I want a sky chariot that can keep pace with a thunderstorm and climb just as high."

"Oh . . . oh no . . ." I said. *This* was the favor she wanted? That she'd been so afraid that I'd balk at she'd been unwilling to give it voice? She wanted me to build aircraft that flew higher, faster, and farther? *The horror.* It was tough to keep the grin off my face.

Every event in my life until now had seemed hellbent on standing in the way of my dreams. The accident, the explosion, being put in charge of a tribe of lunatic goblins. I'd overcome it all and always would, because I was never the type to back down when faced with impassible barriers. Stubbornness to back down and unwillingness to compromise on my goal of being among the few elite astronauts to ever walk on the moon had practically defined every choice I'd made since childhood.

While most people gave up, settling for being accountants or insurance adjusters, the singular goal of *astronaut* remained firmly lodged in the center of my focus. But sometimes the odds seemed so stacked against me. For once, the shoe was on the other foot, and Lura had just handed me a golden opportunity to focus the entirety of our resources on aerospace development.

I saw no reason to tell her that, though.

"Lura, I don't have the materials for a project like that. I don't think I could make you anything fast enough for you to win the Stampede."

"Put the Stampede from your mind. My ambition has elevated, and I will for you secure any materials you require."

"Clearly," scoffed Sourtooth. He scratched his head. Then he shook it, then he groaned. "Argh, I suppose someone had to be fool enough to try it again." He looked at me. "You've ensured the Flock's placement in the Stampede—and with it, your rights to hunt the plains. Without the rudder of vengeance, I now find myself without a path. I should like to see this folly to its end, if you'll have it."

"Sourtooth, I have a feeling this folly is just getting started. Having your smithing skills and knowledge of Rava is something I'd welcome with open arms," I said. And then, to Lura, "Like you said. We have an accord. I can't promise you the sky, but I can promise that I'll do whatever I can to get you flying as high and as fast as this sky devil."

Lura nodded. "Good." She leaned back as one of her orcs riding next to her team's Keeper whispered in her ear. "The other teams are on their way. The day is yours, Apollo. Orc tradition dictates your kill you ought share. Will you honor our ways?"

I looked at the massive length of the whistler. There was enough meat on it to feed the whole tribe for *months*. And if the meat was as nutrient-packed as a smaller-scale grub, then as far as I was concerned, our food shortage was at an end. We could afford to be generous.

"When in Rome," I said. And then added quickly, "Er, that means yes. I'll share."

Many of my goblins had already started to tuck in, and my mouth already watered at the scent of the flash-barbecued whistler meat. Still, there was something else that caught my eye.

The ridged armor on the whistler had seemed more like rock than bone. But as I approached it, I could see a dull, metallic luster where we'd cracked the surface of it, and in the cross section of its decapitation. Sourtooth followed me, eyeing me curiously as I broke off a piece with a small hammer I kept in my pouch. I looked at the material. It didn't look like iron or zinc.

"Sourtooth, how does this thing get so much metal build-up on its carapace?"

The old orc pointed up at the spires. "During storms, thunder calls the dust up from the earth, and when the bolt strikes the whistler's tail, holds fast the metal to its hide. This whistler has been growing for centuries, getting tougher all the while."

I hummed to myself. Strange. This world's version of electroplating? Galvanized carapace? I'd seen plenty of broken steel parts since unlocking the boom furnaces, and this didn't have the right grain. Plus, it was too lightweight. Despite the whistler's size and strength, it still had to be able to move fast and strike hard. But there were other metals that you refined with electricity. I knelt down, picking up a few more pieces of the pinkish gravel that covered the floor of the canyon.

I whistled, getting the attention of every goblin in the canyon.

"Collect as much of this shell ore as you can!" I shouted. "And find me the tail!"

Sourtooth scratched his head. "Pointless," he muttered, kicking his prosthetic against the hide. "This ore is far too brittle for weapons and armor. It serves only to lend weight to the whistler's strike."

"Maybe," I said. "And maybe, we just found ourselves a gold mine."

"A metal of equal worthlessness," said Lura, approaching. I brought my head around. "You don't use gold for coinage or . . . ?" I looked back at my work. "Right. Orcs. I suppose central monetary systems aren't your forte."

Several goblins ran up, chittering. I followed them, with Sourtooth and Lura trailing behind. They led the three of us up a small slope and through several pillars to where the end of the creature dangled, still wound around a pillar. Some of the legs back here were still clawing at air, not yet having received the signal that the front of the monster was dead, I suppose. The end of the tail had a pair of prongs that were a slightly different luster than the rest of the carapace. They were massive, too. Big enough that a dozen goblins would struggle to heft just one of the tail prongs between them. I took a handful of iron nails from my pouch and tossed them up in the air. The couriers squawked and covered their heads, waiting for the rain of sharp iron to fall on them. But it didn't come. Instead, the nails shot up, holding fast to the surface of the whistler's tail.

Natural permanent magnets—*powerful* ones, too. Neodymium equivalents? Probably not quite that strong, but loads better than lodestones or raw magnetite ore. If I couldn't mine or manufacture magnets, could I pull them off the various creatures of Rava that used lightning on their own, like the thundercleaves and the whistlers? That, of course, meant hunting *more* of them.

Did I really want to think about there being more whistlers that I had to kill for magnets?

No, not especially. Not yet, anyway.

Within a few hours, the other teams began to arrive. Their convoys of oryx and pack beasts made camp in the canyon, and the echoes of tent stakes being pounded and processing knives being sharpened rang off the rock walls. Chuck returned toward the evening, fuel-empty chopper being towed behind a Blood Gorger pack-boar. He grinned when he saw Armstrong and me sitting near Promo's forge grilling whistler meat.

I offered the wrangler a strip of dripping meat fresh from the forge. "How was hunting with the Gorgers?" I asked.

"Boss, you shoulda seen it," he said between bites. "This thing they hunted, it was fast, *fast*. Could barely keep up with the choppers. But they'd have got it. Mark me, these orcs know their trade when it comes to bringing down beasties."

"Let's hope so," I said. "Because we're on the hook to take down the baddest one in the skies above Lanclova with Lura." I tried to poke at the coals in the forge with a stick, but Promo swatted me away.

"How you plan to do that?" asked Chuck. "The choppers don't go that high before they start whining and sputtering." He tilted his head up to where a pair of biplanes circled above the camp. "More of those?"

"Something *like* those," I said, watching their lazy loops in the sky. But one of the planes diverted east, and the other wheeled around soon after to follow it. I tapped Armstrong, who followed the action.

"Think they seen somethin'?" he asked.

A moment later, the *crack* of a signal popper echoed through the canyon, and I scrambled.

"Get to the buggies!" I said, running.

I reached my customary trike, looking between the brass bottle and the engine for the pale blue glow. But I saw nothing.

"Girmaks?" I called out. No response. I gritted my teeth. The Ifrit must have been elsewhere. I'd drive it myself.

I dropped a rockette into the starter and kicked the trike into gear almost before Armstrong and my other Secretive Servants had time to get aboard. Overhead, the green puff of smoke that marked the signal popper was drifting on the breeze. I angled the front wheel toward it and opened up the throttle. Vehicles flanked me, and I wasn't sure what I expected to find. But the orcs were taking note as well, and it seemed like their scouts had spotted something. A few orcs mounted up on oryx. Lura joined me, and a moment later Sourtooth on his motorcycle.

"What comes, little brother?" demanded Lura. "Does something challenge the Stampede?"

"I'm not sure yet," I shouted over the sound of the engine.

In the distance on the hard pack, beyond the edge of the canyon, something approached across the ground—something small, scrabbling toward the camp. I shaded my eyes with a hand, but couldn't quite make it out, until it started waving its arms, and then *tripped* and tumbled across the hardpack, stubby legs waving in the air.

"Is that a noblin?" asked Armstrong.

"I think so," I said, trying to think. "Did we lose a noblin today?"

My scrapper chief shook his head. "Maybe he fell out o' the glider?"

"We'll know soon enough."

We pulled up closer, and I could see the noblin was dressed in frayed and tattered robes and covered in myriad scratches. Even the tip of one of his ears had been docked. But through all that, I still recognized my canoneer chief.

"Luther!" I shouted. I pulled up the trike and jumped down as the canoneer collapsed on the ground outside the canyon. He had a small brass jar wrapped in his hands, and the portly noblin huffed and puffed as though he'd run a marathon—which he might well have done, since we were miles from the edge of the desert.

"What the heck happened to you?" I asked. But it wasn't my canoneer who answered, seeing as he mostly just heaved for breath he didn't have to spare, and sat back on the ground.

"*King Apollo! We were betrayed!*"

"Taquoho?"

CHAPTER 40

PUNCH LINE

Slow down," I said. Even though Taquoho wasn't even speaking fast. My head swam.

"*Haut Voclai Behen Mira Do turned on us once we reached the desert and intends to turn the King of the Ifrit against Tribe Apollo,*" said Taquoho. "*He plans to tell them you have taken our kin captive.*"

I looked at Luther, who nodded and explained further between gasping breaths. "They smashed up all the ceramics, then tried to have the paladins kill me, but they refused. So they tried to do it themselves, and that's when I took Taquoho and ran."

Sourtooth growled. "Honorless curs. Bent words from twisting tongues of flame."

"And you made it here on foot?"

Luther groaned. "Little more than stumps, now!" he complained. I eyed the perfectly functioning feet at the ends of his legs and raised an eyebrow, feeling my sympathy diminish. Luther quickly realized his mistake.

"Your pardon, O King! It has been a trial, these last days. We have been hunted and nipped and bitten and harried every step of the way."

I looked to Taquoho.

"*There were minor vermin—threatening to a goblin's ankles, perhaps. But we were fortunate to escape my kin.*"

I sighed. "I'm just glad he got you both out safe. Thanks, Luther." I straightened. "Still. This is a huge problem. The King of the Ifrit thinks we reneged on our deal and kidnapped half of the Ifrit who came to the village." I rubbed my hand over my face. "I guess that means we can't expect any more help and material from the Ifrit until we get the truth sorted out. Well, if it's not one crisis, it's another. At least food is settled for the moment. We have your friend Girmaks to thank for that," I said.

"*Please elaborate, O King,*" said Taquoho.

"Well, once we got onto the badlands, we found out there's this orc hunting festival going on. Girmaks got us into it so that we could get hunting rights for the tribe. So, we joined up, hunted with the orcs for a bit, and long story short, we've got attack helicopters and tanks now and we've got to help them kill this magic-eating monster."

"*I am familiar with the concept of the Stampede, King Apollo,*" said Taquoho. "*As well as the devouring null devil. But who is this Girmaks you reference?*"

I waved my hand. "Right, familiar brevity. Giral Mal Ksch. The union you said had taken a shine to the buggies." I looked back at the trike. "Normally he's hanging out at the motorpool. I'm actually going to ask if you could borrow his coaxial vessel since he's in an engine most of the time, anyway."

Beside me, Sourtooth stiffened. Lura tilted her head.

"*King Apollo,*" said Taquoho carefully, "*The union I referred you to was named Odo Fortu Val. I know of no union called Giral Mal Ksch, or Girmaks, as you have named them. Those words are not of the Ifrit.*"

Sourtooth stalked off, muttering to himself. Lura held her hands over her mouth and began to shake.

I furrowed my eyes. "That's impossible." I looked at Lura. "You spoke with him."

The Dawn's Light chieftess tilted her head back and howled with laughter. "I spoke with him, yes, little brother. But he gave not his name—for I'd have known it. *Giral Mal Ksch* is an old orc phrase, you see." She gazed after Sourtooth and slapped her thigh, laughing. "One favored by an elder orc of the Flock who passed to the next life. *Last laughter be mine*, it means."

"I . . . what?" I stammered. "Are you sure?"

Lura straightened. "Quite sure, little brother. They were his last. The very words he spoke as I threw him down the gullet of the whistler. I suppose the last laugh is his in having, after all, no? I'm sure a great jest indeed, was binding we three together: to see me kill the beast and yet receive credit not at all. To see you press me to aid, and to see Sourtooth stirred out of his cups. A fool, I've been—for thinking myself so clever. Devil of an old orc ghost." She shook her head. "I've lessons in guile yet to learn, 'tis sure."

She chuckled to herself and made her way back into the camp after Sourtooth as if it were the funniest joke she'd ever heard. I looked between Taquoho, Armstrong, Luther, and Chuck for a time before Taquoho's voice broke the silence.

"*No Ifrit would ever impersonate an orc grandfather spirit,*" he said. Then hesitated. "*Perhaps the reverse is not also true . . .*" he trailed off.

"Got 'is revenge on the beastie wot ate him, though," said Armstrong. He grinned. "That's my kind of sneaky! I like orcs."

"Hold on, now," I said, raising my hands. "Let's not jump to conclusions. Luther, what do you . . . ?"

I glanced over. Somehow the noblin had already managed to produce paper and a charcoal nub, and was hunched over the floor of the desert, filling in squares.

I sighed. I guess it was *histry* now. The annals of Tribe Apollo—Stampede hunters and great artificers, and the apparent butts of a dead orc's joke. But we'd be going to bed with full bellies and the immediate future of the tribe secure from the worry of food scarcity.

So it wasn't *Girmaks* having the last laugh. And if he had impersonated an Ifrit once, I had no doubt he was still somewhere in the motorpool, laughing it up and planning his next prank. The orcs loved speed almost as much as the wranglers did—and there was plenty of it to be had on the hardpack and dusty badland plains. An orc ghost that could apparently work an engine as well as any Ifrit would certainly find use in tribe Apollo.

I helped Luther up onto one of the buggies, and we headed back to the orc camp-slash-party. We'd killed the whistler. This was a night for the Flock, who it seemed would be with us for the foreseeable future, just like our contingent of Ifrit. At least until we took out this sky devil.

I held Taquoho's vessel up to the engine block, and his pale flame slid from one vessel to the other.

"*You have made improvements, I can see.*"

"Prototype, test, iterate," I said, climbing to the controls and kicking the trike into gear. "Ever forward. *Ad Luna*. You should see the choppers."

"*I'm sure I shall,*" said Taquoho. But there was an edge of bitterness in his voice.

I pursed my lips. "I'm sorry about what happened with haughty-von-haughty. We may not be able to manage the desert yet, but I *will* find a way to get you and the other exiles home, Taquoho. I promise it."

"*I believe you, King Apollo. But if the king's mind has been poisoned against you . . .*"

"There is that," I said. I clicked my tongue. "So how would we convince him otherwise?"

"*Defeating the null devil would certainly lend credence. But I fear it is beyond even you.*"

I glanced back at the engine block. "I would think calling a desert-dwelling beast a devil would be crude and reductive for you, Taquoho. What did this thing do that was so bad?"

"*It introduced the concept of mortality to the Ifrit. It did so by devouring the natural magics of our essence and starving our ancestors of all their wellsprings save one. It is the reason the City of Brass has walls.*"

The fur on my neck stood up on end. "Good thing there's only one."

"*Hundreds fell from the stars in a time that reshaped the world, thousands of years before the Great Spirit would whisper its first words. It is the last of its kind here. It has hunted and devoured all of its kin.*"

"Lovely."

So. On the to-do list: Conquer the sky for the orcs so they didn't hunt us down, kill an un-killable magic-devouring super-predator, free the City of Brass from its millennia-old oppressor before they sent their paladins to assassinate us for another Ifrit's lies, and, oh yeah, *land on the moon*.

Neil Armstrong never had to deal with this crap.

CHAPTER 41

BIRDS OF A FEATHER

<Your tribe has increased to 922 members.>

So, what do you do when you successfully hunt a whistler near the end of the Stampede? You party. For the eight days it took to process and carve the bulk of the whistler, the orcs drank and celebrated and cheered both the Flock's kill and their withdrawal from the Stampede. Sourtooth strutted on his new prosthetic blade, wearing a necklace of whistler teeth across his bare chest. His skin was marked with the gray-and-white bands of his hunting team. I thought he would be eager to put both my tribe and the Stampede behind him, given the state I'd found him in. But I learned this was not the case.

Now that Tribe Apollo was officially part of the Flock, the reverse was apparently also true. The temporary partnership between Sourtooth and myself seemed to become permanent.

"Or does this road of kinship but one way travel?" he asked, eyebrow raised.

"Of course not!" I said, waving my hands ahead of me. "I'm just surprised. I'm ecstatic that you want to see the village and help me with Lura's task."

"For the Flock, was the task," Sourtooth reminded me. "The Flock could complete it not, were we not of a mind. Besides, I wish to see more of your artifice."

"And I'll be glad to have your smiths working with my igni. Orc metalworking and composite materials are going to be invaluable in our next generation of tech. Two days by overland travel will see us back at the village. I have tests to run and lots of new materials to work with. It'll take weeks, if not months, to haul everything the Whistler had to offer back to the bluff."

Plus, if there was one way to get back in the good graces of the King of the Ifrit, it was to uncork their city by helping Lura take down the magic devourer. I wondered if the desert would turn back into a verdant area once it was gone. In the meantime, we would send a batch of ceramics as a peace offering, along with an explanation. But Taquoho said the method for arbitrating conflicting information within The City was long, arduous, and resulted in the splitting and reforming of various unions along new political lines—a process that often created more problems than it solved. Haughty-von-haughty had really done us dirty by lying about what he found at the village.

Between the orcs and the Ifrit, we were building a monstrous menagerie of our own. The irony wasn't lost on me that if this were Earth, we'd clearly be the heels of the villainous faction. But then, Sauron was never interested in space exploration. So, we at least had that going for us.

The morning of the fifth day, the Stampede resumed. The various teams went their separate ways, and Lura with them. She still had a tournament to win before she went after the biggest trophy of them all. Tribe Apollo, the Ifrit outcasts, and the remnants of the Flock headed west toward the lakeside waystation—which had already started to become a fuel depot and rest stop for goblins hunting plains creatures and harvesting edible plant life that grew in the grasslands.

The taskmasters of Tribe Apollo were proving deft hands at keeping the logistics lines moving. An innate understanding of the technology itself apparently came with a keen sense of where raw materials needed to go to be processed, and where refined materials and devices needed to go to be utilized. I had shored up a few of those processes myself, but the logistics engine was largely self-sustaining.

A perimeter fence of wood backed by mud bricks was going up to protect the central tower that anchored the site. I spotted a platform jutting out the side of the tower that was definitely an airship dock, though it was currently empty. Just outside the fence, a stretch of relatively flat land had been cleared of brush and small debris to serve as an airstrip, and two small biplanes were fastened down with weighted lines.

Sourtooth looked up at the structure as we stopped for water and shade in the daily eclipse. "Underestimate the size of your tribe, we. Believed it numbered some two hundred or more, did Lura. And perhaps that is true—here on the open steppe. But such a number you could feed in the jungle, if just. Pray, what is the true counting?"

"After eight consecutive days of no catastrophes and full bellies, we've replenished what we lost in the Stampede and then some. We may break one thousand goblins soon, if we don't suffer any huge losses," I said. I pulled up my population window and looked at the various assigned goblins and their tasking. "I can use the System to track them and manage everything from spawn rates to assigned tasks productivity."

Sourtooth looked at the goblins scrambling about the fuel depot at their various jobs. "One thousand goblins," he said. "That is a tribe of troubling size, yet still easily quelled. Err caution, little brother. Goblin kings are feared even upon Kelembog. One such as you that seeks peace, others will yet see as a pestilence."

I took a drink of water. "Are goblin kings typically warlike?" I asked. I didn't want to mention that I only knew of one other. My knowledge of Ravan history was still murky, at best—and neither Ifrit nor orcs kept written records that I could reference. Ironically, my canoneers were making the closest thing to a history book on Lanclova, as far as I knew.

Sourtooth rubbed his chin. "A goblin uprising swept across the Duchy of Habbe—though of *when*, the songs are not clear. Before my grandfather's time. Some thirty thousand ravenous maws descended like locusts, having scraped bare every rock in the mountain of lichen, grass, and grub. Not each on their own dangerous, you see. But in aggregate . . . and starving . . . it left a devastated duchy for some time."

I sighed. "I at least have plans for that. Hunting secures us in the short term. Gives us enough time to maybe start seeding crops and planting orchards for when the tribe grows as big as I need it to be to reach my goal. But the tribe hasn't taken to agriculture. It's like it doesn't even exist in the tree."

Sourtooth laughed. "Pray, little brother, from where will you gather seed to plant? The humans will not trade it to you. Ifrit have no such thing. Even the Lanclovan soil taints and twists whatever is planted in it. You've seen burst-fruit, I assume?"

I took a pause in my drink and raised an eyebrow at the orc. "Those aren't typical elsewhere?"

The old orc shook his head. "Not meant to grow in the shade of the moon, were the beasts and birds and trees of Kelembog. 'Tis a cruel and cunning eye that warps all it watches. Look no further than the creatures of the steppe."

"I see," I said, frowning. Maybe my goblins weren't to blame for the failures of our early farming attempts after all.

We continued on, hoping to reach the village before nightfall. I saw it before we even entered the jungle—or rather, the several globular balloons lofted above the village and the various wooden structures suspended between their lines. Buzz and Javier had been busy at work. Rufus must have arrived with the canvas for my taskmasters to make so many of them, and I spotted glider launch rails, flex-a-pults, windmills, houses, and countless other goblin devices in the towering complex that Buzz had begun to erect. It looked like the floors of a skyscraper under construction, without the benefit of the supporting structure. What's more is that a cloud of orbiting shapes I'd originally taken for birds were in fact goblins on personal gliders transitioning from level to level or dispatching to tasks in the forest below.

"By foul elders," muttered Sourtooth. "Such a sight, eyes never beheld."

It was a village no longer. That much was for sure.

"Welcome to City Apollo," I said, a bit stunned myself.

We continued through the widened roads, passing traffic the other way who stopped to mob the king and see if the new orcs were A) edible or B) good anchors for sleeping mounds. Other goblins took advantage of the opportunity to ditch the buggies and run into the woods to look for grubs or streams to fish in. By the time we got to the base of the bluff, fully half the goblins who had been riding with us had cycled out for entirely new goblins. But such was their way.

The freight elevators had been upgraded. Rather than suspended by cordage and goblin counterweights, they'd been adapted to the wind-powered screws. Although the platforms struggled and creaked against the weight of the buggies and their added cargo, the wind-powered lifts began to climb with slow, cyclical noises. Overhead, two biplanes flew between discrete levels of construction before passing east on their way to (presumably) Camp Canaveral.

I'd worried that the village would stagnate in my absence. But under my taskmasters, it had flourished. That was perfect, because we had work to do. Thirty thousand goblins like the ravenous blue plague that had swept Habbe? I didn't know that I would need that many. Ten thousand? Perhaps ten thousand could do the job.

Either way, we still had a long road to the stars.

CHAPTER 42

BUILDING UP

"We have some larger-scale structures that we built for the Ifrit paladins. Your people should be comfortable there," I told Sourtooth, pointing out the area. The old orc looked around the base of the bluff at the tangle of squat, misshapen buildings lining the southeast corner of the bluff. Large anchors tethered the floating platforms above, which themselves were suspended by balloons crafted from canvas. "Make yourselves at home," I said.

"Hope the smell of the humans has joined them on their southward trek," he said. He shouldered his gear. "Come on, lads. Working doors we'll need, lest any of you should want to wake at the bottom of a goblin breeding mound." He shuddered. Hmph. At least the paladins had let goblins snuggle them.

The orcs hurried after him, and I headed to the central square. It was hard to believe how much and how quickly the bluff had changed. Village Apollo was turning into a proper city. And my goblins were *everywhere*. They worked at hammering together wooden structures, linking up gear assemblages to wind power, working gas-powered lathes to turn raw materials into usable parts, and assembling buggies, bikes, choppers, and gliders in the motor-pool. So much smoke rose from the foundries and furnaces on the north end of the bluff that I thought something *must* be burning. But the blaze was in the hearts of all the goblins working to make our Space Program a reality.

Buzz greeted me with a wave, pulling up in a small flatbed buggy with a plethora of loose construction equipment in the back that nearly became a projectile hazard as he screeched to a stop.

"Welcome back, boss!" he shouted over the roar of the engine. He slapped the side of the vehicle. "Hop in!"

"Good to see you, Buzz!" I said. I waved to Armstrong and Chuck. Armstrong jumped into the back, threatening to crush the primitive suspension, but Chuck waved me off.

"Gonna check on the animals," he said. "See how the paddocks are shaped up."

"Suit yourself," I said. I slapped him on the shoulder and watched him jog off to the west end of the bluff before I slid into the buggy beside Buzz.

"You've been busy," I said.

"Been *crowded*. Only way to go is up, innit? Wotcha think?"

I looked overhead at the concentric ringed platforms staged haphazardly on canvas balloons. Such a feat of engineering would have given architects ulcers and physicists strokes. But it looked perfectly goblin-sane, and the blue furry side of me wanted nothing more than to climb up it.

Buzz shifted into gear and we sped off.

"Is Eileen back yet?" I asked.

"Still up north," said Buzz. He had to shout because his foot seemed weighted down with lead on the throttle pedal. "We had some converts come in. Once they're in the tribe they make gliders and some head 'ere. Most stay put, start buildin' up their own bluffs with the new tech they learn. I send builders out to help. It don't take long to get 'em flyin' but most of 'em don't have a source of metal to make engines. We got more sulfur, rubber, clay, whatever anyone needs. Takes time to send word back and forth of who needs what where, though."

"So I've seen," I said. I'd been using the System menus to keep track of resources in and out, monitoring trends and shortfalls.

Being able to draw resources to central hubs like the bluffs from multiple areas meant a smoother curve of extraction from the forests. One of Eileen's bluffs near the mountains had even come with a source of copper, which was at least as valuable as a new goblin variant.

"Radios are on my to-do list," I said. "Now we've got strong magnets and copper wire, generators will be straightforward. From there we'll build extra equipment to send and receive signals."

"If you say so," said Buzz. More content to wait until I got the tech unlocked than try to work through it in his head, my lead builder put his focus into navigating the bluff at a breakneck pace. He stopped short near one of the lines leading up to the next platform, swerving into a halt that threatened to tip us straight over.

"I sent along the second airship with rotors and other hard-to-make parts, help some of the new lads find their feet and get engines going. Got one of the noblins onboard to spread the canon. Should be back in a day."

"Good thinking."

Buzz hopped down and went over to what looked like a knotted rope loop strung between a small windmill on the second platform and a bearing on the ground. At the top, I could see several aircraft staged and ready to launch. Buzz grabbed the rope and let it pull him up. I jumped on behind him, with Armstrong and a few other bodyguards close in tow.

At the top, I spotted a goblin that was slightly bigger than the others—a taskmaster I didn't recognize—who seemed to be in charge of the air hangars. His jaw dropped when he saw me, and he dashed over.

"Sir, sir! It's an honor!" he squeaked.

I grinned and looked at the air fleet, which had a mix of powered and unpowered gliders staged in lopsided rows. "You in charge with Eileen gone?"

"Yessir!"

"Suppose you'll need a name," I said, racking my brain for an astronaut or pilot name.

"They call me Footsmash, my king!"

Or . . . he could be called *Footsmash.* I looked down at one of his feet, which looked to have been mangled at some point in the three weeks or so since he'd been born. "Footsmash it is," I said. I supposed taskmasters would be popping up all around as the tribe grew, and I wasn't going to be there to name every single one of them. Tribe Apollo was becoming bigger than *Apollo.* Which it needed to do if this logistics engine was going to grow large enough to support the thousands of goblins I'd need to start processing, refining, and manufacturing complex aerospace components.

"Got a bi-glider ready?" asked Buzz.

Footsmash led us to one of the larger models with a big, cast iron engine block. I rubbed my hands together. While helicopters might be cool (they're not), airplanes were my jam. And I'd wanted to get my hands on the sticks ever since Eileen flew the first one over the Stampede camp. I climbed up into the cockpit and familiarized myself with the controls—which had been upgraded from the days of the first heavy gliders that had individual goblins work the control surfaces. These ones used push-pull rods to manipulate actual three-axis controls built into the wings and the tail so that one pilot could steer.

"Strap in, boss!" said Buzz, indicating a harness. I pulled the straps tight and cinched them down, marveling that goblins had actually integrated a safety feature into a vehicle. Armstrong stuck a rockette into the starter, and the engine rumbled to life. We started to roll, even at idle power, and I realized the aircraft wasn't secured or chocked in any way.

"Where's the runway?" I asked, looking around for a place to turn.

"More like a drop-way," said Buzz, tugging his own belt tight.

My stomach sank. *Oh. That* was the reason they'd installed the belts. I swallowed, looked at the quickly approaching edge of the platform, and jammed the throttle wide open. The noise mounted behind me, and I pulled on the pair of ear-cups in the cockpit. Black smoke belched out the back of the biplane, and we built up what speed we could before we shot straight off the edge of the platform.

I gritted my teeth and shoved the stick forward, angling the nose down toward the ground. We weren't going fast enough for takeoff, so trying to stay level would just stall us out. We needed airspeed, and this was the only way to get it. We fell past the edge of the platform, then quickly passed the top of the bluff. The cliff face blurred past us, and the ground rushed up. System's little altitude and airspeed window popped up, one climbing while the other rapidly depleted.

"Uh . . . *boss?!*" shouted Armstrong.

The wings started to shake, and I hauled back on the controls, pulling us out of the dive as the engine screamed. I thought the plane might come apart from the sheer forces, and *then* I thought it might come apart from smashing into the tops of the trees south of the bluff. But it managed to claw back into a climb, and we cleared the tallest branches by a few meters.

I felt Armstrong relax behind me, and I eased my white-knuckle grip on the controls and banked us to the left.

"*That's a proper takeoff, boss!*" Buzz's voice came through the speaker. "*Welcome home.*"

CHAPTER 43

JUST A SWAMP THING

I circled the bluff, joining the pattern of gliders already filling the airspace. We'd been gone a few weeks, and I wanted to see the extent of the changes.

As we climbed, I got a look at the upper suspended platforms where goblins worked at workshops, turned lathes, tuned engines, slept, or crafted. The topmost layer had stockpiles of raw materials and workshops for clothing and armor. The balloons keeping the whole thing suspended were thick canvas, and looked like they had once been a ship's sails. Braziers of scat fed them with hot air. I supposed several hundred goblins created more than enough fuel to keep them lofted, but I wasn't sure what we'd ever do if they needed to come down.

Buzz pointed out various facilities and workshops as we passed. "*There's the paparium, where the canoneers oversee their paper and charcoal production together—it's burnt down twice already. Over there's where we make clifford saddles and plate carriers. That hut there is where we keep jars of bomb fruit juice. Next door is one of the rockette stores.*"

Good to see things hadn't changed. I nudged the stick forward and took us low. The forest had been pushed back even more, now at least half a kilometer from the edge of the bluff in most directions and even more to the west, where the paddocks held dozens of herd animals captured and brought in from the plains. A clutch of twenty or thirty horn hoppers bounded away from our low pass, and near them a dozen oryx drank from a trough. Small packs of cliffords ran freely across the grass, keeping the herds together. Wranglers rode alongside on dirt bikes with prods and clubs.

There was one form I didn't recognize right away, until it raised its head and I saw the large, pronged tusks jutting from the wide, flat face.

"*You captured a thundercleave? Alive?*" I asked, dumbfounded.

"*They come on their own to the scratchy towers. Got a taste for the pulp-slurp. Wranglers say they ain't so bad if you don't startle 'em. More beasts come back every day from the badlands, and we send the vehicles back out with more go-juice and ammo to stage at the lake camp.*"

Having placed in the Stampede, we now had a right by the orcs to hunt game in the plains, and that meant being able to build up our herd animals. But that wasn't the only food project. I angled us north, where we'd cleared all the way to the river for farmland. Though, as I looked at what were supposed to be tilled fields, it seemed more like the zen garden of a dyslexic dog than the ordered rows of an industrial farm. Here and there, an odd plant poked through the surface, and the occasional large hole pocked the area.

"*The lads still don't get the point of sticking food back in the ground,*" said Buzz, "*But we've been stuffing seeds, berries, rocks, eggs, anything we can find on the off chance it grows like you said it would.*"

I grimaced. "*It's looking more and more like agriculture might not be in the Goblin Tech Tree at all. But it still works, it's just regular old science. We'll figure it out,*" I said.

As I flew over, a fountain of dirt shot into the sky a few kilometers to the south, leaving a new smoking hole in the field. The *BOOM* reached us a moment later.

"*I take it you've been planting bomb fruits?*" I asked. Buzz nodded. Our one successful agricultural venture thus far had been the bomb fruit orchard created primarily by accident when trying to create safe storage for the volatile fruits during my first days on Rava. Whatever else they were, bomb fruits were extremely efficient at scattering their seeds. Back then I'd only had a couple dozen goblins in the tribe, and the loss of even a single one was devastating. Now, System didn't even alert me unless there was a significant drop in a short time.

I angled the plane north toward the river, where an extensive network of docks jutted out into the water. Small boats floated up and down, powered mostly by manual impellers and the rare gas outboard engine. The fishermen were using anything from small, three-goblin canoes to the big ten-plus goblin pontoon barges. Upstream, I could see several wooden towers dotting the banks.

I made a low pass by one of the towers. The goblins at the top had fish smoking on racks, and they jumped and chittered and waved as we flew past. I pulled up and around, angling us southwest. The road to Huntsville had been widened and further cobbled, but I stayed above the river, following its winding path until I started to see the towers and furnaces of Huntsville. The river spread and slowed, and then we reached the edge of the marshlands, where I saw boats traversing the brackish water in between peat mounds and goblins wading in the water with prilling knives.

Low to the right, a splash and a hiss indicated the emergence of a croc-knocker, who immediately struck a goblin with his tongue prill. A nearby boat swiveled its mounted weapon, and the *kra-ka-kow* of multiple rifles preceded a gout of black, oily smoke from the deck. The croc-knocker rolled belly-up, and several goblins jumped into the water to retrieve the carcass.

Flying farther in, we passed a screw-pump that looked remarkably like an Earth-style oil derrick—if miniaturized and swarming with little blue goblins. It was also on fire, but that didn't seem to be hurting productivity as goblins cycled in with bladders to collect the fuel being pumped up out of the ground. I spotted a larger taskmaster overseeing the process and offering encouragement in the form of shouts and kicks to goblins who weren't moving as fast as she thought they ought to be.

How many taskmasters are we up to? I asked System.

<You currently have 33 taskmasters.>

Huh. I supposed that shouldn't surprise me. That meant I was on a first-name basis with fewer than half of them. And that ratio would only get worse as our layers of middle managers kept growing. My first variant was the rarest, but also the most critical to the massive logistics engine this tribe was already starting to become.

Still think I should have gone with the hobgoblin sentinels?

<I have no direct input or assessment on the variant choices of a goblin king.>

System was a damn liar. I chuckled. Off to the northwest, I spotted another smoke trail and shaded my eyes. "*Buzz, that's an awfully big fire. What do we have in that direction?*"

Buzz followed my gaze. "*Nothin', boss. That's King Ringo's island. We don't go there on your orders.*"

I frowned, looking at it. Had the wayward king of Daytona managed to burn down his own castle? Somehow, I doubted it. I dipped the wings and angled the glider toward the swamp king's domain.

As we got closer, I could see that there was definite damage to the outer walls and huts of the island. A shredded, untethered hide balloon was draped across the treetops, and several primitive boats were smashed on the shore. The keep's perimeter wall was damaged and smoldering in several places—absolutely not by accident. Someone had attacked Ringo. Of the boglins, there was no sign.

"*I don' like this, boss,*" said Armstrong, leaning so far out of the plane he threatened to throw off our CG.

"*Me either*," I said. I circled around for a lower pass and spotted a group of croc-knockers watching us as we flew by. Which struck me as odd, for some reason. As I passed over, they opened their mouths—despite the fact we were clearly out of range of their prills. Rather than iron, a cloud of red mist streamed up from their nostrils and mouths, taking the form of a narrow lance that shot up toward us.

"*Oh, hell!*" I shouted.

I jammed the throttle wide open as Armstrong scrambled for the rifle under his seat. He fired several shots back at the mist, which seemed to have no effect. But we built speed, and the thing apparently reached the end of whatever tethered it to the crocs, because it doubled back and shot toward the pack of reptiles once more. My stomach just about lurched into my throat, and my heart thumped in my chest. That was the same type of creature or spirit or *something* I'd seen take over the cliffords we brought to Huntsville and wreck our first camp. We hadn't had any problems with them since, but clearly something had changed.

I angled us back toward Huntsville. "*Buzz, can you fly this thing home?*"

"*Sure, boss!*"

"*Good. Tell Sally to get to work on the electric generator project. Tell her to strap bits of the whistler tail to an engine and spin them around wrapped copper wire until a goblin tech unlocks.*"

"*Sure thing, boss!*

I didn't want to delay electric motors and generators any longer, but this situation couldn't be ignored. Ringo was my canary in the coal mine, and he had clearly stopped singing. I wanted to know what he saw, which meant I had to find him.

"*Armstrong?*"

I needn't have asked. The burly scrapper was already uncinching his safety harness and slinging the rifle over his shoulder. He shot me a quick salute, and I nodded. Buzz and I awkwardly switched places, with my lead builder assuming the controls. He wasn't a great pilot—in fact, he was kind of terrible and terrifying—which was why he was in charge of building things instead of running the air fleet. But he got us relatively over Huntsville. I grabbed an emergency glider from the cockpit and scrambled out onto the wing. When I was sure I was clear of the prop, I leapt off the wing and opened the glider, catching the air and starting to circle over the bustling village Huntsville had become in my absence. A few seconds later, several blue, furry forms plummeted past me.

Armstrong and his Secretive Servants hadn't bothered with the gliders.

CHAPTER 44

THE MISSING BEATLE

The first thing Armstrong did on landing was press-gang several Huntsville goblins into the Secretive Servants to make sure I had ample protection. The swamp had long since proven to be a hostile environment—maybe even more so than the badlands. We hadn't conquered it so much as mitigated it, and we'd still only explored a small part of the waterways and islands that made up the big crescent-shaped bog buffering our northwest flank.

But we'd also come a long way since first braving its waters with ceramic-tipped spears, slingers, and small hot-air balloons. Now we had gas-powered engines, steel, guns, and soon we'd have electricity. From what I'd seen, the croc-knockers had become an annoyance at best, rather than a monolithic obstacle that could only be avoided or deterred. But the red mist spirits we'd only run across once before. Which made me have to ask: What changed? Ringo had existed in the swamp for years, and apparently not fallen afoul of them. And the answer was pretty obvious. I'd come. I'd spent the last few months disrupting the balance of power on Lanclova. It was only natural that things were beginning to respond.

I found Hadfield on top of the tower on the north end of Camp Huntsville, directing the flow of iron and oil coming in from the bog through a new canal that had been dug from the camp straight to the waterway, sealed off by a portcullis in the water. In addition to his skull mask, he'd adopted a poncho of woven grass and a wide thatch hat that made him look like a mound of bog peat. I hadn't realized it was possible for a native goblin to go *even more* native, but from his easy grin, Hadfield was clearly loving life in the swamp.

"Welcome back, boss! Yer just in time for the next batch of icky-slicky."

The process of extraction and refining at Huntsville was best described as barely controlled chaos backed by the occasional detonation of a boom furnace producing a piece of workable iron. Totems erected throughout the camp boosted the productivity of the labor pool, and production here had to be diligent to keep the growing fleet of motor vehicles supplied with fuel at the bluff and on the plains.

I told Hadfield about the situation on Ringo's Island while I watched the process. He considered the problem.

"We've steered clear of the place, most-like, as you said. Built a pump for their spring. Leave supplies out for 'em on occasion, and they leave us little stacks of smooth stones and shells, for some reason. But they stopped taking them two days ago. Was about ready to go check on 'em myself."

"So whatever happened, happened very recently," I said, nodding. "Then there's a good chance he and some of his tribe are still out there. We need to find them and figure out what's coming."

With boglins most active at dawn and dusk, that would be the best time to perform our search without disrupting iron and kerosene production to a degree that stunted food collection efforts and tribe defense. We still had Lura's task to accomplish as well, and the huntress didn't seem the sort to rest on her laurels.

"We got plenty of boats and crews, boss. But they get stuck in some of the thicker peat. Boglins could be gone to ground in areas wot we can't reach."

"I might have something for that," I said. "Come with me."

Navigation in the bog so far had been primarily for the purpose of collecting the iron found near the loose river runoffs where rafts tough enough to withstand a croc-knocker attack could maneuver between the peat mounds. We'd need something different to get up some of the smaller, vegetation-choked waterways.

We went down to the forges where the local igni were working with their crafting teams to make impeller craft. Most of them were still goblin-powered via pedal crank, since motors had been reserved for ground and air vehicles—and in fact, the swamp had a pair of helicopters that they'd built because there was no area clear enough for a runway. Taking a small engine with a spare prop from one of the choppers, I had the igni mount them sideways to a pair of canoes strapped together. The result was a shallow-draft pontoon boat with an air fan, and no underwater impeller to get choked by debris.

<Goblin Technology Unlocked: Combust'em patrol boats>

Once the first one was done, the craftsmen got sorted out on making a few more. The choppers would also be useful in the effort, being able to scout through the bog—but I doubted we'd spot boglins from the air, especially if they didn't want to be spotted.

"Armstrong, I want scrappers leading the charge on this. Your boys are natural nighttime trackers."

"Onnit, boss. Trust," said Armstrong. He scratched his chin. "But . . . why do you care wot happens to Ringo? Didn't he stab you? An' didn't you torch him?"

I didn't want to explain that Ringo was the only other person I'd met who might be from my home world and therefore my only link to it. The fact he was a paranoid Florida swamp-man just meant he fit in better with the goblins than I did. But it was a legitimate question. Other goblins had actually stopped working to wait for my answer. I looked around for a canoneer and whistled him over. I pointed a finger in the air.

"What's the first commandment?"

The canoneer reached into his bag and fumbled for a folded scrap of paper. "Be excellent to each other," he said.

I looked at Armstrong. "Goblins help goblins. Ringo got paranoid and scared because for years, he thought he was alone in a world where no one *gives* a goblin anything, they only *take.* Well, he's not alone, and neither are we. We've got orcs, we've got the Ifrit, and we've got the boglins. Maybe they're not all *entirely* on our side, but we're getting there. And we're not giving up any of them. And we're definitely not giving up *on* any of them."

A wave of straighter backs and puffed-up chests passed through the crowd. The canoneer scribbled furiously on a corner of his pamphlet, and even Armstrong nodded.

"Guess we gotta stick together, even with a goblin that tried to stick us," he said. "Right. I'll gather the lads."

By nightfall, we had a handful of boats and two dozen scrappers and their non-variant crews. Hobgoblins were pretty common as far as variants went, making up about a fifth or sixth of the entire tribe. Twenty of them would be a force to be reckoned with. I started to climb onto the lead boat, but felt strong hands pin my arms to my sides and lift me off the gangplank. I kicked the air helplessly.

"Sorry, boss," said Armstrong. "As your Secretive Servants, we're stayin' behind walls 'til we know wot we's dealing with. Leave it to the scrappers. They're good lads."

I relaxed, deflated. "You're right, of course," I said. Armstrong put me down, and with a longing look at the airboats, I wished the scrappers luck and headed back to the safety of Huntsville's walls. The scrapper search and rescue teams set off so they could search into the night. But I still had the diurnal limitations of a non-variant forest goblin, and not long after that, a hot meal put me down for the count.

<Your tribe has decreased to 881 members.>
<Your tribe has increased to 912 members.>

I woke up to a hell of a shock, losing nearly forty goblins overnight. I checked the roster menu and found that fully fifteen of them had been scrappers I'd assigned to the search party. That was *most* of the search party. What was even worse, though, was that a taskmaster had vanished—one responsible for pumping and transporting kerosene from the springs in the swamp. Without taskmasters managing the minutiae of logistics, the downstream effects would start to stunt efforts of everything that required fuel—which now heavily influenced food production and aircraft manufacturing.

I struggled out from the bottom of the cuddle puddle and went up to the north wall, where several goblins were already pointing out smoke trails from farther north, where the pumping station had been. I gritted my teeth. If I'd just been there . . . it probably would have made no difference. As much as I hated to admit it, even more goblins would have died from the Head of the Snake skill, if they really did meet with such a catastrophic result. But the search party survivors hadn't returned yet, so there was no way to know what had happened. Hell, it could have been the red spirits, or it could have just been some other form of particularly nasty endemic life.

It was a couple of hours before two of the scrapper boats limped their way back to Huntsville with dead-tired skeleton crews.

"We never even saw wot was attacking us," one of them said. "It got real dark. Then four crocs jumped out all at once, right onto the boat! And these even bigger things with big claws 'n' teeth. We lost sight of the other lads with us, and when we'd made it out of the fight, they weren't nowhere."

"Didn't you have torches?" I asked.

"Somefink snuffed 'em," said the scrapper. He looked over his shoulder back at the bog. "I could feel 'em watchin' me."

That wasn't good. Something was definitely in the swamp, and it was making a concerted effort to attack goblins. It knew to hit at night, it knew to separate groups of goblins to negate their numbers advantage. Scrappers were great ambush fighters and surprise attackers. What could get the jump on *them*?

I opened the variant spawn control sub-menu and slid the slider for scrappers all the way to the right, prioritizing their reproduction above other variants.

The goblins started squawking and running to the eastern rampart. I closed the menu and followed them. We were greeted by a dark shadow in the sky to the east. A shadow that was drawing closer.

CHAPTER 45

WORKING REMOTE

The sound of motors reached us before the silhouette resolved into an airship—not Gertrude, but one of the others built in the weeks we'd been on the badlands. Like all of the tech that was iterated on after unlocking, this was more refined than our first powered balloon, yet somehow more ramshackle. Two canvas envelopes kept the thing aloft, one fore and one aft, with scat burners beneath. A rampart of wooden planks circled the envelope with patrolling goblins. The rigid structure suspended in a tangle of cords was longer and thinner, and sported sponsons with the barrels of recoilless rifles poking out. I also spotted a belly-mounted missile ready for a rider. No doubt there were at least two dozen goblins aboard with spears and rifles close to hand.

Someone whistled from one of the other towers, and I saw a goblin frantically waving semaphore flags. The airship came in, scraping the edge of the tower before the goblins atop could hook it and tie it down. Most of the crew, not needing to wait for the gangplank, simply disembarked at altitude—including a taskmaster I definitely recognized.

"Sally!" I shouted, dropping off the rampart. I jogged over, where she proceeded to glare at me and then kick me, and flail tiny, angry fists—until Armstrong appeared and lifted her away from me.

"Hey, hey!" I said, trying to fend her off. "That's your king you're kicking."

Glare.

I ran a hand through my fur. "Look, I'm sorry I didn't come to see you when we got back. We just meant to take a tour, and . . . well, excuses won't cut it. I'm sorry, Sally. Can you forgive me?"

She crossed her arms and turned her head, but her posture and expression had softened. Armstrong set her back down. She whipped around and sank her teeth into his leg.

"Argh! Wot'd I do?" he demanded, shaking her off. The diminutive blue ball of chomp rolled away and jumped back to her feet.

"What are you doing here, anyway?" I asked.

Sally pointed up at the airship, where goblins were busy unloading flat, dull-gray plates and the tail section we'd taken off the whistler. My eyes widened.

"Sally, that's amazing!" I said. With magnets and wire, we could start converting the mechanical energy of the motors into electric energy through simple alternators.

Electricity might seem like a big jump, but at its core, if you have angular momentum, and you have magnets and wire, you have electricity. What happens next is the complicated bit, as it's fed through rectifiers, filters, diodes, or regulators to make it safe and practical to apply. But I'm betting *regulator* wasn't even a word in the Goblin Tech Tree. If struggling with the internal combustion motor had taught me anything, the KISS principle applied to goblin tech. *Keep it stupidly suicidal.* The more ways it had to blow up, the more likely it was to unlock the tech.

Sourtooth was struggling to disembark as well with the crosswise flow of goblins competing to unload equipment or rush aboard for something to carry down to the ground, and Taquoho hovered behind him along with a few other Ifrit and Promo.

The old orc scrabbled down the ladder on the docking tower, making good time despite his leg, followed by the ignis taskmaster. "Thinking to dump me off while adventures you seek, hmm?" Sourtooth demanded.

"Wouldn't dream of it," I said. "I'm glad you're here, actually."

Sourtooth looked around at the totems lining the camp. "Not the freshest smelling of the lands I've trampled. Yet neither is it the most foul. I would join in the work, little brother mine."

Truth be told, I was glad to have him. Sourtooth was well traveled. Maybe even as well as Rufus, if in different circles. The old orc might be able to offer insight into the threats currently plaguing the boglins. Of course, we had to find them first.

I turned to my chief ignis and rubbed my hands together. "Promo, let's set up a workspace. I'm going to need wire, engines, cross sections of the whistler tail, and tools." I considered. "We're also going to need sand and metal pipes. We've got a day to work before the next wave of scrappers is born and I want to make the most of it."

"Trust, boss," said Promo. He waddled off, already barking orders like he owned the place. The rest of the goblins snapped to and started dashing about, rearranging the area in a strangely efficient manner. While individual goblins sometimes worked at odds or stepped on one another's feet, the weird semi-gestalt nature of the goblin tribal structure ensured the needle moved consistently toward the *task complete* end of the spectrum.

Sally and I set to work, using a gas-powered table saw ordinarily used to cut wood in order to cut narrow slices of the whistler tail prongs. As I had suspected, they were powerful, permanent magnets—nearly on a level with rare-earth magnets back home. They'd be ideal for applications at all levels of electrical equipment, from portable power generators to walkie-talkies. The material chewed through the sawblades, and not for the first time, I really missed the diamond-coated tools common on Earth. We made up for efficiency with volume, but individual work was still somewhat arduous.

Its tail wasn't the only gift the whistler had given us. Arguably just as valuable was its hide. The stone-hard carapace of the meteor-made-flesh was actually a form of natural metallic chitin, and if my guess was correct, it used the magnetic prongs of its tail to electroplate itself using the ore from the pink gravel of its canyon. The result was a lightweight, bonded composite metal natural to Rava that, if not actual aluminum, was the next best thing. It was clear the Ravan periodic table was more overlap than difference, but I doubted you'd find this ore anywhere on Earth.

While Promo and I spent the afternoon eclipse figuring out how to heat and shape the whistler carapace into thin panels for general use, a small motorcade arrived with yet another surprise. The goblins hauled open the gate on the east side of the settlement to allow the vehicles in, and I saw the squat form of Rufus with his black-and-white badger snout sniffing the air.

"Well, now the gang's really all here!" I said.

The wild-marked merchant spotted me and hopped down from his buggy, fishing in his trouser pocket for a coin, which he flipped to the driver. The driver caught it, looking at it curiously, before popping it in his mouth and swallowing it whole. Rufus spotted me and trotted over, a grim expression on his face. He cast a sidelong look at Sourtooth working at one of the forges, who was quick to return a lopsided sneer.

"I've just returned from the City of Brass," he said. "The Ifrit delegation reported to the king that you took many of their number captive and reneged on your agreement to produce ceramic parts."

"It's not true," I said. I gestured to the Ifrit present in the camp, flying in their coaxial vessels. "They're free to come and go as they please. They've chosen to stay. The delegation leader destroyed the first shipment and tried to abandon Taquoho and kill one of my taskmasters. You can ask Taquoho about it. He'll tell you." I raised my voice and called for the Ifrit, who floated down. Rufus repeated what he'd told me.

"Ah, it pleases us to see you, Rufus—though I wish it bore brighter tidings. I assure you, everything King Apollo has said is the truth."

Rufus raised his hands. "I believe you. I saw the Ifrit at the bluff. They're clearly not prisoners of any kind or under any duress or threat. However, the King of One Thousand Names does not share that view, and because I brokered this exchange, the delegation's lies have damaged my reputation, Apollo. Nothing is more serious to the Ifrit than their own being taken captive. That's why they so rarely leave the City of Brass."

I sighed. "I'm sorry, Rufus. I didn't mean for any of this to backfire on you. We need to get the record straight with the king. We've remade the ceramic parts, and I'm ready to send them along with envoys to make clear what actually happened. I'm going to make this right."

"It's not so simple a thing," he said. He fished in his pack for his flask of liquor and took a sip. "Some may argue that if all the Ifrit do not return, then the threat against those remaining may influence the words of whoever you sent back. Disputes among Ifrit aren't just a matter of evidence and opinion. They get very . . ."

"Political?" I asked.

Rufus nodded. "Ifrit political debates have much in common with civil wars. They're incredibly nuanced and complicated. The king alone is a union of one thousand Ifrit, and you can imagine how difficult it is for such a being to reach consensus with itself."

"Taquoho suggested as much," I said, grimacing. I hated politics. "Still, we can't do nothing. Especially not with your reputation on the line when you've done so much for my tribe. Will you accompany the shipment? It might help to have you deliver them personally, along with your account of what you witnessed."

"I'm not sure they'll let me back into the city," he admitted. "But I'll try. I've invested too much in this deal and have too much to lose if it falls through."

"There's also the cooperation of two nations and the progress that comes from mutual exchange and understanding," I added.

Rufus shrugged. "Mutual understanding and progress won't buy me an estate in Umberbarrow. Trade will."

"Well, I wouldn't want Umberbarrow to go un-estated. We'll fix this, Rufus. I promise."

Somewhere deeper in the camp, someone fired up an engine. The rumble of the engine was quickly followed by a loud *snap* of a high voltage arc and then a brief shriek. I looked over to see an expanding cloud of smoke and smoldering blue fur next to a device tossing off sparks and blue tendrils of electricity.

<Your tribe has decreased to 908 members.>
<Goblin Technology Unlocked: Spinny spark'ems>
<Goblin Technology Unlocked: Spark'em spinnies>

"What under the stars was that?" asked Rufus.

"Progress," I said, rubbing my hands together.

It was time to shock this tribe into the next age.

Ad Luna.

ABOUT THE AUTHOR

Scott Warren is the author of the reincarnation LitRPG series My Big Goblin Space Program, originally released on Royal Road. He has written more than a dozen books in between working as a submariner, helicopter pilot, and international military instructor. While his day job takes him around the world—sometimes in the most austere of conditions—he is never far from a book in progress. Warren lives in Maryland with his wife and their cat, Lady.